The Ripper's Legacy

A gripping archaeological thriller

Nigel Plant

Unearthed Quill

Copyright © 2025 by Nigel Plant

All rights reserved.

No part of this publication may be reproduced, distributed, or transmitted in any form or by any means, including photocopying, recording, or other electronic or mechanical methods, without the prior written permission of the publisher, except as permitted by U.S. copyright law. For permission requests, contact Unearthed Quill Publications.

The story, all names, characters, and incidents portrayed in this production are fictitious. No identification with actual persons (living or deceased), places, buildings, and products is intended or should be inferred.

Book Cover by 100 Covers

First edition 2025

ACKNOWLEDGEMENTS

Thanks to my wife Lynn for her plot improvements, constructive ideas, and support in completing yet another book.

Thanks also to Simon as a top editor for all the impressive editing and discussions over plot directions, even on holiday in Spain.

I've enjoyed writing this novel, but the plot was much tougher than the previous two, so without Lynn and Simon's help I wouldn't have got there. Your patience is very much appreciated.

Finally, to my readers, thank you for your valuable time and I hope you have enjoyed reading the books as much as I've enjoyed writing them.

Also By Nigel Plant

- **Paradox of The Thief** – Reed Hascombe's first archaeological thriller set in the Peaks of England, where the discovery of an ancient scroll leads to a gripping search for buried treasure competing against a rogue artifact dealer.

- **Enigma of The Sword** – the second of Reed's archaeological thrillers set amidst the wild Cornish coastline, where a gold medallion provides clues to the most powerful sword in history involving deep-sea dives and battling a local crime lord.

- **The Ripper's Legacy** – Reed assembles an archaeological investigation team that sets off to London, where a Victorian love letter written by Jack the Ripper leads to a thrilling search for hidden treasure while clashing with a secret cult.

- **The Aztec Pursuit** – Reed and his team travel to America, searching for the lost gold of the Aztecs and end up stranded inside the Bermuda Triangle on an unmapped island, whilst pursued by the Mexican cartel and an eccentric Russian professor.

Chapter 1

THE SHARD, LONDON

MONDAY

BLEAK WINTER RAIN BATTERED the window pane of Madeleine Robinson-Smith's office on the seventeenth floor of the famous office block, The Shard, in central London. The actual address was 32 London Bridge Street, but its distinctive shape had given rise to its nickname. Described as a 'Vertical City' with offices, residential apartments and restaurants, it stands over 1,000 feet tall. Floor space inside these offices was at a premium with a price to match. Madeleine often wondered if she had made a poor decision to sign a ten-year long contract for the head office of her family business. Back then, she felt nothing could curb her passion for the future. Electric vehicles were all the rage, and the batteries required to power them needed lithium. Three years ago, she had secured a deal to purchase all of their lithium requirements from a mine in Venezuela. Her plans were to sell the vital mineral into America, the UK, and China. However, the mine collapsed six months ago, which put an end to that plan. With China's ability to source increased amounts from their own mines, this left her business struggling.

Madeleine became CEO of Robinson's Mining Supplies five years ago. She had worked her way up through the business from shipping clerk to manager, before she became Chief Finance Officer. Her father, Stuart, decided it was time to retire. Her knowledge of the business was impressive, and her father had no hesitation when he passed over control to his only child. At fifty-four, she had plenty of experience, which made her the ideal candidate to become its new boss. Business went well after her appointment. Sales increased and profits climbed until the mine in Venezuela collapsed. She had to cancel big contracts with customers for the supply of lithium with no other source of the vital mineral. The company received fines from some customers, penalties levied because of the supply problems. This had turned profits into losses, impacting the business more than she had envisaged. The business was on its knees, cash-flow was tight and everyone looked at her to solve it. Over one hundred employees relied on her for their monthly income. A weight on her shoulders that increased every day.

A patch of blue sky appeared in the distance as Madeleine gazed across the London landscape. She twirled strands of her blonde hair around her fingers, a relaxation response started as a child, enabling her thoughts to drift off and provide answers to the latest puzzle racing through her mind. Earlier, she had visited the gym in The Shard, part of the facilities available, before commencing her work. A quick blast on the rowing machine had allowed her to free up vital space in her constantly buzzing head to address the issues of the day. She had to admit the facilities at The Shard had been a major reason she had picked this location as their new head office, but perhaps her heart had ruled her head? The clouds appeared to recede as the patch of blue sky increased, which prompted thoughts of winter holidays in the Canary Islands. Her American husband of six years had booked them a two-week break in late February, so only a few more weeks to wait. She needed some sunshine and a break from the daily stress of being CEO, although she knew she couldn't ever switch off as emails and messages from her Personal Assistant would fly through the ether and land on her phone daily. The intercom buzzed.

Madeleine spun round in the affluent office space. A solid oak desk, three filing cabinets, and a large display cabinet, crammed with awards from over the years. Framed photos of mining locations from around the world adorned the neutral walls. They chartered the company's progress during the past five decades. Behind the largest photo, one of a cobalt mine in Yorkshire, which her father had started the business with, sat an integral wall-safe. She pressed the intercom button to connect with her PA.

"Yes, Kathy?"

"Mr Montague is here for your two o'clock appointment."

"Thank you. Show him in, please."

The appointment was vital. Madeleine ran through the key points she needed to communicate in her head. The door opened as Kathy Jones, her PA, entered, followed by Basil Montague.

"Basil, how are you?"

"Very well Madeleine. How are you keeping, my dear?"

"Could be better. How's your lovely wife?"

"She's well. How's Richard and his art gallery?"

"He's very well, already looking forward to our winter break. The gallery is booming since he employed a German girl to manage his social media."

"Excellent news."

"Can I get you a drink, Basil?"

"Coffee with oat milk, please. And a couple of your delicious chocolate biscuits, if I may?"

"Certainly," said Madeleine, pressing the intercom and relaying the requests to her PA.

"Take a seat Basil."

Madeleine watched Basil Montague wedge his portly body into one of the burgundy leather-lined oak chairs. He really needed to lose some weight, she thought, otherwise a heart attack would be on the horizon for her bank manager. He unbuttoned his navy suit jacket as it stretched tightly over his ample stomach, inflated by his consistent indulgence in fine dining at the many restaurants of London. Madeleine didn't dislike the man, but he could irritate her with his pompous nature. His thin grey hair was too long, plastered over his skull with some shiny hair product. The handlebar moustache ought to have gone. It just didn't look cool after turning grey. She spotted a slight yellow stain on the chest section of his white-collared shirt, just left of his necktie. He must have had fried eggs, or a cooked breakfast that morning and dribbled the yolk down himself. Not a pleasant thought.

"Shall we get down to business, Basil?" asked Madeleine.

"Certainly."

"I wanted to run through our business plan with you and discuss future funding. I've prepared a presentation covering the key points," she said. The remote control for the TV lay on the desk, so she grabbed it before clicking the mouse on her laptop. She swivelled her leather office chair to view the TV and plucked up a wireless clicker to begin the presentation. She rattled through the first three slides, confidently belting out her practised sales patter. Then a knock on the office door interrupted her flow. Kathy strode in with a tray laden with drinks and a plate of luxurious biscuits. Her PA could be like a human bulldozer as she bustled to the desk and plonked the full tray on the corner.

"Thanks Kathy. Help yourself to biscuits Basil," she said and passed him his coffee. She watched as he shovelled two double-chocolate cookies into his mouth without drawing breath, like a young bird of prey gobbling a mouse.

"Carry on, my dear," he said and snaffled a third biscuit from the plate.

The next slide appeared on the TV screen as Madeleine pressed the clicker, which showed the cash-flow position of the company. A large deficit in cash-flow needed to be resolved with a further loan from Whitechapel Bank. This was the crux of today's important meeting. She needed to persuade Basil to provide the extra funds whilst they searched for alternative lithium mines. After she completed her presentation, she switched straight to the key point.

"In conclusion, Basil, I'm looking for some extra help from you. We need an extra five million to get us through the next twelve months, then we'll be back on track. What are your thoughts?" she asked the bank manager. She rose from her seat and smoothed the lapels of her jacket, part of her purple trouser suit. She felt it was important to look your best, especially when she had to ask for money. As she waited for his answer, she strode over to the window and noticed the blue patch of sky had now spread to the whole of the horizon. A positive sign, perhaps?

"I understand your position, Madeleine, and the business plan provides an optimistic future, but in all honesty, we can't provide any further funding."

Madeleine pivoted on her heels and glared at the portly bank manager with yet another cookie crammed into his gaping mouth. Not what she wanted to hear. She spun the frown into a smile.

"Why is that Basil?"

"Your debt to asset ratio is already beyond our safe threshold, my dear. I'm sorry but my hands are tied. I really wish I could help you."

"Can you increase our overdraft instead?"

"I can't do that either."

Time stood still as Madeleine absorbed the response. She had expected this answer and requested more funding than she actually required.

"What about if we lower my request to say only three million extra?"

"I can't even offer you one million Madeleine. You don't have enough assets to secure the funding against. Unless you wanted to put up a personal guarantee?"

"You know very well I won't do that, Basil," she said with an edge to her tone. If the bank wouldn't help her, let's get rid of him quick, she thought. "Okay, thanks for your time, Basil. Let's keep in touch." She held out her hand, which showed the meeting was over, as the bank manager hoisted himself from the chair.

"It's been a pleasure, as always. We must organise a night at the theatre for the four of us soon," he responded, shook her hand, opened the door to her office and left her to contemplate her options.

As she paced the office, Madeleine knew that without extra funding she had to downsize of the business, which meant redundancies. Not something she wanted to do.

However, another alternative had presented itself. She moved over to the Yorkshire mine photo and pulled it ninety degrees away from the wall on its hinges. Then she punched in the code for the safe, her son's birth date, 1608. On the top shelf lay a yellowed piece of paper inside a zip-lock plastic bag. She drew it out and examined it for the umpteenth time. Her grandmother, Mavis, had passed away last year. On clearing her small Georgian terraced house, she had discovered a letter hidden inside an old jewellery box. It might have been nothing, but her gut instinct suggested the love letter to her great-great-grandmother was important. Since then, she had devoted hours of her time investigating her ancestry through online websites to trace her family history. But she couldn't comprehend what the love letter meant. It was time to find some professional help, although discretion was vital.

Kathy Jones waved goodbye to the bank manager as he loped off towards the elevator. The bank manager's visit was normal, as he came every six months. However, she knew the business had some cash-flow struggles based on limited conversations with her boss, but she didn't understand to what extent. She would have to ask when the next opportunity arose.

Her thoughts drifted off to the evening. What to watch tonight? She settled on the latest murder box-set she had started at the weekend. She had a real penchant for murder mysteries, with the most infamous one on her doorstep in Whitechapel. Then the following evening, her favourite sport, judo class. Her squat body made her perfectly suited for this type of martial art. She turned her attention back to the computer screen, focussing on her tasks that remained for the day.

Chapter 2

TAPTON, SHEFFIELD

MONDAY

REED HASCOMBE SAT IN his newly kitted out office at home, a four bedroom detached house in Tapton, a suburb of Sheffield, that he and his girlfriend Emily Barrington had moved into a few weeks ago. Since their adventure in Cornwall last summer, they had used their prosperity to upgrade their home. Whilst he had donated some of the money to several charities, he felt they should also benefit from their good fortune. They had spent all of their two-week holiday chasing around the Cornish coastline. He had found a gold medallion hidden inside a pirate's chest, which led them into a search for the lost treasures of a regal legend whilst battling against a local crime lord.

After they had moved house, Reed quit his full-time job as a graphics designer. He had enjoyed the thrill and adventure of searching for hidden treasures so much that going back to his mundane job felt counter-productive. Instead, he launched Sherbet Investigations, a team that specialised in treasure hunting. He launched a website and a presence on the dark web. He devised the name from the initials of the three members of the treasure hunting team: himself, Emily, and his best friend, Euan Spencer, the added 'T' for 'treasure'. Emily continued with her job as a teacher at Sheffield High School, albeit part-time, and Euan still operated his electrical business. This allowed his friend some flexibility when new investigation jobs came in. With a steady stream of investigative work, he was happy, but nothing substantial yet. No lost or buried treasure to locate.

Reed had learned lots of additional skills over the past couple of years, especially about archaeology. He wasn't an expert by any means, but knew the basics. Besides that, both he and Euan were extremely capable rock climbers and had joined a parkour club. They went to meet-ups each week, where they honed their abilities traversing urban landscapes. No city building was out of reach from an onslaught of urban exploration participants, known as urbex's. He finished his online research, rose from the office chair and pushed back his long dark hair behind his ears. He bounded downstairs to get another cup of Columbian coffee and prepared his lunch. A tuna mayo sandwich on granary bread but without cucumber as he hated the limp green mush intensely. Then his phone rang.

"Hi, Sherbet Investigations, how may I help you?"

"Hi, is that Reed?"

"Yes, speaking."

"My name's Madeleine Robinson-Smith, and I need your help."

"Hi Madeleine. What can I help you with?"

"I found an old letter in my grandma's house, which includes a riddle about some hidden treasure. I've read your website and about your two major discoveries, very impressive. So I'm hoping you can help me?"

"Certainly," said Reed. His excitement grew at the mention of hidden treasure, right up his street. "Have you spoken to anyone else about the letter?"

"Only my husband. I did some research into my family history. It suggests the letter is authentic."

"Where are you based?"

"I'm in London. We should set up a meeting. I can show you the letter and we'll discuss the next steps?"

"Sure, when's convenient for you?"

"I need to get moving on this. How does tomorrow sound?"

"I can get there at ten o'clock if that suits you?"

"Let's make it eleven, as I'm blocked out until then. My office is in The Shard. I'll text the address to you shortly. See you tomorrow," said Madeleine. Her authoritative tone was obvious.

"Looking forward to it. Thanks for the call."

Boom, that was what Reed had been waiting for, a juicy treasure case, hopefully the big one he desired. Something to get excited about. He finished his tuna mayo sandwich and checked train times to London from Sheffield. No problem to arrive at eleven, but he needed to get Euan on board. They had been friends since school, when Reed lived with Euan and his parents during the summer holidays after his dad ended up in prison. From that time, they were inseparable and often spent weekends rock climbing in the Peak District. His phone pinged with a text message from Madeleine, which provided the address for the meeting. A quick online check revealed information about his potential client and her company. He had to do some further research, but first he needed to call his mate.

"Euan, we've got a fresh case. Can you come to London with me tomorrow?"

"Of course, mate, I'll reschedule tomorrow's job. What time are we leaving?"

"We can get the seven thirty-four train to St Pancras, which gives us over an hour to reach The Shard."

"That's fine. What's the job about?" asked Euan.

"Madeleine Robinson-Smith is the name of the client. She holds the position of CEO at Robinson's Mining Services. She's found a letter in her grandma's house that contains a riddle about some treasure."

"It could be a hoax."

"That's possible. We should view the letter, then assess the job," said Reed.

"Sounds interesting if it's real."

"Let's hope it is. See you at the train station at a quarter past seven."

"Okay mate, see ya."

Reed didn't mess about. He booked their tickets straightaway and dropped Emily a message, updating her with his plans for the next day. He carried out some further research about his client and noticed some negative financial news about her company after a mine collapsed in Venezuela six months ago. Could that have been what drove her requirement for an immediate meeting? Either way, he felt the excitement grow as he thought about the quest for hidden treasure.

Chapter 3

THE SHARD, LONDON

TUESDAY

REED STOOD OUTSIDE THE Shard and stared upwards. He couldn't see the top of the building as the very tip disappeared into a low hanging cloud. He would have got a cricked neck if he had continued to stare skywards. They had arrived early, with over twenty minutes until the meeting, so they sat at an outside cafe next to western Europe's tallest building. Throngs of people trooped past, headed for London Bridge Station, as another train rattled in departure. Euan came back from the cafe counter with two cups of steaming coffee and a luxury pastry each, and set them down on the grey plastic table with garish bright-green chairs.

"Cheers Euan."

"No problem, boss."

"Stop calling me boss. This is a team thing."

"Someone has to be the boss. You're better at that shit than me. You know, getting people to do stuff for you," said Euan with a grin at his best mate.

As he rolled his eyes, Reed punched Euan on the arm playfully, their bond as strong as ever, a real bromance. He gazed up at the building again, intrigued by the intricate structure with over eleven thousand panes of toughened glass. Impressive, he thought.

"Can you imagine if we tried parkour on this building? How far would we get?" asked Reed.

"Not far. The glass panes look joined."

"The security guys would have a major meltdown well before you reached that first level."

"Probably. Drink up and let's meet our newest client, well hopefully if I can sell our services effectively." Reed fiddled with his hair tie again, his fingers damp with a little nervousness. The idea he had to sell himself to prospective clients didn't come naturally to him.

"You'll smash it!" replied Euan.

They entered the building, checked in with the security team, and Reed punched the button to call the elevator. After they had reached the seventeenth floor, they entered the head office of Robinson Mining Services Ltd. Their client's PA sat outside a large office with floor to ceiling windows.

"Hi, I'm Reed Hascombe from Sherbet Investigations and have an eleven o'clock appointment with Madeleine," said Reed to the inquisitive-looking woman with cropped brown hair.

"Take a seat and I'll check with her," she said and offered them the visitor's waiting chairs. Reed listened to her buzz through to the CEO on the intercom. Then she rose from her chair and beckoned to Reed.

"Follow me. So what's it regarding, Mr Hascombe?"

"Sorry, that's private."

The PA scrunched her face up before opening the door to her boss's office and allowed Reed and Euan to enter.

The waft of a floral perfume drifted towards Reed as he entered the office. His prospective client rose from her chair, smiled, and introduced herself. The professional-looking business woman was immaculately dressed in a royal blue trouser suit, her shoulder-length blonde hair bouncing as she moved. They sat in the plush visitor's chairs facing the extensive windows. He surveyed the sumptuous office with its oak furniture and framed photos of mines plastered across the walls. The view through the office windows was incredible, London's skyline in all its glory. He twisted the silver ring on his finger, keen to plunge into the meeting and secure the job.

"Thanks for coming today on such short notice. How was the trip down?" asked Madeleine.

"No problem. The journey was fine, thanks. You've got an old letter that mentions treasure?"

"Yes. As I said, I found it in my grandmother's attic space inside a jewellery box." Reed waited whilst Madeleine opened one of her desk drawers before laying a plastic zip-lock folder on top. Inside was a yellowed piece of paper that contained a scrawled letter dated 1st December 1888.

'1.12.1888

Dear Beatrice,

I fear I will soon be caught, so now I must declare my undying love for you. The first time I set eyes on your beautiful face, I fell in love, bewitched by your hazel eyes. I wish we could be together, but alas, it's not to be.

I stole something of immense value, and I bequeath it to you, the love of my life. Remember our third night together, the all-consuming passion in our secret place? Go beneath where the bells toll, find the hidden access to the water. Behind the twentieth brick from the ladder, you will find a key to my treasure, just for you.

I regret the bad things I have done, the spilling of much blood. The many women didn't deserve to die, but the mist clouded my thoughts. I must run, as the demons in my head chase me eternally.

Forever yours

X'

Reed passed the folder for Euan to read the letter as Madeleine started her explanation.

"I remember years ago having a conversation with my grandmother, who explained that her grandmother would tell her stories about the man she loved, who had done some evil things. She couldn't remember the name of the man, but said she possessed a love letter written by him. Whilst my grandmother was alive, she never once showed me the letter. After lots of research, I think Jack the Ripper wrote it, whoever he actually was. The last paragraph fits with his modus operandi, and the date aligns with the murder's stopping."

"This could be a clever prank letter, but if it's genuinely written by Jack the Ripper, then there will be tremendous interest ...." he stopped as he realised the PA was standing beside the desk. She held a tray containing coffee and biscuits. He wasn't sure how much Madeleine had shared with her inquisitive PA, but out of courtesy, he stopped until the assistant had left the office.

"Sorry about that," said Madeleine, once her PA was out of earshot. "Kathy's excellent at her job, but she can be nosey."

"That's okay. I didn't know whether she was aware of the letter?"

"I haven't told her. Please continue."

"If the letter's genuine, it'll generate massive interest in the media, so I suggest we keep it under wraps for now. Does anyone else know about it?"

"Only my husband. He's seen the letter."

"My first thought is, have you had it verified?"

"What do you mean, verified?"

"In terms of age. It'll be possible to carbon-date the paper so we'll get that done quickly. You mentioned you've done some family research. Presumably you know who Beatrice is?" Reed said, his earlier nervousness now diminished as he delved into the details.

Madeleine plucked out another sheet of paper from her desk drawer, which showed a family tree, and passed it to Reed.

"She's my great-great grandmother. I found the birth certificate for Beatrice's daughter. It shows she was her mother, but the father's name is blank. It's complicated. You can understand it better from the document."

"So your maiden name was Madeleine Robinson. Your grandmother was Mavis Robinson. Your father is the link between the two of you, Stuart Robinson. Let's take that back another step. Alice Price was your grandmother's mother and the daughter of Beatrice."

Reed sensed Euan was agitating to say something, so he encouraged him with a flick of his hand. "Could Jack the Ripper have been the unnamed father? And are you descended from him?" he asked, running his fingers through his ginger hair.

The puzzled look on Madeleine's face surprised Reed, as she clearly hadn't considered that.

"Oh gosh, that never occurred to me," she replied, twirling a few strands of her blonde hair in her fingers, clearly finding that possibility peculiar.

That response gave Reed a boost, Euan often thought outside the box, considering improbable things that shook up the thinking. He grinned to himself, pleased he had brought Euan with him. The letter intrigued him and he hoped it wasn't a fake, which had originally felt the most likely.

"We'd love to help you. If we assume your theory is correct, then first, we'll verify the age of the paper. Second, identify suspects who might have been Jack the Ripper and thirdly match them with locations based on the contents of the letter. This won't be an easy search. The treasure mentioned might be nothing more than a bracelet he stole from a victim. In my experience, anything particularly valuable always takes a lot of time to find. I may not be an expert on Jack the Ripper, but I believe there was a long list of potential suspects at the time."

"From my research I'd say there are around twenty credible suspects, so I'm under no illusions how difficult this task is," said Madeleine.

"How long have you had the letter?"

"About six months."

"Would you like us to begin the investigation for you?" asked Reed.

"What are your fees?" she asked, as the businesswoman in her switched on.

"We charge one thousand a day plus expenses plus ten per cent of the value of any major discoveries, a finder's fee," said Reed.

"That sounds reasonable. When can you start?"

"Is tomorrow quick enough?"

"Perfect. Send me the contract today and I'll get it signed."

Reed sipped his coffee, grabbed a chocolate cookie and placed their business card on to the table for her. Now they just had to deliver. Pleased with his ability to seal the deal, he took several photos of the letter and the family tree document, then cut a one inch square off the corner of the old letter for the carbon-dating process. He could get the age testing completed in Sheffield and then begin their work. They said their goodbyes, and he promised regular updates to Madeleine before departing the office, eager to catch their train back to Sheffield. Although he had doubts about the true value of any treasure, especially as it surfaced in Victorian times, the client was paying them well.

When she took coffee and biscuits to Madeleine's office, Kathy had heard the words 'Jack the Ripper'. This piqued her interest and once the men had left, she burst into her boss's office, intent on finding out the full details.

"Can I see the letter you were talking about please Madeleine?" she asked.

"It's private, nothing to do with the business."

"I'm what you call a Ripperologist and have written an article on Jack the Ripper, so I'd love to see it."

Madeleine exclaimed, "I didn't know such a thing existed!"

"It's a fascinating case in the world of murder mysteries. I've watched documentaries and read lots of books about him."

She spotted the letter on Madeleine's desk and picked up the plastic wallet to examine it. Her eyes glazed over, her fingers trembled. Oh wow, this is incredible, she thought.

"Can I take a photo?"

"No, it's private, and the investigators told me to keep it under wraps for now," replied her boss, as she took back the plastic wallet and placed it inside the wall safe.

Kathy felt annoyed as she had so badly wanted to share this with her fellow Ripperologists. They would have been over the moon. She retired from the office without another word. The stories of the Victorian serial killer had absorbed her since school, when studying the history of the case. She had thought she would become a detective but failed to meet the requirements for joining the police force. She planned to post about the letter on the Ripperologist blog that evening, even if she couldn't share a photo about it. It would be massively interesting to her fellow bloggers.

Chapter 4

TEN BELLS PUB

TUESDAY

BERNIE JOHNSON STRODE INTO the Ten Bells Pub in Whitechapel, London, five minutes late. He was always five minutes late for the Ripper Guild meetings. He held the key, besides; the secret club of Ripper enthusiasts was his brainchild, and this was a display of his seniority to the others. A buzz of chatter greeted him from the pub's patrons, many just there to sample the wide selection of real ales and elaborate cocktails. The pub owner had kept the Victorian architectural features and added a splash of modern colour and lighting. The pub, spread over three floors, always bustled with a wide demographic of free-spending customers. Tonight was no different. For well over ten years, he had held the meetings at the Ten Bells Pub, a monthly retainer ensuring they had their own private space. Not in the rooms above the ground floor, but below in the cellar area. All under lock and key, his key. Even the landlord didn't have access to their private space, just as well, as he might have changed his mind about the monthly retainer if he knew the sordid reason for their weekly get-togethers.

The other three members sat apart in the busy pub, pretending they didn't know each other. Once Bernie passed through the bar, they would join him, one by one. He wrestled with the padlock on the aged door with one broken hinge, making a mental note to get a new lock. This one had become seriously worn over the years.

He entered the room, about the size of a large bedroom with two brown sofas, and in the corner stood a wooden display unit, their trophy cabinet, with its Ripper memorabilia, displayed proudly. He turned the wall heater up high as his breath created a trail of vapour in the chilly air in the underground hideaway. The cold didn't bother him as he was a tough East End character, having built his own car repair business with a tasty sideline. the Georgian townhouse where he lived with his wife contained his own gym, allowing him to alternate between a rowing machine, cross trainer, or weights for daily exercise. He liked to work hard and keep fit. He had passed his life ethics on to his son, Ryan, who had joined him in the family business. However, as he was at the wrong end of his fifties, his hair couldn't keep up with his active lifestyle and now he elected to keep his head bald with regular shaving. This gave him an air of menace, which he revelled in.

The door opened and in walked an old school colleague, Basil Montague, although Bernie didn't like the bloke. He was too pompous and had grown lazy in his later years. He had to endure the bank manager, though, as his evidence of a family connection to Jack the Ripper was indisputable.

"Bernie, I nearly couldn't make it with such late notice."

"The situation's changed. We need some action."

Bernie watched the overweight bank manager sink into one of the tattered sofas, almost spilling his pint of beer.

"I had to convince the wife I was meeting a client with an emergency cash-flow situation. You know she can be difficult, so I'd appreciate more notice for a meeting next time."

"I told you the situation's changed. We need to act now."

The creak of the door alerted Bernie to another member entering their meeting room. It was Jakub Kosminski. Despite Jakub's sullen demeanour, he still liked him and often relied on him for situations that required extra muscle. Although the lad worked as a barber, he kept fit by working out at the gym. He changed his hairstyle often, always with a shaved section. Bernie knew Jakub had a history of violence, as the police had arrested him twice for grievous bodily harm. Being of similar age to his son Ryan, he had a good bond with the Polish descendant.

"Jakub, take a seat."

"What's all the rush?"

"The situation's changed."

"How?" said Jakub as he rubbed his hand over his head, which displayed a snake tattoo weaving its way through his hair.

"Let's wait until Sophia gets here."

Bernie sipped his beer, placing it on the edge of the wooden display unit and admired his favourite item in there. A silver ring with an encrusted obsidian jewel purported to have belonged to Jack the Ripper. His father had told him of their family link to one suspect and the folklore that Jack had also stolen important jewellery, but history books omitted this information. He was so convinced by the folklore he had started the secret guild, which functioned with the purpose of finding treasure that Jack had hidden across the East End. Whatever that was. When Bernie started the Guild, membership was only possible with irrefutable evidence of a family link to a suspect who could have been Jack. The door burst open.

"Geez guys, it's freezing in here. Why didn't you warm it up earlier, Bernie?" said Sophia Meyer as she bundled in and sat down next to Basil.

"I didn't have time! Perhaps you should have worn more clothes," responded Bernie, glancing at her choice of clothing: thin leggings, converse boots, and a tiny black leather jacket over a top. He couldn't help but admit she was pretty, and she had worked her magic. She had moved to London six months ago from Berlin and landed a job as a social media manager at an art gallery. Apparently, she had become obsessed with Jack the Ripper in her teens, after her grandmother had told her about their family history.

Sophia was the newest member of the Guild, which had yielded a substantial bonus, as she worked for Richard Smith, Madeleine Robinson-Smith's husband.

"But if I didn't look a bit sexy, then Richard wouldn't fancy me and we wouldn't know about Jack's letter, now would we, Bernie?"

"But you still haven't discovered the contents of the letter yet, have you?"

"I'm working on it. There's an art exhibition at the weekend and I'm planning on chatting with Madeleine."

"Too late for that now."

"Why?" interjected Jakub.

Bernie stood against the display cabinet, blocking the glazed section, as the other three eyed him from their positions on the tattered brown sofas that used to be in his living room ten years ago.

"Madeleine's PA posted in one of the blog's we track. She's seen the letter, so I messaged her directly, and she blabbed everything. She told me the letter referenced treasure, and that Madeleine has now recruited a team to find it. Your seduction route is out of the window, Sophia. We need to take action now."

"I said that a few weeks ago. I've had enough of that old bloke drooling over me with his stinky breath and lank grey hair," retorted Sophia, flicking her long blonde hair forward, catching Basil in the face. The bank manager didn't seem to care and beckoned Bernie to continue.

"We're aware she keeps the letter in her office safe. That's what Richard said, Sophia?"

"That's what she told him. He was unimpressed. He couldn't see why she didn't bring it home," said Sophia in response to Bernie's question as she zipped up her jacket.

"Right, we'll need to break in and blow the safe. Did she say anything yesterday about the letter Basil?"

"No nothing. The business needs extra cash, which I refused totally. I could have lent her more money, but after our discussion last week, putting the squeeze on would be more productive for us. It looks as though that's worked."

"Not really, because we still haven't learnt the contents of the letter!" said Bernie as he snapped at Basil, such a pompous idiot full of his own self-importance.

Jakub shifted in his seat again before he asked, "when do we break in?"

Bernie smiled to himself. The Polish lad always wanted to get involved in any action, "I'm thinking Thursday evening. It'll be you, Ryan and Mikey whilst Davey tracks down this investigation team she's recruited. We'll need some explosives, sort that for me, Jakub. I'll talk to the lads first, then text you with the arrangements."

"What do I do?" asked Sophia.

"Nothing yet. Carry on with your plan and we'll see what happens on Thursday. Once we have the letter, you can cool it with the husband."

Sophia nodded her approval as Bernie took another mouthful of beer, keen to wrap up the meeting.

"We don't know if the treasure is actually worth anything, it could be just a silver bracelet. But if the letter yields anything valuable, we'll divide up the proceeds four ways, unless we identify Jack the Ripper. If he's from one of our families, then that person gets half. All clear?" said Bernie.

The other three confirmed their agreement. They had decided on the plan of action. Time then to put it in place. For Bernie, this opportunity had been a lengthy wait, nearly forty years after he had established the Ripper Guild. Now he planned to take full advantage, even if it meant back-stabbing his fellow members.

Chapter 5

YORK LAB

WEDNESDAY

To run SHERBET INVESTIGATIONS, Reed required a suite of contacts with special skills. With some help from the artifact dealer in Cornwall, Alistair Edgeworth, who he had met last summer, he had compiled a list of professionals that he could call upon. Among these was a lab equipped for carbon dating. Which is exactly what Professor Johnny Beckett supplied from his laboratory in York. After returning from London the day before, Reed had scheduled to meet the Professor in order to get the age of the letter established. The case would fall flat on its face straightaway if the paper wasn't at least one hundred and fifty years old.

Reed arrived at the reception to the laboratory, unsurprised by the sterile appearance of the space. It was akin to a new hospital, but with the clutter removed. He checked in with the young receptionist and waited for the professor to collect him. His thoughts turned to his client as he pondered her motive for paying him to investigate the letter. She appeared to have money, but was the company in financial trouble? The family tree she had provided was extensive and must have taken months to compile. At the beginning, maybe it was just curiosity that drove Madeleine to delve into her family's past. Now she had verified the addressee of the letter, perhaps it had become a genuine interest. Anyone would get excited with potential treasure at stake, he mused. It was possible the treasure mentioned in the letter could be worthless, but the client was paying him to discover the truth. A tall, smartly dressed man in a blue pinstripe suit approached him and interrupted his thoughts.

"Reed, pleased to meet you. I'm Johnny Beckett."

He had never met Johnny, just seen a nondescript headshot on the laboratory's website, but recognised him from that. Reed put out his hand as the professor shook it.

"Hi Johnny, thanks for seeing me today."

"You're welcome. I'm happy to help any friend of Alistair's," said the professor. "Follow me and we'll get started."

The professor strode off into a clean, empty corridor. Reed struggled to keep pace with the professor, whose long legs glided effortlessly across the grey vinyl floor. They turned immediately left, then right, before he gestured to Reed to enter an office directly in front of them.

"Take a seat. We need to get the paperwork sorted before I set the machine running," said the professor.

"Thanks."

Reed watched the professor pull out a form and start writing. After he had answered all the questions, the professor jumped up and beckoned Reed to follow him again. This was like a follow my leader game, hustling around corridors that looked identical. How did the professor remember his way around this rabbit warren? They arrived at a wide glass window overlooking a room that contained an impressive-looking machine. The professor unlocked the door and ushered Reed inside.

"Have you got the sample, please?" he asked Reed.

"Sure," replied Reed. He pulled out the small plastic pouch that contained the small square fragment of paper from the letter and passed it to the professor, who placed it onto a slide in the machine's body. It didn't take long for the machine to whirr into action after the professor tapped on the touch-panel control screen.

"Let's leave it running and grab a coffee in the canteen. It takes about thirty minutes. You can tell me all about your adventures with Alistair," said the professor as he locked the carbon-dating machine room door.

Reed chased after the speedy professor as he strode purposefully around more empty corridors akin to one of those mice runs seen in lab experiments before reaching the canteen.

"What can I get you Reed?"

"Strong coffee, milk, no sugar, please."

"Is that a latte or cappuccino? Our machine does fancy coffees?" asked the professor.

"Cappuccino please."

As the coffee machine spluttered and bashed out two cappuccinos, Reed glanced around the canteen. Just like a large, clean corridor with metal tables and chairs, he thought. The professor selected a table in the middle of the canteen and nodded a greeting to a white-coated lab technician sat nearby.

"Alistair was very complimentary about you. He referred to you as a young Indiana Jones, but without the whip," said the professor, laughing at his own joke.

"That's too kind of him. I seem to have a knack for finding treasure."

"Your find in Cornwall impressed him. What's special about this letter?"

Reed paused as he remembered that client confidentiality was now a key part of his business. "Oh, a client discovered a letter addressed to her great-great grandmother. She wants to check if it's real."

"Pretty boring stuff then."

"Nothing to get excited about," he said, feeling uncomfortable with the white lie.

"Give me the lowdown on last summer's adventure. Alistair didn't have time to divulge the details when we spoke, although he was pretty excited about it."

Reed used the chance to avoid more questions about the letter. He presented Professor Beckett with a full account of their Cornish adventure. The discussion led to his Peak District adventure the year before. Then the professor's wristwatch beeped.

"Perfect, the machine should have finished the process," said the professor as he pressed the alarm off button on his wristwatch. "Let's go."

And so another rush around the warren of white and grey tunnels, masquerading as corridors, started. The machine had indeed finished its task and spewed out several reams of paper. The professor snatched up the sheets and scanned them before he focused on the key point.

"There we go Reed. The age of the wood used to make the paper is between eighteen-fifty and nineteen-hundred. We provide a range of dates, as there are many factors that affect the aging process. I won't bore you with the details. So the letter is Victorian."

"Brilliant. Thanks Johnny. I appreciate your help."

"No problem. I'm here whenever you need any of our services. Keep these printouts. It's your authentication. I'll get an invoice emailed across in the next couple of days."

"Fantastic."

"I'll show you back to reception. I can't let you wander around on your own. You might get lost," laughed the professor as he shot off down the corridor with Reed hustling behind. They shook hands at the reception and said their goodbyes.

Reed jumped into his waiting red VW campervan, perfectly kitted out for weekends away adventuring. He had constructed the interior himself with its double bed, two ring stove, and minute washbasin. There was plenty of suitable storage space and a travel safe bolted to the chassis of the vehicle. He made a quick call to Euan, letting him know the results, then dialled Madeleine's number. She picked up straightaway.

"Hello Reed."

"Hi Madeleine. We carbon-dated the paper and verified that it's Victorian. I just wanted to keep you up to date with developments."

"Excellent. What's your next step?"

"We have a full day scheduled tomorrow to review suspects and formulate a strategy. I'm hoping we can get to London on Friday to begin the investigation on the ground. I'll call you late afternoon, early evening."

"Okay, thanks. We'll speak tomorrow."

"Bye," said Reed as the line went dead. She was very business-like, although a little cold, he thought. He pushed the key into the vehicle's ignition, turned over the engine, and headed back to Sheffield, pleased with the carbon-dating results. It meant they had at least two weeks of well-paid work ahead with the possibility of hidden treasure being involved again.

Chapter 6

HOXTON CAR REPAIR SHOP
WEDNESDAY

BERNIE SAT AT HIS battered desk in the practical office of his business, on the mezzanine floor of the car repair shop in Hoxton. He had run the business for over twenty years since his dad had passed control over to him. Soon Ryan, his son, would take over the reins, but the lad still had important stuff to learn. The next few days presented an excellent test for him. Overnight a new order had come in, a BMW M sports car in Calypso Red to the Czech Republic. The colour didn't matter, that was all part of the scam. They would find a car for sale, steal it and then respray it at the repair shop. The real reason he had purchased one of the new-fangled automatic paint sprayers several years ago, which sat in the flat-roof building in the unit's backyard. All they had to do was mask off the wheels, windows, and trim properly, as the machine sprayed the cars in two hours normally. A great sideline that generated substantial cash. He confirmed receipt of the deposit payment and printed the details. Time to summon the team.

As he rose from his chair, the overhead strip light flickered again. This annoyed him, so made a mental note to fix it later. He banged on the glass window that overlooked the two-bay workshop area below, but with the radio blaring out, the lads didn't hear it. Instead, Bernie wrenched open the door, the glass rattling in the frame, and leaned over the steel balustrade at the top of the metal stairs.

"Lads, I need you all in the office. Close the shutters," he shouted over the noise of the radio and the electric wrench as one lad removed stubborn wheel nuts from a customer's car below.

Bernie slipped back inside the office and waited for them. He employed all three lads in his legitimate business, but his car thief gang, the Hoxton Hot Rods, only operated on the dark web. He had chosen the name as it linked to the family history from Victorian times when his great-great-grandfather belonged to the Hoxton High Rips, a well-known street gang.

The team comprised his son Ryan, who brimmed with self-assured, boyish charm and optimism, a key member of the group, always bouncing through life. One of Ryan's interest was Urbex, where his son met up with mates to investigate derelict buildings in London. He had never understood the attraction. Then Mikey Chandler, all muscles and East End chat who indulged in backstreet bare-knuckle fight clubs. The lad adored boxing and would spend his earnings on fight nights, of which there were plenty in London. And finally, Davey Warren, better known as Mouse because of diminutive stature and a nasal twitch, like a little rodent sniffing out food. He had become vital to Bernie's plans, having the technology skills to set up a website on the dark web and keep it secret from the authorities. The lad had also helped him with Ripper information gathering, tracked leads and monitored blogs for anything of interest. He kept Davey fully motivated with discrete cash payments from time to time.

The door burst open, disturbing Bernie's thoughts as Mikey entered with his dark blue overalls tied at his waist. Any opportunity to flash his muscles, he thought. He waited until the other two had arrived before he started.

"Right, lads, a few busy days ahead. We've a new order come in for a BMW M in Calypso Red. Mouse, stay in the office and find one up for sale. You'll each get the normal ten per cent of the sale price, so I assume you can all manage a collection tonight?"

"I'm supposed to be meeting the missus tonight. Can we make it tomorrow?" asked Mikey.

"No. I have another job for tomorrow evening."

"Two cars in one week?" asked Ryan.

"No. I need you to break into an office to retrieve an important letter. It may involve blowing a safe."

"Geez dad, that's hard core."

Bernie hesitated before replying. He knew his next words wouldn't go down too well with his son, although they were all familiar with the Ripper's Guild's past.

"I haven't mentioned this before, but someone has discovered a letter written by Jack the Ripper and I've been trying to obtain it. Unfortunately, it's become public knowledge and I need to get it quick. This is the plan. Mouse, I want you to get hold of the schematics of The Shard, specifically the seventeenth floor where Robinson Mining is located. The safe is inside the CEO's office, a Madeleine Robinson-Smith. Ryan and Mikey, you'll meet up with Jakub and carry out the raid. Break in, blow the safe if necessary, and bring me the letter."

Ryan rolled his eyes as he faced his father. "Not bloody Jakub, he's off his head. I can't work with him."

"You'll have to. He's in on it. I'll speak to him beforehand, rein him in."

"On the previous job, he nutted some guy for no reason and smashed another geezer with a crowbar. He's got no control, he just goes mental."

"I know, but it's better he's on our side," said Bernie as his son shook his head.

"What shall I say to my missus if I'm out two nights on the trot?" asked Mikey.

"Say something plausible, Mikey. Both things need to happen. Just sort it!" Bernie's agitation spilled over with the complaints. What was a matter with them? He turned to Davey. "I also need you to research artifact investigators and treasure hunters. A group is apparently working on behalf of the CEO woman, searching for a hidden treasure that belonged to Jack the Ripper mentioned in the letter. Stay in the office until you've completed both."

Davey nodded at his boss and settled at the spare desk, pulling out his laptop from his backpack.

"So me and Mikey have to do all the work between us?" whinged Ryan.

"Geez, Ryan, would you quit your moaning and just get on with it? I'll come down and help soon. Can't have you youngsters work too hard, can we? Right, let's crack on."

Whilst the other two wandered off downstairs, Bernie stood beside Davey as he passed on his requirements for the list of tasks he had set for the tech lad. He planned to scout out The Shard tonight while the others stole a vehicle for the order. He could analyse the security and do a reconnaissance trip on floor seventeen if he went before the end of office hours. The letter was vital. He felt it in his bones.

Chapter 7

SHEFFIELD

WEDNESDAY

EUAN HAD SPOKEN TO Reed earlier, who confirmed the letter was from the Victorian era, meaning they had a meaty case on their hands. He completed the rescheduled electrical job by lunchtime and hurried home to get on with his next important task. To finish the drone upgrade. He was a self-employed electrician who loved to build electronic devices in his spare time. His favourite and most effective design was a drone with a high definition camera. It had helped them on their two previous adventures in the Peak District and Cornwall. He had also designed an unmanned ground vehicle capable of firing mini bolts and plumes of smoke for distraction. But today it was the drone that needed an upgrade.

Six months after his breakup with Lynsey Dewhurst, he was in a much better place mentally. He felt back to his normal bubbly self. She clearly wasn't right for him. Perhaps he had forced the relationship too much. That was history, time to look forward. Sat at the workbench in his sparse second bedroom, he fiddled with another wire as he connected an upgraded camera to the base of the drone. This one had infrared and thermal image capabilities, the former being restricted to just five yards. Coupled with the thirty times zoom function, Euan's upgraded drone gave them the perfect surveillance machine for all situations. After he had connected the final wire, he slotted the camera into place on the metal base of the drone. Darkness had descended whilst he had been busy tinkering with the machine, but that gave him the perfect conditions in which to test it.

Euan wandered downstairs with the drone and walked into his basic kitchen with blue cupboards to grab something to eat. His two bed terraced house provided a haven, his bachelor pad. He rarely entertained any female company, but had several dates with the pretty blonde daughter of an important customer last month, but the relationship had fizzled out. It didn't matter; he had enough other interests to keep him busy, although during the winter Reed and he wouldn't venture out to the Peak District rock climbing, as it could be quite dangerous in the rain or with ice around.

Reed was like a brother to him. They had been very close since the age of twelve, when Reed lived with his family during the summer whilst his best friend was homeless, which cemented their friendship. They had lived together in a rented terrace house in their early twenties for several years before Reed moved in with Emily. He loved the time spent with Reed rock-climbing in the Peak District, the highlight of any week. Theirs was a bromance with years of real depth to it. They had known each other for over fifteen years, and being part of Sherbet Investigations meant they spent plenty of time together.

He finished the last slice of cold pepperoni pizza he had saved in the near-bare fridge before slipping outside in his warm climbing jacket. The earthy scent of the recent rain increased as he approached the green space close to his house. Once inside the park area, Euan fired up the drone and sent it skyward. The drone rose above the oak trees that fringed the park, as a lone runner burst past Euan on the tarmac pathway. He activated the thermal imaging, which worked a treat, pinpointing people out walking their dogs. He zoomed in on an individual, using the infrared option, which provided a focused image. That all worked fine. He sat on the weathered wooden park bench and plucked out his phone before calling his best friend.

"Aye up mate."

"I've sorted the drone. The thermal imaging works well, although the infrared function is patchy beyond five yards."

"That's amazing!"

Euan smiled to himself. Reed's praise always made him happy inside. He looked up to his friend, so any compliments meant a lot to him. "Thanks. I'll bring it over tomorrow and show you."

"Brilliant. Come over for eight, Em said she'll cook us breakfast, then we can crack on with looking at the suspects," said Reed.

"Sounds perfect. I'll see you tomorrow."

A cat screeched behind him as he gripped the drone and strolled back to his house, avoiding the bulldog straining at its leash as he passed another dog walker. Happy with his day's work, his thoughts turned to the Victorian letter. How were they going to decipher which suspect was Jack the Ripper?

Chapter 8

DULWICH

WEDNESDAY

Ryan Johnson had called the car owner earlier, arranging to view the BMW M sports car for sale, priced at forty thousand pounds. Although Ryan planned to get it for free. He had used a burner phone to call the man and given a false name. Mikey Chandler sat beside him in their battered white work van with two black balaclavas in hand and a Bowie knife at his side. The tools of their trade. He fidgeted in his seat, glanced at his watch, and decided it was time to make a move. He had parked two blocks away to reduce the risk of tracing their illegal activity. They left the vehicle, locked it, and Ryan passed the keys to Mikey as he would drive the stolen vehicle back to the car repair shop. The lads checked for pedestrians or dog walkers as they approached the house, but being winter and close to eight o'clock in the evening, no-one passed them on the way. Both wore baseball caps, so it would have proved difficult to identify them.

"There's number sixty-seven and the car's in the driveway," said Ryan as he pointed to the large house ahead of them. The district was typical of a wealthy leafy London borough, detached houses and expensive cars. The street lights lit up the pavements, the light circle of each one just touched the next, similar to a theatre stage.

"I can squat behind that grey van, then you lure him to the front of the car so I can jump him."

"Brilliant plan," said Ryan as he ambled up the driveway, casting a glance at the BMW.

As Ryan approached the house, a sensor light switched on with his approaching movement. He pulled his baseball cap down further just in case there was a CCTV camera on the wall. He pressed the white doorbell. A chime rang inside the house as he waited for the car owner to appear. Seconds later, the man answered the door.

"Hi, you've come about the sports car?" the man asked. His clean-shaven face contrasted with his slightly podgy appearance in a stained black sweatshirt.

"Sure have," said Ryan. He often used a poor American accent on heist jobs. All part of the ploy to disguise himself.

"You're American?" asked the podgy man.

"Sure am. I moved over two months ago. I absolutely love England. But I need some smart wheels."

"We can take the car for a test drive."

"That sounds great, man. I've scanned it. The car looks super."

The man shuffled out of the door in his green crocs, pulled it shut and jangled the keys. Ryan then pretended to scrutinise the vehicle, inspecting the wheels before he made his way round to the front of the car. He bent over, used the torch function on his mobile phone and rubbed a finger over the bonnet.

"Hey man, look at this. There are some scratches."

The podgy man wandered over to Ryan, facing the house. He looked at the area of paintwork Ryan pointed out.

"You're going to get the odd stone chip mark. It happens to all cars."

"I need a reduction in the price. I can't be spending more money repairing it if I'm paying full whack. Can we say two thousand off?"

"That's way too much, I'm thinking five ....."

The man stopped speaking as a hand snaked around his neck and held a sharp knife to his throat.

"What's going on?"

"Give me the keys," said Mikey in a deep, gruff voice, his balaclava pulled over his face.

Ryan acted his part in the scenario, pretending to not be involved.

"Whoa man, what the fuck are you doing? I'm oughta here," he said and ran past Mikey before hiding behind the grey van. He watched Mikey grab the keys, who then battered the man until he was unconscious. Between them, they dragged the podgy man out of sight, into the evergreen bushes at the side of his lawn.

Ryan took the keys, tugged on his balaclava and jumped in the sports car, gunning the engine as Mikey ran off back to their van. Speed was of the essence, as he had to secure the vehicle inside the Hoxton Hot Rods lock-up before the man or his family called the police. He had twenty minutes at the most. He drove fast on the estate roads with no traffic or onlookers and stuck to the speed limit on the main roads. The car drove beautifully, sliding round tight corners before he accelerated out of them. When he was half a mile away from the car repair shop, he heard some sirens. He saw flashing blue lights in his mirror in the distance. Could it be the police searching for him?

They always had to follow the same route into the car repair shop to avoid the ANPR cameras scanning the main roads. He whizzed round the corner onto the unmonitored route and sped up on a straight section. The lights had spooked him and he didn't notice a bearded man eating a kebab underneath a lamppost until too late, as he raced past doing fifty in a thirty zone.

His heart raced as he braked hard for the approaching junction. The braking felt troublesome as the car veered slightly to the right. That had to be corrected before shipping the stolen vehicle abroad. He whipped the car round the next junction and took a sharp turn towards the car repair shop. He drove it right up to the roller shutter doors of the paint shop building, where they hid the stolen cars ready to paint. The sirens were still audible but sounded further away, he thought, whilst waiting for the door to complete its ascent.

His pulse slowed as he sat in the leather driver's seat, running his hands round the steering wheel and taking gulps of air to calm himself. It was the most stressful heist yet. He recalled the man eating the kebab, hopefully he wouldn't remember the speeding sports car.

Chapter 9

Sheffield

Thursday

Emily had prepared a cooked breakfast for the three of them before furnishing both Reed and Euan with a list of Jack the Ripper suspects. She had created the list the previous evening after reviewing many Ripper websites. With twenty odd names to delve deeper into, they set aside four hours until lunchtime to carry out the research. Each of them would then choose their two most likely candidates, giving them six suspects to investigate. Since their adventures last summer, Emily had changed her hours to part time in her history teaching job. This allowed her to help Reed with Sherbet Investigations as she enjoyed the puzzle-solving element of the work. With a real flair for bringing clarity to the location conundrums, she was a vital part of the team. She nudged her wavy brown hair back behind her ears and focussed on the suspect she was assessing.

Two hours later, Emily rose from her chair and stretched for a bit, easing the cramp in her calf, sustained during her karate class recently. She had now moved up to red-belt grading, about halfway towards the ultimate master's black belt. Two years ago, she just wished to improve her self-defence skills, but enjoyed it so much, she carried on training. She and Reed had lived together for several years and loved every second of their relationship, although he hadn't popped the question yet. That was okay, though, as she felt a sense of contentment, knowing they were both happy. She sat back down, examined her list, crossed out another name, and moved on to the next one.

Emily completed her research and rose to prepare some sandwiches for the three of them. They had conversed little during the morning, all focussed on getting the research complete, as they needed to leave by three o'clock to get to London. Reed had booked them into the New Road Hotel, mainly because it was close to the area they would work in and also because he and Euan planned to join a parkour event happening on Saturday morning at the hotel. She wandered through to the kitchen of their detached four-bedroom house with its glossy grey cupboards and integrated appliances. She looked in the fridge, then the cupboards, and with little choice, she made tuna mayo and cucumber sandwiches, although Reed's was minus the cucumber. He hated cucumber and called it the slug of the plant world. Several years ago, he had food poisoning from a sandwich purchased at a railway station. He believed the limp cucumber was rotten because it felt slimy in his mouth.

"Lunch is ready," Emily shouted upstairs to the two lads ensconced in the office. Within seconds, the bounce of feet on the stairs showed Euan was on his way down. He enjoyed his food, especially pizza.

"Awesome, Em, what have we got?" asked Euan.

"Just tuna mayo sandwiches."

"Oh. I was hoping it might be pizza."

"You ate a cooked breakfast. Surely you can't want more fattening food."

"I'm a growing lad!"

"I doubt you'll be growing anymore. Where's Reed?"

"Just finishing up. He said he'll be down in five minutes."

"How did your research go?"

"I've got two prime suspects," Euan said with a smirk on his face.

Emily rolled her eyes.

"Okay, let's eat lunch. Afterwards, we can discuss our findings."

Reed appeared, gave Emily a quick peck on the cheek and the three members of Sherbet Investigations tucked into their tuna sandwiches, no cucumber, with a packet of prawn cocktail crisps. They washed it all down with another cup of Columbian coffee. Emily gestured to the other two to join her in the lounge, relaxing into the corner of the green mottled L-shaped sofa. She grabbed her list, notes, and had a pen at the ready.

"I'll start. My first suggestion is Francis Tumblety. He was an American and police had arrested him twice as a Ripper suspect, but released him each time. He worked as a doctor at Royal London Hospital, so had access to surgical knives. There were rumours he offered women's body parts to the black market, but that appears to be unfounded," Emily said, before taking a breather for the others to digest her comments.

"My second suspect is Aaron Kosminski, a Russian born Jew who defected to Poland before coming to London. The DNA found on the shawl of the fourth murder victim points to him as the most likely Jack the Ripper suspect, and several key websites highlight this. He worked at a barbershop, so had access to razors and frequented the Ten Bells Pub on Commercial Road. People knew this as *The Jack the Ripper Pub* and has strong links to the women murdered."

"He sounds more likely than the doctor," said Reed.

"Yes, he's my number one," she said. "Did you want to go next?"

"My first suspect is Walter Sickert, a German artist whose DNA was on two letters supposedly written by Jack the Ripper. Also, Patricia Cornwell has written a convincing book about him being the killer. She maintains his paintings contained clues. He had painted St Paul's Cathedral Crypt, All Hallows by the Tower and, more importantly, Jack the Ripper's bedroom. He has to be considered, but the paintings appear a little too convenient compared to my second suspect."

"Who's your second suspect?" asked Emily.

"Thomas Cutbush. He's English, worked as a clerk and was also part of the Hoxton High Rips street gang. Apparently, they kicked him out when he displayed signs of mental illness. Some years later, authorities detained him in Lambeth Infirmary. But he escaped and later attacked two women. The Sun newspaper subsequently named him the prime suspect. A senior Metropolitan Police officer went to great lengths to deny this, claiming there were other suspects. When you consider Cutbush had an uncle who was also a superintendent in the Metropolitan Police force, it seems like a bluff to protect themselves. He eventually died in Broadmoor a few years later. I think he's more likely than the artist."

"Yes, I agree," said Euan.

"We have Cutbush and Kosminski so far. What are yours, Euan?" asked Emily.

"My least likely is Montague John Druitt, an English barrister and part-time teacher. He's listed as a suspect because he drowned in the River Thames early December in eighteen eighty-eight. Authorities recorded it as a suicide, and no further murders followed his death. Investigators found a suspiciously large amount of cash on him. There doesn't appear to be any other information linking him to the murders. I think he's the least likely out of the suspects we've considered so far."

"Totally agree. And your second one?"

"I'm quite excited about this one. If you can be excited about serial killers. His name is James Maybrick, an English cotton trader who also worked at the Whitechapel Bell Foundry. He's supposed to have kept a diary detailing all the murders and, apparently, in his handwriting. He travelled between Liverpool and London regularly and also had several affairs. A few years previous, he had lived in America at the time of the Servant Girl Annihilator case. The perpetrator murdered eight people over a two-year period.

Although this seems a stretch to relate him to that case. He also owned a Victorian watch engraved with the words *'I am Jack, J. Maybrick',* complete with the initials of the five women murdered. What do you think?"

"I think the diary and the watch make him our initial target," said Reed, then checked the photo of the letter on his phone and added, "plus he has links to bells, which is a clue in the letter. If we can gain a copy of Maybrick's diary, we can compare the handwriting with the letter."

Emily shuffled in her seat, tucking her hair behind her ears. "I agree, Maybrick first, then either Cutbush or Kosminski afterwards. Okay, let's assemble our gear and set-off to the big smoke," she said, checking the time.

The three of them trundled off and loaded up Reed's VW Campervan with small suitcases, climbing gear, and Euan's drone. Emily felt a buzz of excitement fizzing away inside her. She enjoyed their adventures, even if this case had a sinister edge in the backstory. However, that belonged to the past, didn't it?

Chapter 10

WHITECHAPEL

THURSDAY

NEWS OF THE JACK the Ripper letter had steered the person's thoughts down a particular path. They always knew about their ancestor's dark deeds, but could they have been the serial killer? The feelings from years previous surged forward, but could they go one step further? Evoke fear in another human being and then execute the most severe attack? The sight of a shaking body, the stench of human sweat, and the chilling sensation of power coursing through their veins.

The sun dipped over the horizon, the slither of orange light slipping away, bringing darkness to the city, even though it was barely four o'clock. A major downside of living in a northern hemisphere country at this time of year. The upside for unscrupulous people, darkness, masked their illegal acts, like the sale of drugs or the killing of an unlucky person. As the night descended upon London, it transformed into a maze of shadows and secrets. A city where danger lurked in every hidden corner, mingled with a deep sense of unease.

The person peered from the window in the room's shadow and cast a glance at a single man walking along the pavement. The blade was sharp and drew blood as the person ran it along their thumb, checking its suitability. Was tonight the time?

Cut-outs of Jack the Ripper stories lay buried in their hidden scrapbook. A table of names scribbled on the inside cover, but the only one that mattered topped the list. Their relative from Victorian times. The hint of treasure in the letter focused their thoughts. They would steal it once discovered; after all, it belonged to their ancestor. Let the investigators do the hard work.

They wandered into the back of the building, grabbed the bottle of liquor from the nearby workbench, and swigged back another mouthful. The fire of the premium vodka burnt their throat as an incense candle flickered in the corner.

All their preparations had led to this point in their life. As the would-be killer stood at the threshold of their evil exploits, the sight of their meticulously prepared tools lain on the workbench evoked a mix of anticipation and nervousness. The unsaid thoughts hung in the air and mingled with the rusty aroma of freshly drawn blood. A rush of emotions surged through their veins, a potent cocktail of justice, determination, and a touch of pleasure. But tonight wasn't the night. Maybe tomorrow would be?

Chapter 11

The Shard, London

Thursday

THE GLOOMY WINTER'S NIGHT settled in about two hours ago as Madeleine reviewed her email inbox. Just one more response to send before going home, although to an empty house. She had called Richard three times in the past hour, but he wasn't answering. He must be busy organising the last displays for Saturday's art exhibition, which he expected her to attend, even though she hated the casual chit-chat with airy-fairy arty types. They could waffle on for hours about a proverbial stain on a piece of cloth and how it exploded their minds with creativity. She struggled with anything that wasn't business focused. The thought of stains reminded her of Basil Montague, her bank manager, who would be in attendance. No doubt he would prattle on about wine and drill her about the business. She desperately needed a solution for the cash flow problem.

That last thought revolved around her mind and prompted an immediate internet search for emergency business loans. Two new options had appeared. An invoice discounter and a third tier business loan provider. After further investigation, she decided that both were viable options, albeit expensive. She cobbled together some notes and contact numbers, ready to phone them in the morning. As Madeleine rose from her plush leather chair, she glimpsed her reflection in the window as London's nightlights twinkled far below her office. She looked tired and slightly gaunt, but at least she still looked presentable. Then her phone rang. She glanced at the display, expecting it to be Richard calling her back. Instead, it was the one glimmer of hope on the darkening horizon. Reed Hascombe.

"Reed, hopefully you have some good news for me?" she asked.

"Hi Madeleine. We've arrived at our hotel in London, the New Road Hotel in Whitechapel. We're making some progress and have six suspects to examine."

"Which ones?" Madeleine said, being well informed on the list of Jack the Ripper suspects, having spent some time analysing them herself.

"The first one we're looking at tomorrow is James Maybrick."

"Why Maybrick first?"

"Several reasons. He supposedly kept a diary that detailed the murders, so we're hoping to gain a copy to check the handwriting against the letter. He also had a watch with his name engraved on it, saying he was Jack, plus the initials of five women murdered. The last important connection, he worked at Whitechapel Bell Foundry. This links with the letter, so we're planning to investigate the place tomorrow."

"Isn't that a derelict building?"

"Yes, but that's not a problem."

"Don't get caught trespassing."

"Don't worry, we won't."

"Call me tomorrow if you find anything."

"I will do, bye."

Madeleine placed her mobile phone on the oak desk and stared out of the office. The floor to ceiling window offered a generous view of London, stretching for many miles. The sprawling cityscape, with its iconic landmarks, the London Eye and Big Ben, dazzled in the distance. Standing by the window, a sense of awe washed over her with the vastness and energy of the capital city laid out before her. It stirred a sense of wonder tinged with concern. She thought about the letter in the safe and considered the comment about treasure. It was highly unlikely, it could just be a silver ring, but she had to hope. She glanced at her phone, almost six thirty. She called Richard for the fourth time. Voicemail once more. The suppressed thoughts raised their ugly head again. He couldn't be that busy. She had felt for several weeks he was a little distant from her and wondered if he was having an affair with Sophia, his new social media assistant. Madeleine had met her once, beautiful and confident with her swirling blonde hair. She rebuked herself and planned on an Indian takeaway for the both of them, intending to collect it on her way home. She gathered up her handbag and phone just as a movement at the other end of the office caught her eye. Who was that?

She slipped out of the office and turned to lock it. But seemingly out of nowhere, three men appeared wearing black balaclavas and carried knives.

"Get on the floor!"

Madeleine's heart raced as she dropped to the grey carpet, clutching her phone, and frantically tried to open it one-handed to make an emergency services call. The man in charge spotted her action and swooped down to claim the phone.

"What's your name? Why are you still in the office?" he said, breathing into her ear.

Panic rose in her gut as the thought of being kidnapped ran through her concerned mind. "Kathy. Kathy Jones," she said.

"Pleased to meet you, Kathy Jones," laughed the man. "What're you doing in the boss's office?"

"She told me to stay late and finish an important email. I'm her secretary," babbled Madeleine.

"She must pay you well, Kathy. This suit of yours is Saville Row," said the man, flicking over the lapel to peer inquisitively at the powder blue jacket's label. He pulled out his phone, tapped away and a few seconds later presented her with an image of herself.

"Amazing what the internet can reveal, isn't it Madeleine?" he stated. "Let's start again, get up."

Madeleine's fears of being kidnapped had become real as the man in charge guided her into her own office, pointing to the guests' chairs. He positioned himself across the other side of her lavish desk in her leather chair, whilst one man patrolled the office door. The other searched the display unit. Perspiration formed on her forehead as she considered the circumstances. She would have been home if only Richard had answered earlier. Wasn't it ironic that his preoccupation with his attractive assistant might have caused her kidnapping? She noticed the man at the desk rifling through her drawers. Perhaps they were just thieves?

"Where's the safe?" he asked.

They are thieves, after all. A bit of clarity came to her mind, thinking she wouldn't get hurt if she co-operated.

"What do you want?" she asked.

"The letter."

This surprised her. It wasn't the answer she had expected. How were they aware of the letter? Only Richard and Reed Hascombe knew about it. Oh and Kathy, maybe she had blabbed to a friend? The letter itself held no value, but the clue to a potentially high-worth item might be of enormous significance. Her mind raced with thoughts, should she feign ignorance? Would they find the wall safe? Then the man's steely voice broke through her meandering thoughts.

"Don't pretend you haven't got it, Madeleine. We know all about it. It's in the safe. Where's the safe?"

She was dumbstruck by their level of knowledge. Again, three people came to mind. It definitely wouldn't have been Reed Hascombe, as he had taken a photo of the letter, hadn't he? She questioned her memory and rebuked herself. Of course he had. She had spoken to him earlier, and he had mentioned the bells comment. So that left Richard or Kathy. Richard appeared to have no genuine interest in the letter, passing it off as a prank, because of so many fake Jack the Ripper letters over the years. But he had questioned why she kept the letter in her safe at work. Kathy had requested a photo of the Victorian letter on Tuesday. The leak had to be her. Could she hold out until security detected her predicament? Without her phone, how would she possibly alert them?

Her hesitation provoked a response from the man who had been searching the display cabinet crammed with awards. He grabbed her hair from behind with his gloved hand, snapped back her head, and held a knife to her throat.

"He asked you where the safe is," the aggressive man said, with a slight East European twang to his distinct gravelly voice.

Madeleine's heart beat like a big bass drum, threatening to explode from her chest. She had no choice unless she wanted to die or get hurt. Plus, Reed had a photo of the letter; therefore, the situation wasn't totally hopeless.

"In the wall. Behind the photo of the cobalt mine," she gasped under the pressure of the knife against her throat.

The man in charge leapt to his feet and scanned the multiple photos adorning the wall before he laughed in her face.

"How do you expect me to select the correct one? Show me."

The man behind Madeleine released her hair, enabling her to stand as she steadied herself on the arm of the chair. Her legs had turned to jelly with the ordeal. She walked tentatively towards the integral wall safe, holding on to the edge of her desk to steady herself. Wearing heels didn't help in this situation. Then a thought pulsed through her mind as her foot nudged the floor-standing machine beside her desk.

"The safe needs a code. I'll get the letter for you. But it won't mean anything to you," she said.

"Don't you worry about that. Just get me the letter."

Madeleine pulled back the photo of the cobalt mine and punched in her son's birth date. She eased open the safe door, knowing she had to be swift with her next movements. The adrenaline rushed as she plucked up the Victorian letter encased inside its plastic wallet. She swivelled on her heels, took three quick steps towards the man in charge, and pretended to catch her foot on the carpet, plunging to the floor. She shot out a hand to press the power button and slammed the wallet into the hungry teeth of the shredding machine. The letter was in pieces in seconds.

"What have you done?" screamed the man in charge.

On all fours beside the desk, Madeleine felt exposed and grasped the edge of the desk to pull herself up. Something hard hit her temple as she stood and everything went dark.

Ryan Johnson stared at Jakub Kosminski in disbelief. Why did he always succumb to anger? He had told his dad that the guy was a loose cannon and now he had complicated the situation further.

"Why did you do that, Jakub?"

"She deserved it after destroying the letter."

"We could have asked her about it, you idiot."

"She wouldn't have told us," said Jakob.

"She might have done. Or we could have kidnapped her, but now she's unconscious. How're we supposed to carry her past the security guard?"

The lack of an answer from Jakub infuriated Ryan, but he didn't fancy an argument with him as the guy was a capable fighter and prone to random acts of violence, as just shown. Earlier, they had sneaked past the security guard when he wandered to the men's toilets. They had reached the seventeenth floor and hid in the men's toilets, all squashed into one cubicle. Now, their plan lay in ruins. He considered how to retrieve the situation. He grabbed the woman's Versace handbag and emptied it on the desk. She was clearly wealthy. The Porsche key fob sparked his interest, perhaps they could steal her car? Then a bright yellow business card caught his eye, with the words Sherbet Investigations splashed across it. Hadn't his dad mentioned something about investigators? He tugged out his phone and called Bernie.

"Dad, we have a situation," he said, hearing a sigh in the background.

"Have you got the letter?" asked Bernie.

"No. The woman was still working, so we persuaded her to open the safe. She grabbed the letter, dived to the floor, and shoved it through a shredding machine. So unfortunately she's destroyed it."

"Geez, Ryan, how the hell did you let that happen? Can't you beat the information out of her?"

"No. Jakub's knocked her out," said Ryan, perturbed by the silence from his father. "But I've found something useful. She had a business card in her handbag for an investigator. She has a Porsche, which I've found the keys for. Perhaps we could steal it?"

"Leave the Porsche, it'll be on a camera recording, too risky to steal it. Bring the business card and the shredding machine contents, that gives us something to work with. Don't get caught on camera when you leave the building," said Bernie.

"Okay," Ryan said, as he ended the call.

"What should we do with her?" asked Mikey, the third member of the group.

"Let's leave her here. She might not report us to the police. She wouldn't want to mention the letter to them."

Ryan led the way as they left the office, choosing to take the stairs as the elevator could alert the security guard to their presence. The outcome of the evening had been a big disappointment, and again Jakub had proved he was a considerable liability. Ryan had known how much the Ripper stuff meant to his dad, but never fully understood the family history link. Perhaps he should ask him?

Chapter 12

WHITECHAPEL BELL FOUNDRY
FRIDAY

REED HUDDLED CLOSE TO Euan as they squinted at the drone's control screen. It displayed the roof of the Whitechapel Bell Foundry; the location linked to James Maybrick. The foundry matched with the clue in the letter that mentioned access to water where the bells tolled. They had checked into the New Road Hotel yesterday evening and now they squatted in the hotel's roof-garden, behind some ornamental hedging. The roof garden offered stunning views of the city skyline as the sounds of bustling traffic drifted upwards. A cold gentle breeze brushed their skin. Even though it was early morning in February, the sunshine burst through the grey winter clouds. The sunshine affected their ability to see the screen properly, so Reed shielded the unit with his hands. The distance between the two properties was well within range for the drone. He had chosen to assess the abandoned Victorian foundry from above before walking to the building.

"Look Euan," he said as his finger pointed to the corner of the screen. "It looks like a gap in the roof."

"I can't quite see it?"

"There," said Reed, his finger jabbed at the unit once more.

"In the corner? At the join between the rooflines?"

"Yes, can you drop the drone any lower?"

"Hang on a sec. Is that any better?"

"Perfect. We should be able to enter through that gap. It'll be a tight squeeze, but it's possible."

"I agree."

"Right let's go."

With the drone packed into its aluminium carry-case, they returned to the hotel room where Emily waited. Both grabbed their backpacks and put on their climbing harnesses. They intended to scale the high brick wall at the rear of the foundry and climb to the roof, so their climbing gear was essential.

Reed led the way as the three of them departed the hotel and walked to the Whitechapel Bell Foundry in six minutes. Positioned on the opposite side of the road, Reed viewed the three-storey building, with its painted green wooden windows, Georgian entrance access, and a green and red winch locked against the wall. It had a distinct look with the name splashed across a plaque prominently placed near the entrance. Years of accumulated dirt surrounded the bricked-in windows on Plumbers Row, where graffiti marred the walls. The dilapidated building had seen better times. Euan had mentioned in his research that it was the foundry that constructed Big Ben's bell centuries ago, a now historical event key to the character of London. He imagined the clang of metal against metal and the intense glare of the foundry furnace in the building's heyday. What a sight that would have been. Bells had certainly tolled here, but did it have access to underground water? His mobile phone rang.

"Hi Madeleine."

"I've some bad news, Reed. Three men accosted me in my office yesterday evening and forced me to open the safe. They wanted the letter, but I shredded it before they knocked me out. They knew it was in the safe and clearly want it as they took the contents of the shredding machine with them, plus your business card."

"Are you okay?" asked Reed.

"I'm in hospital at the moment, but they're releasing me this afternoon. Just a mild concussion, but I'm fine. I wanted to let you know to expect trouble."

"Thanks for letting me know. We're used to aggressive opponents. Take it easy for a few days."

"I've got Richard's art exhibition tomorrow, so I'm resting up today. I've mulled over who knew about the letter in the safe. It was just Richard, Kathy, my PA, and yourselves. I haven't spoken to Kathy yet, but Richard assures me he hasn't mentioned it to anyone, although he looked a little sheepish. Kathy asked for a photo of the letter after Tuesday's meeting when she spotted it on my desk. Apparently she's a Ripperologist."

"We came across Ripperologists in our research. They're people with theories about who Jack the Ripper was, hence the lengthy list of suspects. Maybe she posted something online about the letter. We'll be extra vigilant in our inquiries."

"Okay, thanks Reed, good luck."

"Thanks, bye."

He told Euan and Emily the details of Madeleine's ordeal. The turn of events surprised neither of them.

Reed observed the increasing number of passer-bys as the clock ticked towards rush hour. He hadn't expected so many people wandering around. This was vastly different to Sheffield. He scanned the outside of the ramshackle building, searching for a suitable point to ascend to the roof. The building was three storeys high and required a rope to access the roof, but attempting it above a busy pavement was risky, as someone could easily call the police. A pair of blue battered steel gates adjoined the corner of the building in Plumbers Row. He decided this was the best option. He handed Emily one of the two-way radios before he and Euan wandered over to the gates, leaving her sat on a bench underneath an elder tree. They waited for a lull in passer-by's and then boosted themselves over the gate, which provided suitable cover from passing pedestrians. The other side of the gates led to a building plot, albeit overlooked by large tower blocks, but there had been no other option.

Reed attached a retractable grapple hook to the end of a rope, flung it up the wall and secured it on the roof's ledge. He shimmered up, followed by Euan, and then hauled up the rope. They found the roof's perceived gap, which proved to be a repair with a different material. He scrambled over to a nearby roof-window, tugged out a crowbar from his backpack and eased the window upwards on the ratchet system. With a six-inch gap, they broke the lock between them and opened it fully, allowing them to access the building. Reed spotted a metal gantry about eight feet below. He tied a short rope to a window ratchet, and they both descended to the gantry, their feet clanging on the platform.

The building had been an immense warehouse with large roof lights, but now only pigeons roosted in the eaves with trash strewn across the empty floor. A musty smell filled the air, a mix of old wood and decaying debris. The sound of fluttering wings echoed through the vast space as pigeons perched in the rafters cooed and shuffled around. Sunlight filtered through the dirty glass of the roof lights, casting a dim, hazy glow on the scattered rubbish below. The emptiness of the warehouse felt both eerie and intriguing, its abandoned state inviting exploration. Reed bounded down from the metal gantry to the floor via a series of steps. He surveyed the space, about the size of a basketball court, looking for any access underground. Nothing. He pressed the button on the two-way radio.

"Em, we're inside."

"I couldn't see you on the roof. Have you found anything?"

"No, not yet. We need to check the other areas."

"Take care," said Emily.

Reed hustled to the exit door of the warehouse area. Perhaps this was where they had stored the finished bells, ready for shipment? He found the exit door locked and used the crowbar to gain access to the next area, which looked like the foundry area, where they had constructed church bells. With an enormous furnace bolted to the floor, a hint of ash tainted the concrete floor. Discoloured metal and layers of dust gave it an almost burnt out appearance. He cautiously weaved between the towering machinery dotted with engrained oil spots. His fingertips brushed against the cold, rough surfaces as he searched for a trapdoor or a hidden ladder access. Still nothing. He pivoted to search for Euan on the opposite side of the furnace area, who immediately tripped over a length of protruding metal and crashed to the floor.

"You okay mate?" he shouted across.

"I've banged my knee. That hurts."

"You're always tripping over."

"But I bounce up every time, like a fairground target," laughed Euan. "Over here. There's a wooden door with maintenance department scrawled across it. We should look inside."

"Now coming," said Reed.

Once Reed had reached the maintenance door, he again used the crowbar to gain access. Inside was a large panel of controls with different size levers and push buttons. Thick black cables ran from the panel upwards and downwards, like a myriad of phone lines in an old call centre. It felt like they had stepped back into Victorian times as they analysed the control panel. No mention of water, though. He then noticed a wooden half-size door, painted in green with a black lever latch. A padlock secured it. He used the crowbar to break it and opened the door.

The space in front of him looked restrictive, so he pulled on his head torch, dropped to his knees, and crawled into it. Just enough room with his backpack. He edged along slowly and froze when he heard a scurrying sound as an enormous rat ran over his hands. The sound of dripping water reached his ears, encouraging him to move forward to reach the edge of a pit. The beam from his head torch illuminated a rusty ladder descending into the darkness.

"I've found something," he shouted back to Euan.

"What is it?"

"A ladder dropping into a pit with water dripping to the bottom."

"Great mate, I'm right behind you."

Reed gripped the top rung of the rusty metal ladder as he lowered his legs over. His heart rate increased as he slowly descended into the dark void as the sound of dripping water intensified. The air grew colder, his breath coming in wafts of vapour. Suddenly, the ladder moved outwards, away from the wall, as a couple of bolts shot out from the top. He hung on to the ladder, annoyed with himself for not using a rope. Reed rotated his head, his eyes scanning the dimly lit pit, and spotted the bottom. The sight before him was a mixture of chunky gravel, old brickwork covered in a carpet of damp moss and water pooling in the corners. With a sense of urgency, he quickly clambered down the remaining rungs as his fingers grasped at the rough edges of the pit wall. Finally, he stood on the ground, feeling the dampness seep through the soles of his shoes.

"Euan, the ladder needs fixing at the top before you come down," he said.

"Okay mate, I'll sort it with a couple of climbing cams."

The bottom of the pit was actually a tunnel, akin to an old underground railway. Reed scanned the area and spotted many metal bolts strewn across the floor. As Euan joined him, he realised someone had removed the old train tracks. They shuffled southwards and came up against an imposing brick wall that blocked their progress. He remembered the letter and pulled out his phone to check the wording, the twentieth brick from the ladder was the crucial point. He counted twenty bricks from the ladder southwards, but nothing obvious or any loose bricks. Similarly, he searched to the north, finding no hiding place. Disappointed, he pressed the radio button to speak to Emily, but it didn't work. He was out of range so swivelled round to his mate.

"Should we go back? Or we could see where this tunnel leads?" he asked, knowing full well the answer before Euan spoke.

"Let's investigate whilst we're here."

"Spot on, I knew you'd say that."

They laughed together and trudged off northwards, avoiding the loose bolts and scurrying rats that appeared every few feet. As Reed observed the defined brick structure, he marvelled at the contrast between this man-made creation and the natural caves he had explored in the Peak District and Cornwall. The sound of their steady footsteps echoed off the walls, filling the air with a rhythmic cadence. Dampness lingered in the air, a reminder of the history and age of the Victorian structure.

"Where are they now, Davey?" asked Bernie, holding his phone as he had Ryan on the other end. It had been easy for his tech guy to find the details of the investigation team and track the phone number of Reed Hascombe from the business card they had gained. Bernie rose from his chair in the car repair shop's office and strode over to view Davey's laptop.

"They're in the gym," he said to his son.

"Why would they be in the gym?"

"Getting fit. Isn't that what you do?"

"How can I find them in there?"

"Wait outside."

"Hang on a minute," interjected Davey. "They've moved next door to the hotel. That's strange. It's like they've ghosted through a wall."

Bernie peered at the screen, perplexed, as the flashing blue dot moved into a section of wasteland where the old St Mary's station used to be. Then he realised.

"They're underground in the old train tunnel!"

"How did they get there?" asked Ryan.

"It doesn't matter, just seize them."

"Okay, we're on it."

Bernie ended the call and studied Davey's attempt on the desk to paste together the strips of paper of the letter. Aligning the minuscule strips proved impossible, which rendered the image incomprehensible. He just had to hope that Ryan and Mikey could catch Reed Hascombe and interrogate him. He had to know the letter's contents. It could be the clue to Cutbush's stolen object his father had talked about.

Chapter 13

ST MARY'S TRAIN STATION
FRIDAY

REED HEARD THE RUMBLE of traffic overhead as he spotted an opening in the tunnel ahead in the light of his head torch. As they approached, an abandoned train platform became clear. An old London Underground plaque identified the location as St Mary's, with colourful graffiti sprayed across the platform wall. A distinct red splash caught his eye. *'Jack lived here'*, it said, as droplets of red created a blood dripping effect. Discarded wrappers swirled in a corner as the whistle of wind whipped them into the air. Another immense brick wall ahead blocked any further progress as Reed clambered from the tunnel floor onto the platform. They had a simple choice: find an exit here or return to the foundry. He sighted an opening in the platform's wall and strode over to it. A series of stone steps ascended, dirt ingrained in the rough texture from years gone by. Behind him, Euan's head torch flickered, creating a rave-like effect.

"Let's head up those steps."

"That's quite spooky," said Euan as he pointed to the blood red graffiti. "People clearly still remember Jack the Ripper."

"He's infamous in London, and probably worldwide."

A chilly wind blew down the steps as Reed ascended, avoiding the rubbish blowing towards him. The light from his head torch illuminated more explicit graffiti, some of it unintelligible, and the odd discarded needle on the steps. It was an intensely desolate place, not somewhere to be alone, he thought. They reached a heavy steel door, wedged open with a broken brick. He had to remove his backpack to squeeze through the gap as Euan followed close behind. At the end of the corridor, he spotted iron bars with daylight penetrating the gloom and traffic fumes hit him as they closed in on the gap. Fortunately, someone had cut and bent one bar inwards, allowing them to wriggle through the hole into an area of wasteland. Uneven shingle and abandoned waste littered the area. Barricaded by grey building site fencing, they couldn't see where they were, just tower blocks surrounding them. Reed pressed the two-way radio button, and it worked this time.

"Em, are you there?"

"Where are you? I was getting concerned."

"I'm not sure. We've been searching an old underground tunnel and reached St Mary's abandoned station. Can you come here?"

"Will do. Did you find anything?"

"Unfortunately not."

"Okay. See you in a bit," said Emily.

Reed trampled across some sodden cardboard and reached the edge of the fencing. He swung round to check Euan was behind him and noticed a couple of guys clamber over the grey fencing on the opposite side of the wasteland. He heard a shout.

"Stop," shouted Ryan as he recognised Reed Hascombe, his long black hair trailing in the wind as the ginger lad alongside uttered some words.

"Come on, Mikey," he said to his accomplice. "Let's grab them before they climb over the fence." He sprinted hard across the gravel before his foot caught on a grass divot, causing him to stumble. Mikey pulled him up, and they bolted towards the two lads clambering over the fence. He jumped up and grabbed a trailing foot, pulling it hard before he got kicked and let go. He clambered over the fence, jumped to the pavement and spotted their two targets running across the busy road, dodging traffic. Ryan pulled out his phone from his jeans pocket.

"Found them," he said as Bernie answered.

"Find out the letter's contents."

He struggled to speak whilst running across Whitechapel High street as he narrowly avoided a passing bus. "I will when we catch them."

"Stop wasting time talking and get them."

Ryan loved his father, but he was demanding, especially with Jack the Ripper stuff. He sensed important information written in the old letter. This would explain his father's focus. He pounded down a side road, trailing behind Mikey, unable to spot the two targets.

Reed glanced over his shoulder and noticed Euan was lagging behind him as they hurtled into an alleyway. His mouth dropped open when he spotted a ten-foot brick wall ahead with a wrought-iron gate leading inside a building. A dead end. Orange wheelie waste bins and piles of flattened cardboard boxes lined the alleyway, as a drainpipe splashed water onto the cracked tarmac, where moss had accumulated. Battered rear doors to restaurants gave no route for an escape, so with their backs to the gate, Reed spoke.

"Looks like we'll have to fight our way out. I'll take the lead, and you use the crowbar."

Reed gave the metal crowbar to his best friend, just as the two men chasing them appeared in the alleyway's entrance. He stood his ground, ready in a fighting stance as they approached. The muscular man threatened first, fists raised, which exuded a boxer's stance. That's okay, thought Reed, my signature move will take him out. The second aggressor snatched out a Bowie knife, waving it in the air with a grin plastered across his face.

"You're cornered, so let's make this easy, Reed," said the knife man.

He immediately understood the use of his name. These men had attacked Madeleine in her office and wanted Jack's letter. "You know my name. What's yours?" he asked.

"That's not relevant."

"You stole Madeleine's letter, so I think it's relevant."

"She shredded it. Anyway, I want to know the letter's contents. Otherwise it'll turn ugly."

"That's not relevant," said Reed as he mimicked the knife man.

The boxer took a step towards him and threw an uppercut punch, which Reed avoided with a dip of his shoulder. He followed it up with a kick to the boxer's shin. The grimace on the boxer's face showed it hurt. Reed bounced on his toes, ready for the next attack, biding his time. He caught the flash of a blade aimed at Euan, which his mate swatted away with the crowbar. The boxer approached again, snapping in a couple of jabs as one caught him on the chest. He stumbled backwards as the knife man spoke.

"Don't mess with the Hoxton Hot Rods, you'll lose. Last chance. Tell me the contents of the letter."

"That's not relevant," said Reed, goading him deliberately as he filed away the gang identity for later.

The knife man stepped forward, jabbing his blade at Euan, and nicked him on the forearm. The crowbar was useful, but difficult to manoeuvre in close combat.

"Step back Euan, you can swing it easier," he said.

The chilly wind whistled through the alleyway as empty carrier bags swirled in the corner. The four men opposed each other menacingly, so Reed took the initiative against the boxer lad. He feigned a stomach punch and swivelled with a drop kick to the man's chest. Surprised by the kick, the boxer stumbled backwards, allowing Reed to perform his signature move. A leg sweep takedown, which smashed the boxer onto the floor. A quick kick to the head dazed the boxer on the floor as he struggled to regain his footing. This allowed Reed to turn his attention to the knife man. Euan swung the crowbar, which Reed followed up with a punch to the knife man's head, causing him to stagger backwards. This was the escape opportunity he had hoped for.

"Quick, let's go."

Reed spun around and leapt towards the ten-foot wall that blocked their exit. He had seen an escape route earlier, and now they had the time to execute it. He clambered up the wall, jerking Euan up behind him. Stood atop the wall's ledge, they jumped across the five-foot gap towards a metal fire escape and grasped the edge. He hauled himself over the railing and scurried up the staircase with Euan close behind. Their parkour training had come in useful. Once they reached the rooftop, the escape route opened out in front of them. He pressed the talk button on the two-way radio to speak to Emily.

"Where are you, Em?"

"Outside the fencing at the St Mary's station."

"Sorry. We got chased and had some trouble. We're on the rooftops. I can see Truman's Brewery nearby. Can you meet us there?"

"Of course. Are you both okay?" asked Emily.

"Yes, we're fine. We'll be there soon."

His phone buzzed, but it was just a message from the hotel confirming their participation on the parkour course tomorrow. From the rooftop, Reed leaned over, his gaze searching the alleyway for the attackers, but they weren't there. He jogged across the flat roof and spotted them down below on the road adjoining the alleyway, the boxer being helped along by the knife man. It was safe to resume their escape, so Reed leapt across the small gap to the next roof and studied their descent to ground level. It appeared straight forward. He had learned who the lads were, but not why they coveted the Victorian letter. Presumably they had to know it mentioned treasure?

Chapter 14

WHITECHAPEL

FRIDAY

HIDDEN IN THE SHADOWS of the charity shop, the would-be killer watched the revellers leave the pub at closing time. Newspaper articles were fresh in their mind, read from their secret scrapbook. That night, they would pay tribute to their Victorian ancestor. A February mist drifted in and the streetlights flickered as a blanket of darkness settled over the city. The unseen person's heart raced with a mix of excitement and trepidation. Adrenaline increased, causing a surge of energy that sharpened their senses. Goosebumps prickled their skin as their hands clenched and unclenched. Fingers twitched, restless with what lay ahead.

Their eyes darted from one person to another, appraising each passerby. A mixture of anticipation and fear consumed their thoughts. This person wasn't merely an unseen observer, but a force to be reckoned with. Fuelled by the intensity of their passion. They watched an individual separate from the last crowd of pub-goers drifting off into a cobbled side street. The time had come.

As the would-be killer approached their target, time slowed to a crawl. The air pulsed with tension as shadows danced around the street, magnifying their presence. They withdrew a sharp knife, grasping the handle with dishonourable intent. With a sudden surge of strength, they lunged forward, their movements fluid and precise. The would-be killer grabbed the victim's head, jerked it back, and dragged the blade across their prey's throat. Arms flailed as a gurgled cry of help went unheard. Blood spilled, turning the cobblestones into a mosaic of crimson. The victim's body lay beside a brick wall, left to drain of life. Their mission accomplished, they had become a killer as their chest heaved with victorious pride. The storm of emotions that had consumed them now subsided, leaving only a sense of fulfilment.

As the killer melted into the shadows, a modern legacy was born, forever etched in time. Jack's spectre had risen. The scrapbook would include new cuttings, adding their heinous acts to those of their ancestor. The story of the infamous Victorian murders continues nearly two hundred years later. Whispered in hushed tones throughout the land.

Chapter 15

COMMERCIAL STREET POLICE STATION

SATURDAY

IT WAS STILL DARK when Detective Chief Inspector Clara Loxstone had left her modern two-bedroom apartment over-looking the River Thames earlier. She glanced out of her office window at the car park and noticed daylight slowly petering in. Dead bodies in London had become commonplace over the past few years. The on-duty desk sergeant had called her at four am on the orders of her boss, DS Browne, to pick up the case. A hardened police officer with twenty years' experience, she had wanted nothing else than to be a detective in the Metropolitan Police. Her dreams came true a few years back and since then she had progressed to DCI on account of her abilities and strong work ethic. Her abrupt style could annoy people, but got results with her peers and team members. She sipped on her third cup of earl grey tea, while she waited for DI Charlie Page to arrive.

Clara erased the whiteboard contents in her cramped office. Experience taught her they would shelve all open cases until they had solved this murder, as it would likely dominate news coverage for days. The Commissioner of the Met Police would probably get involved, so she needed to get ahead before the whispers and rumours started. The door to her office burst open as DI Page entered, his mid-length hair still bed-tangled and half a jacket lapel flapping upwards.

"Sorry ma'am, the traffic was dreadful."

"More like your bed was sticky, Page. Let's view the body."

"Yes, ma'am."

"We'll walk. That'll wake you up."

A grunt from her subordinate was the only response, but she didn't care. Clara grabbed her bag and marched out of the police station at record speed, with DI Page struggling to keep up. For forty-seven she was reasonably fit, because she walked to work most days and attended weekly yoga sessions. Yoga allowed her to switch off from work, as she often endured long hours. Fortunately, her husband was understanding about it and with no children to worry about, their lives had been career oriented. They strode past Spitalfields Market where the hub-bub of the day's activities had just begun. Past the church, they turned left into Wentworth Street before slipping into Gunthorpe Street where uniformed police had cordoned off the narrow, cobbled street at both ends.

Halfway down the street, the corpse lay completely drained of blood. Crimson fluid tinged the cobbles as the forensics team took samples. Clara turned to the man in charge.

"Anderson, what've we got?"

"Caucasian male, age around twenty-five, reasonably fit. A sharp knife slit his throat from behind. That's a guess based on the unusual angle of cut. Carotid artery severed, which led to the rapid bleed out."

"Estimated time?" asked Clara.

"I would suggest midnight, give or take an hour."

The forensic man lifted the blanket covering the corpse for Clara and DI Page to view it. She tied her wavy black hair up before squatting, then observed the clean cut across the dead man's throat. As she was about to point this out to DI Page, she heard him throw the contents of his stomach into a storm drain.

"Geez, Page, get some steel inside you. It's becoming

embarrassing when you throw up at every dead body!"

A gurgled "yes ma'am," emitted from her sub-ordinate.

"Any thoughts on the type of blade, Anderson?"

"Possibly a scalpel. It's a clean incision. Or a machine sharpened hunting knife with a top curve section."

"Okay, thanks. Get your report over asap."

"Will do."

Clara instructed Page to speak with the uniform officers patrolling the entrance whilst she searched the area. This also gave her the opportunity to have a few quick blasts on her vape kit. As an ex-smoker she had transitioned to vaping several years ago and preferred it now. She loved the salted caramel flavour, coupled with the blast of nicotine, it kept her sane most days. Rubbish littered the area, but as she moved another empty sandwich wrapper with her foot, she noticed a black leather covered button. It appeared clean and possibly freshly placed there, so she advised forensics of its existence. Her next step was to get the tech guys to analyse CCTV footage in the area and uniform officers to do a house-to-house on all properties in the road. She caught up with DI Page, who had nothing useful to add, so they headed back to the station.

Right now, they had no leads. The investigation couldn't start until all the data streams had filtered through. This had been a callous murder, not the normal gang fight. Revenge perhaps? The killing had looked premeditated based on Anderson's initial thoughts.

Chapter 16

WHITECHAPEL

SATURDAY

REED BENT OVER, STRETCHING his legs to loosen his hamstrings ready for the morning's exercise, then banged out ten press-ups for good measure. He had been looking forward to this parkour event ever since he booked the New Road Hotel last week. Another of his and Euan's activities they enjoyed together, along with the rock climbing. The event excluded Emily, but they had planned lunch for later, where the three of them would decide on the next suspect. The chief instructor came forward and gathered the eight participants around him to run through the safety protocol before the three-mile activity begun. Reed tied up his long black hair into a bun on the top of his head. He didn't want this impeding jumps, flips and hand-offs whilst traversing the course.

"Ready mate?" he asked Euan.

"Yeah, I'm looking forward to it. Plenty of famous landmarks to see."

The chief instructor left the hotel frontage as he jumped onto an eight-foot brick wall and bounced along amid gasps of surprise from people walking past. At the end, he flipped off, using his hands on to an orange wheelie bin before landing on a lower brick wall. Reed, Euan and the other six participants followed the route whilst a second instructor brought up the rear. The group headed towards the tobacco docks, alternating between walls and railings with plenty of flips and handstands thrown in. Most passersby stood and watched the group perform their tricks, especially through the gardens. Once at the docks, they managed several wall-walks off the side of two time-worn ships docked there before they grabbed a well-earned breather.

"Wow, that's so cool," said Euan.

Reed pulled out his phone and gestured to Euan to stand beside one ship as he took a photo. "One for the scrapbook."

"Everyone ready to go again?" asked the chief instructor.

Murmurs of consent rippled across the group.

"Great, Tower Bridge next."

Reed slipped in ahead of Euan behind the chief instructor and followed his lead around more car park walls. They came across a derelict building covered with graffiti. The group ascended an external fire escape, racing to the top. Each participant took in turns to flip down vertically between the levels like a human centipede chain, all legs and arms. It wasn't long before they arrived at Tower Bridge and dodged through the throng of tourists to reach the wall of the first Victorian tower. The river ran beneath the magnificent structures with their ornate windows and curved edges. Religious crosses adorned each corner, golden centre pieces at the pinnacle of each tower glistened in the winter sun.

The chief instructor jumped onto the four-foot railing and immediately weaved between the bridge struts, using his arms to spin around each one. Reed leapt onto the guard railing and peered at the one hundred and forty-foot drop into the cold water of the River Thames. Amid shouts of protest from the tourists, the parkour group weaved their way along the railing with arm spins, before a handstand off at the end. The instructors hurried everyone along afterwards and raced towards the Tower of London for another breather. Euan caught up and blurted out,

"That was exhilarating."

"Superb, but my arms ache now."

They gazed up at the limestone walls that protected the crown jewels of the monarch of England, reputed to be priceless. The immensely thick walls were a thousand years old and exuded a profound sense of security. Reed doubted anyone could breach them without being caught. In the distance stood the Shard, where they had visited Madeleine a few days earlier. He reached inside his backpack for a couple of gels, passing a black cherry one to Euan. They quickly consumed their energy boost before the chief instructor was off again.

An old red telephone box repurposed with a defibrillator stood in front as they took it in turns to clamber atop and jump across to a huge oak tree branch. One lad missed it by inches and landed awkwardly on his ankle. The group traversed more railings before they headed towards the Brick Lane neighbourhood. This area, rich in Jack the Ripper connections, was the section of the course that Reed was most interested in.

Reed followed the chief instructor through the throng of Spitalfields market-goers as they jumped from post to post between the various stalls selling fruit, clothes, and knick-knacks. A few more wall jumps and hand flips before the group paused for their final breather outside the market on Commercial Road.

"It's the Ten Bells Pub," pointed out Reed to his mate.

"Emily mentioned that Aaron Kosminski drank there."

"Let's make that our next target now we've seen it."

"I agree," said Euan, taking a sip of water from his bottle. "How are your bruises?"

"Fine, mate, how's your cut?"

"Just a scratch. It takes a lot more than a mouthy East End villain to take me down!"

"Yeah, yeah. If I didn't tell you what to do, you'd be mincemeat."

Reed laughed as they headed off on the last leg of the parkour tour which took in Brick Lane. Before they headed back to the hotel, there was still time to use a nearby park's skateboard area, which provided multiple opportunities for back flips. Two hours of exertion had left both lads lathered in sweat and hungry for some recovery food. They said their goodbyes to the instructors and rushed off to find Emily, eager to discuss the next leg in their quest to find Jack the Ripper's missing treasure. Perhaps if they had doubled-backed to the Ten Bells Pub, they would have had a clearer understanding of the forces in play.

Chapter 17

Ten Bells Pub

Saturday

THE FEEBLE HEATER IN the basement dribbled out warm air as the four members of the Ripper's Guild looked to keep the chill off. Sophia and Jakob sat on one tattered brown sofa, scrolling through their phones. Bernie sipped his pint of real ale and watched as Basil, the bank manager, pontificated about what the hidden treasure could be. He quickly became bored with hearing Basil's posh voice and hijacked the conversation.

"Let's get down to business. Is everyone aware of the awful murder last night?" he asked.

Murmurs of surprise rippled from Basil and Sophia whilst Jakob just grunted something unintelligible.

"According to my sources in the police force, there's been a murder close by on Gunthorpe Street. A slit across the throat with a sharp blade. Similar to Jack's modus operandi, but I didn't mention that to my source."

"Oh my, that is interesting," said Basil.

"Was it a prostitute?" asked Sophia.

"No. Mid-twenties male."

"It can't be a copy-cat killer then."

Through the WhatsApp group chat, he had disclosed their futile attempts to retrieve the letter from Madeleine Robinson-Smith on Thursday. But he now had to update them on the failed attempt to apprehend the Sherbet Investigation team.

"We didn't get the letter from Madeleine, but did Richard say anything yesterday?" he asked.

"He told me everything when he came into work. Well, everything he was told by his wife. He waved it off as a stupid letter that meant nothing. He's too wrapped up in the exhibition tonight to care."

"So your plan is to talk with Madeleine tonight?"

"Yes. That's assuming she comes. She may not feel up to it with concussion," said Sophia, glaring at Jakob. "But if she does, I'll definitely corner her."

"I don't think your female charms will work on her like they seem to on her husband."

"Don't be stupid Bernie. She'll get more than the edge of my tongue tonight!"

Bernie disliked her tone and arrogance, after all, he was in charge. "We wouldn't be in this position if you had done your job properly sooner!" he retorted.

"If it wasn't for me, you wouldn't even know about the letter. Remember that Bernie."

The atmosphere had turned frosty, as it often did. They were a mismatch of individuals who would never socialise outside of their group. A clear common goal united them, and Bernie wanted to achieve it as soon as possible.

"I have another update. Yesterday, my tech guy tracked the mobile phone of the lead investigator. My lads cornered them in an alleyway. Unfortunately, he and his mate got away as he's some sort of ninja freak, according to Ryan."

"That wouldn't happen if I were there," mumbled Jakob.

"It was too short a notice to call you," said Bernie. "They disappeared into the old tunnel near St Mary's but didn't appear to find anything. When you have your little chat with Madeleine tonight, get some more information on them."

"Okay," Sophia responded with annoyance.

Bernie sensed the Guild was becoming a little fragmented with their differing attitudes. He needed to pull them around.

"We're in this together to gain what is rightfully ours. Let's focus and all do our bit."

He heard grumbles of agreement before silence reigned. Each person sipped their drink, lost in their own thoughts, before they all drifted out of the room.

Bernie phoned Davey for an update on what Hascombe had been up to today. Sophia's plan for the art exhibition had to be the top priority. Hopefully, she would be successful and gain some information about the contents of the letter.

Chapter 18

REFLECTIONS ART GALLERY
SATURDAY

MADELEINE PEERED AT HER tired face in the cloakroom mirror, noticing more wrinkles on her forehead than the previous week. The aging process wasn't kind. Perhaps Botox would help, she thought? Apart from that, she scrubbed up well, considering her ordeal two evenings ago. A splash of make-up and a royal blue velvet gown adorned with a gold chain made her look quite glamorous. She channelled her inner strength, ready to face the throng of art critics and casual painters. This was Richard's big night. He had been so busy with the art exhibition he fell asleep on the battered sofa in the back room last night and didn't come home. Richard had persuaded a well-known artist, Smirks, to display a selection of their work, along with some by local artists from the East End. Madeleine stepped out of the ladies' cloakroom into the spacious art gallery and scanned the diverse range of sculptures on display in the main exhibition area.

The place thronged with people browsing the artwork, each piece emphasised with its own spotlight. Her husband had certainly done a fantastic job setting up the exhibits. In the centre of the room was a unique piece, an arrangement of used rubber car tyres with painted stick people both on a beach and in mountain scapes. This was Smirks pièce de résistance, simply titled 'Future'. It had won many awards and was already attracting the most attention.

Madeleine surveyed the crowd searching for her husband and spotted his shoulder-length grey hair on the far side, chatting with Basil Montague, her bank manager. A swirl of long blonde hair flashed beside Richard as Sophia appeared and laid her hand on Madeleine's husband's arm. This garnered churning emotions inside her. They were too cosy. She desperately hoped he wasn't having an affair with the pretty German girl. It was time to find out.

Madeleine meandered across the gallery, nodding at various acquaintances, before she reached the group.

"Basil, how are you?" she said.

"Oh my Madeleine, you look absolutely divine," he gushed, his handlebar moustache twitching like a rat whiskers.

"Well, thank you."

Sophia's hand rested firmly on her husband's arm as she turned her attention to her. Fury bubbled inside her.

"Sophia. Good to meet you again," she said, putting out her hand to encourage the girl to remove her hand from Richard's arm. Sophia obliged and shook her hand.

"Oh, I agree with Basil. You look incredible, Madeleine," said the German girl.

"Thank you Sophia, you look pretty amazing yourself."

"Thanks. Can we have a chat later? There's something I wish to discuss with you," asked Sophia.

"Of course. There's something I wish to discuss with you as well."

"Nothing bad I hope?"

"Not at all. Can I steal my husband away for a few moments?" she asked.

"Certainly. I need to mingle and encourage some sales. Get out my best sales patter." At that, the German girl swivelled on her dangerously high heels, swished her long blonde hair and caught Basil across the shoulder as the bank manager gawped at her walking off.

Madeleine still seethed inside but didn't feel the time was right to get all hot under the collar with Richard about Sophia's hands-on approach to her husband. The pair spent the next hour browsing the pieces of art and chatted to prospective clients and acquaintances. She held Richard's arm whilst also keeping tabs on what Sophia was up to. She certainly didn't trust the charming German girl.

Sophia ran through her plan many times as she checked and double-checked the script would work. Now she had to implement it. She spent the past hour giving out flattering comments to clients in the hope they would purchase some artwork. Frankly, that didn't matter a jot, as the only thing that mattered was getting information from Madeleine. Once accomplished, her husband could shove his pawing hands elsewhere. She had her whole life ahead of her, and finding Jack's treasure would open up the avenue she craved. Back in Germany, whilst a teenager, her grandmother had told tales of their family history and bloodline back to Walter Sickert. He was an alleged suspect in the Jack the Ripper murders back in Victorian England. This had sparked her curiosity and led to her obsession with the serial killer as she spent hours upon hours researching his history. She became convinced that Walter Sickert was Jack the Ripper and came to England to trace her bloodline further. She had been in contact with Ripper fanatics in England prior to her relocation through Ripperologist websites.

Bernie Johnson had been her most important contact, and she convinced him of her family history, which resulted in her invitation to join the Ripper's Guild. Soon afterwards, she landed a job at the art gallery, working for Richard Smith. It was strange how it had worked out. When she had the interview with Richard, he asked why she moved to England and briefly explained her reason. He said his wife had a letter she believed belonged to Jack the Ripper, with Sophia then working her charm on him to get the job. For months, she probed for more details, even putting up with Richard's advances, although she had stopped short of making it more than the odd kiss here and there. Was it sheer luck, or fate, their lives had crossed? Was she destined to uncover her family's history?

Another glance over at Madeleine confirmed the woman had watched her all evening. Sophia planned to exploit the woman's clear suspicions to get the information she wanted tonight. She slipped into the cloakroom, sprayed a mist of perfume onto her neck, checked her make-up and flipped her long blonde hair to one side. Ready to click her plan into action. She wandered over to Madeleine and Richard at the rear of the main display area, slipping in between them stealthily.

"Hi Richard, any sales yet?" she asked.

"A couple so far. What about you?"

"Several people have expressed an interest, so I'll check in with them later on. It would be so good if we could generate some solid sales."

As Richard turned away to speak to someone else, Sophia nudged Madeleine.

"Can I have that chat with you, Madeleine?" she asked.

"Yeah, sure, fire away."

"Can we go somewhere more private? It's a delicate subject," she said, slowly running her hands through her long hair. "Come through to the office." Sophia took Madeleine's arm and guided her towards the archway into the smaller display room with water-colours exhibited on the walls. A young couple studied an ocean landscape painting as they wandered through. She needed to keep Madeleine engaged.

"Sorry about this Madeleine," she said, adopting a fake friendly approach.

"What's this about Sophia? Surely we can discuss it here?"

Madeleine stopped at the office door entrance, disguised as part of the wall.

"It's about Richard. It would be better inside the office, please."

"What about Richard?" came the abrupt response.

Sophia dropped her voice to a whisper, having expected this answer from Madeleine, and planned for it. "He's been getting too friendly."

This brought the desired response as Madeleine pushed the handle down and entered the gallery's office. Sophia followed close behind, paused with her back to the now closed door and twisted the key to lock it. The office was a mish-mash of racks laden with artwork and a workbench loaded with tools. The lack of a window meant the stark lighting highlighted everything in fine detail. Another door led into the rear room that served as a mini kitchen and Richard's crash pad. She swiftly stepped over to a storage rack that consumed one whole side of the chaotic office and picked up a scalpel hidden underneath a cloth. Now she was in control. No need for any charm now.

"Actually, it's about the letter." She brandished the scalpel, making her intentions clear. The surprised look on her boss's wife's face was priceless. She couldn't help but smirk.

"So, this isn't about Richard?"

"No. I need to know the contents of the letter you so cleverly shredded?" she asked.

"You instructed the thieves to break into my office?"

"I might have done. Tell me what the letter said."

"So you aren't having an affair with my husband, then?"

Sophia laughed. "Not yet, but he keeps trying!"

"You won't get away with this. I'll get him to sack you."

"Oh, I don't think so, Madeleine. He likes the taste of my lipstick too much!"

Madeleine lunged forward at the incendiary comment, so Sophia lashed out at her shoulder with the scalpel, cutting the fabric of her velvet gown with ease. The blade also drew blood and seeped through the royal blue fabric. She spun behind the older woman, grabbing her hair and held the scalpel to her throat.

"Next time, I'll cut your pretty face," she snarled. "Now tell me what the letter said." She felt the older woman shaking.

"It's a love letter to my great-great grandmother. I think it was from whoever was Jack the Ripper and mentions treasure."

"Yes, I know all that. Your fumbling husband has told me that. I want to know about the location of Jack's hidden treasure." Sophia applied a little pressure to the scalpel and created a trickle of blood down Madeleine's throat. This spurred the older woman into divulging further information.

"I can't remember exactly what it said, only to search for the hidden access to the water where the bells toll."

"Is that it? There must be more?"

"No, I promise, there isn't anything else," said Madeleine.

"There better not be, otherwise I'll pay you another visit. Or better still, let your husband have what he wants," said Sophia, laughing at her torturous words.

"Leave him out of it. You're crazy. Let me go. I've told you what you want."

Sophia pushed Madeleine away from her as the older woman stumbled on her heels. She watched with her hands on her hips as Madeleine struggled to open the locked office door before bolting through it. She had enjoyed the little tango with Madeleine, causing fear in the woman. Now she had something tangible to discuss with Bernie. She wouldn't mention it to Basil tonight, she thought the guy was a buffoon.

Madeleine rushed to the ladies' cloakroom, avoiding everyone. She needed some space to reflect on what had just happened and clean the bloodstains. Now she knew who was the driving force behind the thugs that broke into her office. And clearly she couldn't tell her husband anything else about the letter. Thankfully, she had held back the exact information about the location. If other people were interested in Jack's letter, then it implied some truth. She needed to speak to Reed Hascombe, let him know about the earlier event with Sophia.

After she had cleaned up the blood and wrapped a scarf around her neck to cover up the cut in her expensive gown, she tugged out her phone from her matching handbag. Reed answered.

"Hi Madeleine, I didn't expect a call from you this evening."

"Things have taken a turn for the worse Reed," she said before explaining in depth the events of the evening. Reed then relayed his endeavours from the previous day, including the fight.

"We still have an advantage, as you didn't divulge the wording of the letter about the location, but we'll need to be vigilant. We're used to this type of situation, but you should go to the police about Sophia."

"I might do, but I don't want the police getting involved with the letter."

"We don't have it anymore," said Reed.

"No, but you have a copy on your phone."

"True."

"I think we leave the police out of it for now," she said.

"Okay, agreed. But take care, she is clearly a dangerous person. We're investigating the Ten Bells Pub tomorrow. I'll update you if we find anything."

"Great thanks Reed, speak again soon."

Madeleine ended the call and decided she would remain at the art exhibition. She needed to have a heart-to-heart with her husband, but for now, she wasn't about to let the crazy German girl influence her behaviour; she was stronger than that. Finding the treasure was paramount and could be the key to a secure future. She hoped

Reed's investigation would bear fruit soon.

Chapter 19

TEN BELLS PUB

SUNDAY

As Euan approached the entrance to the Ten Bells Pub, he sidestepped a teenager racing past on an e-scooter. With Reed and Emily close behind, he entered the pub and stood for a few moments, surveying the bar. The muted conversations of Sunday lunchtime greeted him as he spotted real ales on tap. The pub had kept the Victorian decor features, but added some splashes of modern colour. Hung on the far wall, and identified by a plaque underneath, a large wooden mural depicted an artist's impression of Jack the Ripper. Subtle use of lighting enhanced the authentic East End vibe as he sought an empty table, but with nothing available, he strode to the bar to order drinks.

"What can I get you?" asked the bearded barman in a deep, booming voice.

"A pint of Stella, please." He turned to his friends and took their orders. "Plus a glass of white wine and a pint of your London porter. Can we get a table for lunch?"

"There's more tables upstairs. Find one, note the number, and come back to order your food at the bar."

Euan passed Reed and Emily their drinks before they climbed the stairs and found an unoccupied table. The upstairs room contained an assortment of wooden tables of varied shapes and sizes, as though someone had purchased them at different times. There were several framed pictures on the wall, one of which caught his attention.

"Hey, isn't that Walter Sickert's painting of Jack the Rippers' bedroom?"

Emily tapped away on her phone and brought up a photo of the painting. "It certainly is," she said.

"Interesting. The landlord is using the pub's links to Jack the Ripper as a feature."

After they had chosen their meals, Euan bounced downstairs to place their orders and visit the toilet. He followed the sign towards the toilets and passed an opening with stone steps that descended from the dimly lit corridor. On his return, he slipped quietly down the stone steps, making sure he tiptoed to reduce any noise reverberation. This led to another dark corridor with three doors, one sealed with a padlock. He opened a door, which contained cluttered shelves of cleaning materials and boxes of alcoholic drink bottles. The final door led to the keg storage area, but as he stepped inside, a voice boomed at him.

"What're you doing down here?"

Euan turned and noticed it was the barman. "I'm looking for the toilets."

"They're upstairs."

"Oh okay, sorry about that."

The barman pushed past Euan into the keg storage area to change a barrel and, as he did so, Euan spotted an opening in the floor amongst the barrels and pipework. The top rungs of a ladder were clearly visible. This piqued his interest as he quickly returned upstairs to tell Reed and Emily.

"That might lead to the hidden water access," Euan enthused to the others.

"Yes, it might do. We're aware that Aaron Kosminski drank here, so it's perfectly feasible he knew about the ladder," said Emily.

"We need to get down there unseen," interjected Reed.

"I've thought about that. Let's return tonight after the pub has closed."

"You mean break in?"

"Yes, use your lock pick set. We can also investigate the locked room."

"Okay, I'm up for that," said Reed.

"You need to be careful. Please don't get caught," cautioned Emily as she squeezed Reed's hand.

"I'm always careful." He hugged her and smiled his super confident smile.

The meals arrived shortly after; they enjoyed their food as they planned their night-time break-in, agreeing that the pub's name matched the letter's clue.

Davey Warren was bored. He always felt bored on Sundays. No work, but he had spent the morning recoding an important search algorithm for Bernie. His boss demanded a lot of him but he didn't mind, he enjoyed the challenges. His computer technology skills had led to multiple ways to make extra money, all of which had gone into purchasing his terraced house at the age of twenty-eight. London house prices were sky high, but his skill set paid handsomely.

In order to relieve the boredom, he diverted to check on Reed Hascombe's current location, something his boss asked him to do and provide regular updates. His nose twitched as he identified the current location. The Ten Bells Pub. He realised Bernie would be extremely interested in this, so he picked up his phone and called his boss.

"Have you got some news, Davey?"

"Yes, boss. Reed Hascombe is at the Ten Bells Pub."

He heard a groan from his boss. "Oh shit. What's he doing there?"

"I don't know. He's been there for an hour. Perhaps he's having a drink?"

"Yes, I suppose he could be. Thanks Mouse, I'll head over myself and take a look," said Bernie.

The call ended, and Davey returned to being bored. He expected his boss to call if he needed further help once he had eyes on Reed Hascombe.

Chapter 20

TEN BELLS PUB

SUNDAY

REED STOOD IN THE shadows of an immense oak tree beside the Christ Church in Spitalfields, with Euan beside him, as they surveyed the hybrid block of buildings that contained the Ten Bells Pub. Euan hovered the drone above the buildings, all grouped together around an internal courtyard. The thermal imaging didn't detect anyone in the courtyard, but with the odd individual that walked past the front of the pub, Reed had formulated his plan. Many CCTV cameras affixed to the buildings on the main road meant breaking in at the front entrance was difficult without being caught on camera. Not something he wanted to happen. Earlier, after their visit for Sunday lunch, he had scoped out the buildings using Google maps overhead functionality. Access had to be less risky via the inner courtyard. The drone had provided them with a suitable approach point to the courtyard, a vine-covered ten-foot wall to clamber over. He instructed Euan to drop the drone into the courtyard to double-check all was clear. It was. Time to move.

With the drone packed away, Reed hustled around the ornate sixteenth-century church before he darted across the quiet side-street and round into Puma Court. He quickly found the low wall covered in greenery with its gate access. He checked the handle and surprisingly, it was open. That made things easier. They slipped inside, keeping in the shadows, away from the slivers of light emanating from nearby windows. Reed wound his way around a willow tree, past a wooden bench, and some wheelie bins, before he stopped in his tracks. The back door to the pub had a conspicuous camera above it that threw his plans into disarray, so he scanned for other options. Crouched beside an evergreen bush, he spotted a suitable opportunity. One sash window on the third floor of the pub was ajar, presumably someone hadn't thought to shut it. An adjacent building's drainpipe offered a route upwards. He pointed this out to Euan and shuffled over, being careful to avoid the CCTV camera.

Reed grasped the rusted metal drainpipe and climbed upwards, then shimmied across the stone window ledge to the corner of the Ten Bells Pub. From there, he leapt across a gap to reach the partially open sash window on the third floor. He nudged the window upwards and slithered in, careful to land quietly on the floor. It was another dining area of the pub with tables and chairs akin to the second floor, where they had lunch earlier in the day. A discarded slice of carrot stuck to his shoe as he stood. Their parkour training had come in handy. He turned to help Euan, who passed through the lightweight aluminium case that contained the drone before assisting his friend inside. They squatted on the floor and listened for any sounds of movement. There was another floor above them, which presumably was where the owners lived. After five minutes of silence, they worked their way down the stairs towards the ground floor with their head torches in place, lighting the way through the dark pub.

"Which way is it?" whispered Reed.

"This way," said Euan, as he led his friend down the narrow stone steps.

"Here's the padlocked door."

The brass padlock glimmered in the light of Reed's head torch as he fumbled in his backpack for the lock pick set. He selected a pair of suitable levers and within seconds the shank popped.

"That was quick!"

"No flies on me."

"It's surprising how much shit comes out of your mouth," laughed Euan.

Reed lightly punched his friend on the arm before he removed the padlock, then slowly eased open the door. Safely inside, they scanned the dark space, and it soon became apparent it was a shrine to Jack the Ripper. Inside, there were two worn brown sofas and a wooden display unit that contained Ripper memorabilia. Cuttings of old newspapers, grim murder drawings, a silver necklace and some bracelets. Perhaps the killer had removed the jewellery from his victims? He plucked out his phone to photograph the items and newspaper excerpts. There were four suspects mentioned in the old newspaper cuttings: Aaron Kosminski, Walter Sickert, Thomas Cutbush, and Montague John Druitt.

"It's a meeting room for Ripperologists," said Reed.

"It's gruesome."

"What about the four suspects?"

"We've got three on our list."

"Clearly, someone else is searching for the real identity of Jack the Ripper."

"The landlord?"

"Maybe. We should ask Emily to research the landlord tomorrow."

"Interesting jewellery," said Euan.

"There's nothing worth much. Let's get to the ladder."

As they left the room, Euan stubbed his foot on the protruding leg of a sofa and yelped. Reed turned to him and put a finger to his lips as Euan hopped out of the door on one foot. Reed swiftly clicked the padlock back in place and listened for any noise. All was quiet, so they sneaked down the dark corridor to the final door, the one that accessed the keg storage area. With his lock pick set, he soon had the door open, and they slipped inside. The jumble of beer pipes and barrels blocked their access to the ladder, but they skilfully manoeuvred through the spaghetti-like tangle to reach it. Reed shone his head torch down into the dark area before clambering down the metal rungs. The climb down was short-lived as his feet hit the bottom after about eight feet, so he spun round, but there was nowhere to go. The only item in the pit was a large water pipe with a circular metal valve that resembled a stopcock. What a waste of time. He quickly climbed back up.

"It's a deadend, nothing there but a water valve," he said.

"Oh, that's disappointing, but another location to cross off our list."

"Yep, let's get out of here."

Reed locked the door to the keg storage area before they ascended to the third floor, ready to climb out of the window. He surveyed the courtyard below and thought he spotted someone skulking in the shadows. Then a second person. He silently pointed this out to Euan and whispered,

"Can you get the drone up?"

"It'll make too much noise."

"I'm sure I saw two people sneaking around in the courtyard."

"Where?"

As Reed pointed out their location, one moved, confirming his suspicions.

"We could use one of the front windows to drop out of, but we'll get caught on camera," he said.

"Or wait here until they disappear?"

"What if they don't go soon?"

"Then we'll have to fight them. Perhaps it's those two lads who accosted us in the alleyway Friday?" asked Euan.

"It might be. How'd they know we're here?"

"Perhaps they saw us and have been waiting?"

"Unlikely. How did they realise we were at the pub?"

"They must be tracking us. Perhaps from the location of your phone?" suggested Euan.

"Has to be. I've had an idea. Why don't we climb to the roof and descend elsewhere?"

"Yes. There are no cameras in Puma Court. Let's do that."

Reed led the way through the window gap, proceeding with caution, and shimmied back across to the metal drainpipe before scaling it to the roof. He paused to search for the shadowy figures below, but couldn't see them. Both lads clambered over the rooftops and reached an overgrown jasmine plant that stretched to the roof from the ground, which would allow them to wriggle down safely. It appeared they would escape with no trouble.

Earlier, Bernie had visited the Ten Bells Pub after Davey's tipoff and watched Reed Hascombe, with his two companions, consume their Sunday lunch. He had waited until they left and double-checked his Rippers Guild room was properly padlocked. It was. He had phoned Sophia to get the happenings of Saturday evening at the art exhibition and, for a change; she had achieved something worthwhile. Now they understood the letter's contents. *Search for the hidden access to the water where the bells toll.* His immediate thought was the pub, but he was aware there was no hidden ladder access to water, having spent a lot of time in the building. He could see why someone might consider it as Aaron Kosminski, Jakob's great-great-grandfather, had frequented the pub regularly. Coupled with one murder that occurred close by, it was a serious consideration. But Bernie knew otherwise.

His thoughts had gone into overdrive since his conversation with Sophia. His brain didn't stop whirring and kept him awake. Then, at nineteen minutes past midnight, his phone blipped with a text message from Davey.

Davey: *'Reed Hascombe is at the Ten Bells Pub again, right now'*
Bernie: *'Thanks Mouse'*

Perfect. The treasure investigator clearly thought the pub was a relevant location and had been scoping it out earlier. Bernie clasped his phone as he silently slid out of the bedroom, careful not to wake his sleeping wife. He slipped downstairs and rung Davey.

"I'm going there now Davey, make sure you stay up and text me every five minutes with Hascombe's location. I plan on apprehending him."

"Yes, boss."

He needed some help, but both Ryan and Mikey were still recovering from their injuries from two days ago. Only one choice remained. He called Jakob and explained the situation. The Polish lad immediately agreed to meet Bernie at the pub. Now the two of them were crouched under cover of the willow tree as Davey's latest text pinged on his phone.

Davey: *'He's moved to The Dermatography Clinic'*

Bernie already knew this, as he had spotted Hascombe and his mate slithering across the rooftops. He beckoned to Jakob to follow him out of the internal courtyard into Puma Court, a glorified alleyway with bollards and a couple of elaborate streetlights. As he rotated to his left, he spotted both escapees descending a massive jasmine plant to reach the ground. He fingered the Bowie knife in his pocket whilst Jakob flexed his arm with a baseball bat. He stalked towards the two lads and let out a guttural laugh.

"We meet at last Reed."

The surprised look on the long, black-haired lad generated a buzz inside. He enjoyed being in control and had caught out the sneaky investigator.

"I hope you weren't breaking into any properties, otherwise we'll need to get the police involved," Bernie said, although the police were the last people he would call.

"Just out for some rooftop scrambling, and this large climbing plant looked really interesting."

"Don't get cocky with me son, we've cornered you."

Bernie could feel Jakob behind him itching to get involved, but he wanted some important information first.

"Tell me what the letter says and we'll let you go."

Hascombe didn't speak for almost a minute, which annoyed Bernie.

"I asked you a question."

"Yes, I heard it, but I've nothing to say to you. I'm guessing you work for the blonde woman, Sophia Meyer, at the art gallery?"

This incensed Bernie. He couldn't help himself and blurted out, "She works for me! We know about the hidden water access and the bells. What else is in the letter?" asked Bernie.

"That's it," came the abrupt response.

Bernie edged forward and gave Jakob the nod to attack. The Polish lad flew in with his baseball bat swinging, but Hascombe ducked beneath the bat easily and jabbed Jakob in the ribs twice. Bernie snatched out his Bowie knife and flicked it at the ginger lad, who defended himself by swinging a case in front which batted away each thrust. Bernie twisted, dodged, and lunged, his movements a blur of lethal precision, but the ginger lad's case became a shield, deflecting the sharp blade with a resounding clang.

Tension increased as the four opponents circled each other, locked in a fiery dance of combat. Bernie spotted Hascombe kick Jakob in the leg, who grunted in pain and stumbled back as his bat fell to the ground. Hascombe lunged forward, so Jakob drew a knife from his belt as the two foes circled each other, their breaths heavy with anticipation. With a swift motion, Jakob thrust the knife towards Hascombe's chest, but the seasoned fighter effortlessly avoided the attack. Both streetlamps suddenly turned off as the time hit one o'clock, the designated time that the local council plunged the neighbourhood into darkness. Bernie stood back, but the change in the lighting caught Jakob off guard as the Hascombe swept the Polish lad's legs from under him. Then a shout.

"Run Euan."

Both of the protagonists pivoted on their heels and sprinted down the alleyway. Bernie chose not to chase them. He wouldn't be able to catch them, especially with Jakob on his backside. He cut his losses. His time would come for revenge. He wondered if they had broken into his Rippers Guild room and made a mental note to check in the morning.

Chapter 21

COMMERCIAL STREET POLICE STATION

MONDAY

CLARA LOXSTONE TOOK A final blast on her salted caramel vape before she headed inside the police station, ready to start her day. She had spent her day off yesterday with her husband after an hour's yoga session, her release mechanism. Deep breathing, unconventional poses and stretching all calmed her mood. She had woken fully refreshed that morning, ready to tackle the murder case. All the information and data streams should be available in her inbox. She checked her watch. Not yet seven o'clock. She had always been an early bird. The police station felt eerily quiet for a Monday morning as Clara hustled to her cramped office.

The whiteboard in her office had one name heading it up: Dean Withers. Underneath, DI Charlie Page had written all the facts unearthed about the victim. Male, Caucasian, twenty-six, five foot nine, lived in the southern part of Whitechapel with his girlfriend and had been out with work friends Friday night. The victim had no money troubles and no apparent enemies. Charlie had interviewed the victim's work colleagues, who confirmed he was on his way home.

Clara's desktop computer had eventually finished its startup process, so she logged into her emails. There sat the autopsy report, forensics analysis of the crime scene, and some CCTV footage to view. She printed off the two reports and studied them whilst she waited for Charlie Page. The lad never arrived on time. It had become annoying, and now she would deal with the issue. Seven minutes later, her junior DI blustered into her office, mumbling more excuses for being late.

"Enough Page. It's too many times. You'll get a written warning. Sort it out or get another job."

Her abrupt nature often caused junior detectives to wilt under the pressure. She hated tardiness. Charlie flushed pink as he apologised again.

"I'm not interested. Get onto reviewing the CCTV footage and let me know once you've found anything."

Clara returned to studying the reports and eventually stood to add more comments to the murder case notes on the rather bare whiteboard. Everything confirmed the forensic expert's initial thoughts at the scene. The victim had been killed from behind with one single cut to the throat with a sharp blade, possibly a scalpel or hunting knife. No bruises or any other sign of bodily harm, which suggested the killer had lain the body on the floor rather than let it fall haphazardly. Time of death around midnight. The victim had five times the legal level of alcohol in his blood, so had clearly consumed plenty of drinks during the evening. No footprints found, just the small black leather-covered button she had picked up at the scene on Saturday morning. Unfortunately, no DNA was found on either the victim's body or the button, so the murderer had probably worn gloves. Overall, she had very few clues to assist her investigation.

She wandered out of her office into the cluttered work area for junior detectives and sauntered over to Charlie's desk. He gazed at the computer screen.

"Anything yet Page?" Clara asked.

"I have one thing to show you, but can I finish reviewing this video first?"

"If you must, but make it ten minutes max, in my office."

Clara strolled over to the automatic drinks machine and pressed the button for an Earl Grey tea. Whilst it churned and gurgled, she checked the time. Only two hours before her meeting with DS Browne, her boss, to run through progress on the murder case. Page better hurry as she needed something concrete to present to her boss. As her mind rattled through the facts, she sipped her tea, forgetting it was freshly brewed and subsequently burnt her mouth. She yelped out in pain. Why did machines make tea so damn hot? She rushed back to her office and waited for Page to appear.

Charlie bundled into her office thirteen minutes later, so Clara reiterated his lateness issue by looking at her watch.

"Three minutes late."

"Yes ma'am. That last video took longer than expected," he said, his face bright pink again. He needed to toughen up, she thought.

"What have you got?"

"There's a camera at the primary school on Gunthorpe Street but it's blocked from seeing the road by the tall green fencing. The block of apartments has a camera, but it's facing inwards onto the stairs ...."

"I'm not interested in what you haven't got. It's wasting time, just tell me positive sightings."

"Yes ma'am. Only one camera picked anything up at the top end of Gunthorpe Street. Click on the second video. It's ten minutes in. You can see the victim clearly walking down the road before disappearing off camera. Ten seconds afterwards, there's a glimpse of another person walking past in the shadows. They're wearing a hooded jacket, so not a clear view. Around similar height to the victim."

"Something positive. Add it to the whiteboard. Any thoughts on MO?"

"It wasn't a robbery. The victim's wallet and mobile were still in his pockets. Revenge for something?"

"That's a possibility. I'm bothered by the throat cut as it's unusual to be knifed from behind. They must have sneaked up quietly."

"He was drunk, so perhaps he didn't hear?"

"Very true. We meet with DS Browne at ten o'clock, so can you put together a killer's profile from what little we have?"

"Yes, ma'am."

Clara contemplated the evidence, which lacked vital clues. Had an altercation occurred during the victim's drunken night out? The murder seemed pre-mediated. Had the victim done something that warranted such severe action? They needed to dig into his past and check for a motive to connect the two.

Chapter 22

ST PAUL'S CATHEDRAL

MONDAY

THE WHITE STONE CATHEDRAL was an impressive sight, with its subtle cornices, figurines, and a golden cross atop the dome. Euan stood outside the tour guide's entrance, waiting for Reed to conclude his conversation with Emily. She had returned to Sheffield yesterday for her three days of teaching and promised to carry out research on the Ten Bells Pub landlord. He surveyed the tourists in the ticket queue, a throng of individuals from across the globe gathered in one spot. The bitter chill of the wind meant most people wore winter coats and scarves. The team had chosen their next suspect to investigate last night, Walter Sickert, after seeing his portrayal of Jack the Ripper's bedroom in the Ten Bells Pub. Another of Sickert's works was a painting of St. Paul's Cathedral. They decided it was the next location to look for the hidden ladder accessing water, as the cathedral had plenty of bells to toll.

After Reed had wrapped up his *'check-in'* call with Emily, both lads joined the tickets queue and followed the crowd ready for the tour. The idea was to assess the likelihood of a hidden ladder and then determine how best to gain access to it unseen.

"Turn your phone off, Reed. That way, those four thugs can't track our activity," advised Euan.

"Oh yes, I forgot. It's going to be a pain remembering to keep switching it off," said Reed as they advanced inside the cathedral.

Euan had marvelled at the architecture of the building outside, but once inside, he gawped at the ceiling. The golden hue above his head glowed in the weak winter sunshine as it streamed through the windows that punctuated the dome structure. He wondered how long it had taken the builders to construct such a wonderful sight and glanced at his tour companions, their eyes twinkling in amazement.

"This is incredible," he said to Reed.

"Just amazing."

The tour guide led the way to a stone staircase leading down to the crypt. Euan snapped a few discreet pictures. For the tour, he had to photograph all the rooms and record all the CCTV camera positions on a layout for later. Whilst he had been doing this, Reed had assessed their likely entry point and route to the crypt because they felt certain any hidden ladder was probably there. The crypt had been much bigger than Euan had expected, with several CCTV cameras focused on the significant burial displays. Lord Nelson's coffin took pride of place, topped with a black marble sarcophagus, whilst The Duke of Wellington's impressive casket made of Cornish granite stood further away. Memorials to other prominent British luminaries, including Sir Winston Churchill, Florence Nightingale, and Sir Christopher Wren, were present. Whilst he had been impressed with these, he wasn't interested in them. The locked doors had been of greater interest. Was there anything below them? He fired off more discreet photos using his mobile phone and edged around the crypt, noting each camera on the tour map. Reed nudged him.

"I'm not seeing anything obvious at the moment."

"Perhaps behind one of the locked doors?"

"Let's hope so."

The tour guide continued with their practiced speech as Euan edged around the OBE Chapel with its memorials to noted scientists, artists, and musicians. This definitely was a dead-end. No doors or windows. He lingered at the back of the tour group and managed a few more photos before following the group ascending into the main cathedral area with its golden ceiling and vast dome. The last section of the tour led them up a winding circular staircase with hundreds of stone steps. Two hundred and fifty-seven, to be precise. The older members of the group struggled, so Euan had no choice but to join Reed earlier than expected in the Whispering Gallery. The internal balustrade spanned the circumference of the dome and gave splendid views to the floor below. But they weren't interested in this. The next level up was the important one. Reed had told Euan earlier to spend as much time as possible there, as it was his preferred access point into the Cathedral.

Euan bounced up the next set of stone steps behind Reed, who stood discussing architecture with the tour guide. He knew it was a distraction technique, allowing him to take discreet photos of the Stone Gallery. He zipped up his padded grey jacket as the wind whistled through the open doorway leading onto the external walkway. The view from the Stone Gallery gave a three-sixty degree view of London's skyline. He spotted the Shard, the London Eye, and Tower Bridge from the outside gallery that encircled the dome. Whilst Reed kept the tour guide occupied, he shot more photos and noted the lack of cameras up there. Perfect. He winked at Reed. His mate got the message.

They swapped positions as Euan distracted the tour guide with a discussion on the visible landmarks. Out of the corner of his eye, Euan watched Reed slip back inside the doorway after all the remaining tourists had climbed the staircase and moved to the outside gallery. His best friend stood behind a window and fiddled with the locking mechanism. The plan was to provide an access point into the cathedral during the hours of darkness.

The final part of the tour was the Golden Gallery, the zenith of the dome. From there, the panoramic views of London were breathtaking. After he had absorbed the view, Euan descended the stone staircase, which wound down to the ground floor.

"Did you mark all the CCTV cameras?" asked Reed.

"Hopefully, I got them all."

Euan analysed the layout of the ground floor again and then traced the route to the crypt in his mind, stored for later use. Tonight would be tricky. They had to ascend the outside of the building to access the Stone Gallery, where, hopefully, they could enter the building undetected. Then the tough part, locating any hidden ladders in the crypt when nothing had been obvious during the tour.

Chapter 23

HOXTON CAR REPAIR SHOP

MONDAY

BERNIE DOODLED ON THE booking-in diary open on his desk in the office of his Hoxton car repair shop. He had successfully shipped the BMW M sports car in Calypso Red to the Czech Republic this morning, the last order in his chop-shop sideline. Thirty grand profit after Ryan and Mikey had stolen the car. His thoughts turned to Jack the Ripper's hidden treasure whilst he waited for Sophia to arrive. He had phoned her earlier and suggested they meet to discuss his plan, so she agreed to come over to the workshop. The diary contained scribbles of coins which he had absent-mindedly drawn. He actually didn't know what the hidden treasure could be, and mulled over his links to Jack.

The name of his lucrative sideline was the key as he had named it the Hoxton Hot Rods, a nod to the street gang Hoxton High Rips his great-great-grandfather had belonged to. The story his father told was that Thomas Cutbush had been a member of the street gang and, after a daring heist, where they stole some extremely valuable jewellery, Thomas became greedy. He swiped a significant piece from the heist, apparently the highest worth item. Thomas's great-great-grandfather's greed caused the gang to exile him, and he took the treasure with him. Later he was identified as a suspect for the Jack the Ripper murders. Bernie had spent a large part of his adult life trying to trace the missing jewellery that he felt belonged to his family. Based on the assumption that Thomas Cutbush was indeed Jack the Ripper, the discovery of the letter had become crucial to his search.

A loud wolf-whistle alerted him to Sophia's arrival. He slipped outside the office, hung over the metal railing and observed Ryan and Mikey attempting to chat up the tall blonde German girl. No chance of that lads, he thought, knowing how dangerous she was. Eventually Mikey pointed out the staircase, her heels reverberated on the metal steps as she ascended. He watched the two lads gawping at her backside in tight, shiny black trousers as she reached the mezzanine floor.

"Come in Sophia. It's not the plush standard you would normally expect, but it's my office," he said in a patronising tone, but this was his turf.

"It's fine Bernie, I've seen worse. What's so urgent we needed to meet here?"

"I have an idea which needs to remain between us."

"Oooh, I like the secrecy. Shouldn't we bring Jakob into it? I couldn't care less about Basil, though."

"We will at the right time, but he is dangerous and prone to random, violent acts, plus he got whipped last night."

Sophia flicked her long blonde hair, as she was prone to do when unsettled. "Really? What happened?" she asked.

"Those investigators that Madeleine Robinson-Smith is using appeared at the Ten Bells last night, so I went over there with Jakob and we surprised them. The main bloke, Reed Hascombe, the one I've been tracking, is also a bloody ninja warrior. Jakob used a baseball bat and knife but ended up on his backside."

"Wow. Jakob normally handles himself brilliantly. I bet his pride was hurt."

Bernie said, "He was really upset."

"So what's your plan?"

Bernie stood to close the door before continuing with the

conversation. "The sidekick in the investigation team isn't anywhere as strong as the key guy, although he repelled my knife attacks with a metal case. There must be another clue contained within the letter. More than you extracted from Madeleine, so let's change tact and target the ginger lad."

"Target him how?"

"Get friendly with him. You're terrific at that," said Bernie as he pandered to her ego.

"You mean seduce him?"

"I wouldn't go that far. Make contact, go on a date, then extract something useful from him."

"Ooooh, can I inflict some pain?" asked Sophia.

"Up to you. Mouse has found out they are staying at the New Road Hotel. We know the dark-haired guy is called Reed Hascombe, but I know nothing about his mate. I'll leave it for you to decide the best plan of action."

Bernie's phone rang. It was just a regular customer. Afterwards, he bade farewell to the German girl and listened as she endured more flirting, confidently batting it away with ease. She had a definite skill for handling the male species. He felt confident she could infiltrate Sherbet Investigations with her charms.

Chapter 24

St Paul's Cathedral

Monday

THE WINTER SUN HAD dipped below the horizon about an hour ago as Reed finished his spicy pizza, laced with fresh chillies. He used the paper napkin to wipe his mouth as Euan ate his last slice of chicken bbq pizza. They had fuelled up early, as tonight could be a long one. His plan was to wait until two hours after the cathedral had shut its doors before attempting their break-in. The pizza place hummed with conversation in different languages as the waitresses buzzed around, loading food and drinks onto customers' tables. Reed glanced around the room at the bland decor and checked his watch again. Another hour to kill.

"Fancy another drink?" he asked Euan.

"Sure, I'll have a chocolate milkshake. I'll need the calories for our climb."

"That's a great idea. I'll join you. What about a dessert?"

"Now you're talking. Chocolate brownies for me."

"Mmm, I fancy the toffee cheesecake."

Reed waved at a nearby waitress and placed their orders. She rushed off to greet the latest group of customers that streamed through the double doors of the pizza restaurant. Whilst he waited for their desserts and shakes, Reed checked his backpack to ensure everything required for tonight's adventure was included. It contained: harness, head torch, balaclava, climbing gloves, rope, grapple hook, crowbar, lock pick set. He hadn't checked in with Madeleine since Saturday so called her.

"Hi Madeleine. I just wanted to update you on yesterday's events," he said to the mining company's CEO, before recounting what had happened.

"Have you found anything yet?" she asked.

"Sorry, no we haven't. We'll be searching St. Paul's Cathedral this evening. Walter Sickert has painted it and he is one of our prominent suspects."

"That's sounds dangerous, just don't get caught."

"We don't intend to. I'll speak with you tomorrow if we get lucky."

"Thanks Reed."

Their desserts and milkshake orders arrived and within minutes, they had consumed them. The extra calories were the perfect fuel for their evening activity. Reed paid the bill, and they ambled towards the cathedral.

Euan's CCTV camera mapping had provided a clear route for them from a tiny garden with tree cover. With his balaclava and gloves on, Reed attached the grapple hook to his climbing rope and launched it up two levels, aiming for the stone balustrade. It dropped short. The second attempt was no better. On the third throw, Reed put maximum effort in, the grapple hook sailed high in the air and flipped over the balustrade's edge. The prongs of the hook caught on the protruding lip and engaged the stone wall. He tugged the rope several times and swung on it to secure it. Satisfied with his efforts, he put on his harness and attached the rope with a belay device and carabiner. He ascended, scrambling up the first level to a slender stone ledge before taking a breather.

Darkness provided the required cover, unseen from sightseers strolling past. Once he had swung over the stone balustrade, he waited whilst Euan made his climb. They sat atop the cathedral, their backs against the stone wall, after retrieving the rope, conscious of the camera on the wall in front of them. They didn't know if it had night vision capability. Or if security staff monitored the cameras in real time.

Traffic noise wafted up on the winter's evening breeze with snatches of words from people walking past the cathedral. Reed was used to the relaxed noises of nature in Sheffield, but London presented a different ambiance. Hustle and bustle. Everyone rushed around. He began the next step of their exploit and crawled alongside the stone balustrade, out of sight of the camera. He positioned himself, ready to make his next throw of the grapple hook up to the Stone Gallery. This proved to be easier and within minutes, both lads sat on the cold floor of the gallery. Reed counted three windows from the doorway. He pushed against the window's lock and it opened. Earlier he had taped a slim strip of metal against the inner lock so the window appeared securely closed, but wasn't. A clever idea of his. They clambered inside and closed the metal-framed window.

Reed slipped on his head torch and shuffled down the stone staircase to the Whispering Gallery. It felt awkward in the dark, but strangely familiar. They needed to be conscious of the CCTV cameras, referring to Euan's map to plan their route to the crypt. The main area of the cathedral didn't give off the golden hue that daytime sunlight provided as their footsteps echoed slightly on the stone floor. They walked, crouched and slithered on their stomachs across to the stone stairs that descended to the crypt, avoiding the cameras.

"That didn't take too long," said Euan as he brushed fragments of dirt off his black jacket.

"Hopefully we didn't get caught on camera."

"Even if they captured some movement, they shouldn't recognise us."

"When we get into the crypt, I'll try the locked doors whilst you scoot around searching for any other options," instructed Reed.

"Okay mate, let's go."

In the crypt's darkness, Reed shivered, knowing that many dignitaries were buried there. Their bones encased in all manner of stone and wooden receptacles. He hustled over to the first door, picked the lock, and checked inside. It was just a cleaning cupboard! The second and third doors offered nothing better. One contained bibles, the other held racks of robes. All three were just insignificant storage rooms. The fourth door opened to some stone steps that descended, but after he turned a corner, he faced an uneven block of concrete blocking his passage. He returned upstairs, locked the door, and sought Euan, who squatted beside Lord Nelson's coffin, peering at the floor.

"Anything Euan?" he asked.

"Look here, on the floor. There's guide rails embedded in the stone."

Reed shone his head torch to the spot his mate had pointed at. The beam reflected off narrow metal rails that ran underneath the stone plinth holding the coffin. They extended out around four feet adjacent to the massive plinth.

"Yes, I see. What're you thinking?"

"Does this plinth move?"

"The rails suggest it should. Let's try pushing it."

With their backs to the heavy plinth's end wall, they shoved hard, but to no avail. It didn't move. Reed scratched his head and examined the bottom edge of the plinth, searching for a lock or lever. Nothing. This must be a secret entrance. How could they reach it?

Chapter 25

New Road Hotel

Monday

Sophia sat in the reception area of the New Road Hotel, a quite unremarkable space, just like the exterior of the building. All rectangular lines, akin to a government building. The windows had lead strips which split the panes into small square sections. Even the wall lights looked unremarkable, just perfunctory bulbs to light the space in the evening's darkness. She pretended to check her watch again, then adjusted her blonde hair once more, having tied it up into a bob-style earlier. Her intentions were to bump into the ginger-haired lad and entice him for lunch or a drink. She had researched Reed Hascombe and found some photos from two years ago taken at a homeless shelter in Sheffield. The photos included his mate. She waited for nearly thirty minutes but didn't see either of them. Time to action her plan, so she wandered over to the reception desk.

"Hi, I'm meeting Reed Hascombe, who's staying at your hotel, but he's nearly half an hour late. Can you phone him, please?" she asked.

"Let me check," said the young receptionist as she punched some keys on the black keyboard underneath the screen before picking up the telephone handset. "Who shall I say is waiting for him?"

"It's Sybil Deveroux from Big Boxes," lied Sophia.

The young receptionist punched in 231 on the desk phone as Sophia eagerly noticed the room number. After ten rings, the receptionist replaced the handset.

"There's no answer. Shall I pass on a message?"

"Yes, please. Ask him to ring this number."

Sophia provided a false number, thanked the girl, and wandered off to the ladies' cloakroom. She contemplated her next step. The empty hotel room presented an opportunity for her to learn about the two protagonists. After she had placed several whole toilet rolls into one pan and flushed it several times, she created a blockage. She rushed outside and waved at the young receptionist.

"Help! The toilet has overflowed!"

She waited until the receptionist raced past her, then she dashed over to the reception desk, grabbed a master keycard and bounded up the narrow staircase to the second floor. It took seconds to find room 231, and she swiftly entered. A quick search revealed nothing of interest, just clothes and men's toiletries. No bag except an empty suitcase in the corner. No ID or electronic devices, nothing to help her. She had no more information on Reed Hascombe, so what about his mate? What room would he be in? She chose 230.

Sophia stood in the corridor, her ear to the door and, not hearing anything, she entered. It was empty; the bed was made and everywhere tidy. Ready for its next guest. A few rapid steps took her to room 232, and she gained entry. The room was messy. Clothes strewn across the floor, the bed unmade, and she almost tripped over a pair of blue trainers near the door. Different to his mate's room. She even spotted a pair of Transformers pants atop the suitcase. That's pretty juvenile, she thought. This bloke would be easy to seduce and extract information from. A flutter of her eyelashes and a flick of her hair would probably suffice, she thought. She rummaged around the messy hotel room for several minutes but found no ID. Underneath a discarded t-shirt on the floor, she then discovered something particularly interesting. Hand-written notes, which detailed two Jack the Ripper suspects.

The initial section described James Maybrick with various

comments, all of which had been crossed out. The second related to Montague John Druitt. This was of special interest, as the last comment read, *'extremely unlikely'*. Her mind whirred with intensity. That was the suspect that Basil, the bank manager, had hung his hat on and convinced the others in the Ripper Guild could actually be Jack the Ripper. Bernie would be extremely interested in this, she thought. She was about to send a photo of the notes to Bernie when she overheard male voices in the corridor. Oh shit, they're back.

Sophia rushed into the compact bathroom, and part closed the door, leaving a tiny gap. Her mind raced with workable options to explain why she was in the room. The best option would be to declare she had muddled up the room numbers. The male voices from the corridor continued their discussion. She could enter the corridor, pretend to be a hotel worker, and claim she was needed in room 323 to fix a problem. That would explain why she carried a master keycard. She brazenly slid through the hotel room's door and swung around towards the men.

It wasn't Reed Hascombe at all. The men were twenty feet away, further down the empty corridor, and they didn't even cast her a glance. That was close. She sent the photo to Bernie and hustled downstairs, taking care to avoid the young receptionist when she left the hotel. Her plan to bump into the ginger-haired lad hadn't worked out, and she still didn't know his name. But she had his room number. She would revisit the hotel and work her magic on another day.

Chapter 26

St Paul's Cathedral

Monday

REED SAT SLUMPED BESIDE Lord Nelson's enormous stone plinth and considered their options. Return to the hotel and accept the cathedral wasn't Jack the Ripper's hidden access or search again. He chose the latter. He scanned the cold stone plinth walls, but they were smooth, no switch or lever. The black sarcophagus atop the stone plinth reflected the narrow beam of his head torch but didn't have a hidden button. Surely these metal floor rails had meant the plinth moved in the past? He held his breath and listened for any audible clues, but the air was still with all sounds from outside blocked by the thick walls of the crypt.

"There has to be a hidden switch or lever somewhere," he said to Euan.

"Perhaps there's a concealed cover on the floor?"

Whilst Euan fumbled around on his hands and knees, Reed moved to the white columns interspersed around Nelson's coffin. He searched every inch of all five thick columns without success.

"Reed, over here."

He moved to the other side of the stone plinth, where Euan held a mosaic hand-sized stone in his hand, squatted beside the metal rails.

"This was slightly loose, and it blended in with the floor design, a brilliant piece of craftmanship. I levered it free with my penknife.

There's a switch. Shall I press it?" asked Euan.

"Go for it."

As Euan pressed the button, Reed heard a motor whirr, then the whole stone plinth slowly slid across the floor on the metal rails. He gasped in astonishment as it gradually revealed an opening. He peered over the edge and shone his head torch into the pit of darkness. Steep stone steps descended as a slight breeze wafted from below, tinged with the stench of decay.

"Brilliant Euan, this could be it," said Reed, with a growing knot of excitement bubbling inside him.

"It smells like the tunnel underneath Robin Hood's Stride from two summers ago."

"Oh, you pussy, let's investigate."

"Right behind you," laughed Euan, knowing full well his best friend always took the lead.

"I should let you lead for a change."

"You're the boss. Let's get on with it. We don't want to get caught."

"I'm not the boss, we're a team! Hold your nose if you can't bear the smell and don't throw up," said Reed.

"Yeah, yeah."

Reed took a few tentative steps with his hands pressed against both rough stone walls. After about twenty steps, he reached a flat, earthy tunnel about five feet wide, but tall enough to stand upright. He listened for a few seconds, hoping to hear sounds of water, but nothing, so he strode out purposefully. The tunnel took a sharp turn, which led to some broken wooden planks installed across the width of the tunnel. As he stood on the middle plank, it gave way under his weight, let out a scream, and his legs disappeared into a hole. He scrabbled to hold on to the planks with his hands as Euan appeared and grabbed his climbing harness.

"Don't drop me Euan."

"I've got you. Let me tie a rope on to your harness."

Reed's heart rate had lurched upwards as he clung on desperately, while Euan fumbled in his backpack for a rope. His fingers slowly slipped off the worn wooden planks until he felt a tug on his harness. Euan had securely tied the rope and was pulling him upwards. He swivelled his head to get a look inside the dark pit and spotted several wooden stakes planted upright. The foul stench of death had increased in intensity, and he immediately saw why. The sharp stake ends held decaying rat bodies in various stages of decomposition. Euan's efforts meant he had stronger handholds on the wooden planks and eventually hauled himself free of the pit of death. He sat on the cold earth as he gathered his composure and the adrenaline drifted away.

"Thanks Euan, you saved my life."

"No problem. What's in there?"

"Stakes with rats impaled on them. They must have fallen through the cracks in the planks," said Reed.

"You were lucky. Shall we head back?"

"Not yet. The tunnel continues. Let's carry on."

Both lads leapt across the dangerous pit and continued along the tunnel as their head torches cast dancing beams of light on the rough hewn rock walls. Their footsteps echoed through the narrow passage as the cool touch of the ancient rock against their fingertips added a sense of adventure to the exploration. Reed stopped as the tunnel came to an abrupt end. In the rock wall sat a rusted iron casket on a rough ledge around six inches deep. He pulled the casket out and prised open the lid with his swiss army knife. It creaked and revealed an inch layer of dust with a gold-coloured coin peeking out. Perhaps this was Lord Nelson's ashes? He removed the coin, brushed it off, and noticed the date imprinted on it: 21.10.1805.

"Look at this," he said as he waved the timeworn coin in front of his head torch beam for Euan to scrutinise.

"As we're under Nelson's coffin, could it be his date of death?"

"Possibly. Let's leave it here. It's not the treasure we're looking for."

"I agree."

Reed replaced the coin inside the casket, returned it to the ledge, and they headed back up the tunnel. They jumped over the dangerous pit and climbed back up the stone steps to reach the crypt. The whole exploit had taken only ten minutes, but upon rejoining the crypt, they noticed a torch light at the far end. It rotated across the walls as though someone was descending the stairs. Oh shit, he thought, that's our escape route. Quick as a flash, Reed pressed the button on the floor and the plinth slowly covered the opening. He slammed in the mosaic tile and tugged Euan towards the robe storage room. He fiddled rapidly with the lock, opened the door and they slipped inside before the flickering torch light reached them. They switched off their head torches and Reed watched through a tiny gap in the doorway. It was a security guard in a brown uniform.

The security guard wandered over to Lord Nelson's coffin and scanned the stone plinth with his torch, which was now fully back in position. Reed considered their options. Stay hidden or slip past the guard? He decided the best option was to get ahead of the guard, as the main cathedral area was a wide open space and much easier to be seen. He waited until the guard meandered around the opposite side of the stone plinth, which blocked his view of the doorway, and then they slipped out of the robe storage room. There was no time to re-lock the door, so he quietly closed it. They tip-toed around the edge of the crypt, keeping to the shadows, until Euan tripped on a wayward electrical cable. His mate bundled into a stack of chairs, pushing them across the stone floor, which generated a screech.

"Who's there?" shouted the security guard.

"We need to hustle," Reed whispered as the guard's torch light spun in their direction.

Reed bounced up the steps to the main cathedral area and scanned the area for other dangers. No other lights or security guards. They retraced their way back to the circular stone steps that led up to the Whispering Gallery with less caution than earlier. He bolted up the two hundred and fifty-seven stone steps and waited until Euan joined him, gasping for air. Whilst they took a breather, the main cathedral area suddenly burst into life as lights illuminated the entire section. Reed dived to the floor and pulled Euan down with him. They couldn't get caught now.

"We need to get to the Stone Gallery quick. Are you ready?" he said.

"Not really. But we need to escape," said Euan.

The next stairway was a dash across the open gallery, so Reed sprinted flat out and slammed into the wall as his foot slipped negotiating the corner. Both lads bounded upwards amid shouts from below. A second voice punctuated the silence. He clambered through the open window, removed the slim strip of metal and slammed it shut once Euan had landed on the Stone Gallery floor. Now to descend. He tied a rope to an ornate stone spindle that was part of the Stone Gallery's balcony and abseiled downwards, using his feet to bounce off the walls. Euan followed suit whilst Reed tied the second rope onto the balustrade overlooking the final descent into the tree covered garden area below. Within seconds, he landed on the ground before his mate dropped beside him. Although the ropes remained attached to the stone balustrades, they left no trace of themselves, as they wore gloves.

Reed leapt over the metal spiked fence and slipped into the shadows of a shop doorway. Fortunately, there were few people milling around, so they removed their gear and stuffed it inside their back packs. That exploit had been another dead end. The quest for Jack the Ripper's hidden treasure had proved to be more difficult than he expected. Time to assess their progress, meet Madeleine, and review what they had learnt.

Chapter 27

THE SHARD, LONDON

TUESDAY

MADELEINE GAZED OUT OF her office window as she sub-consciously touched the cut on her throat beneath the pink neck scarf she wore to hide it. The events of the past week had certainly been more dramatic than she had planned. Dark clouds drifted across London's skyscrapers, with the morning's weather forecast promising snow in the afternoon. Her PA suddenly disrupted her thoughts by knocking on the door and burst in with her two visitors. She swivelled to greet her potential saviour.

"Reed, Euan, come in, take a seat. Kathy, can you get us some drinks and biscuits, please?"

"Yes, of course," said her PA and scurried off with the drink's orders.

"It's been a dramatic week since we last met. I shredded the letter, someone knocked me out, and threatened me. Not exactly what I expected."

"These things happen when valuable treasure is at stake. Everyone wants it and not always for good reasons. There are many criminals floating around our country," said Reed.

"I'm hoping you can find it first, obviously."

"We're trying our best, but I thought it would be useful to catch up after the past week. Plus, I'd like to ask you some questions."

"Okay, fire away."

"Let me recap our activities first. From our initial six potential suspects, we've struck off James Maybrick as there was no sign of any hidden treasure. Aaron Kosminski is a dead-end also, but we're keeping him on the back-burner just in case. We discovered a strange cellar room at the Ten Bells pub that contained a shrine to Jack the Ripper. Emily is investigating the landlord, so hopefully that'll provide a new lead. We've just searched St Paul's Cathedral, assuming Walter Sickert as a suspect, which was also a dead-end. Next we intend to explore the All Hallows by the Tower church this afternoon, another of Walter Sickert's paintings. Montague John Druitt is a non-starter which will then leave only two remaining suspects. Thomas Cutbush and Francis Tumblety," detailed Reed.

"You're halfway through your list and nothing yet. I'm disappointed by that, but the fact we're both being targeted with violence suggests there's truth in the letter."

Madeleine fiddled with her blonde hair, twisting it around her finger. She knew Sherbet Investigations were taking risks on her behalf, but desperately wanted a successful conclusion to the search. Her PA thumped her office door open with the drinks. Once the cash flow problem had been resolved, she needed a new PA. Kathy was just so disruptive. Conversation around their progress halted whilst she fussed around with each person's drink.

"Thanks Kathy."

Once the door closed, Madeleine started the conversation again.

"You wanted to ask some questions?"

"Yes. What else do you know about Sophia?"

"Not much. She is clearly manipulative and has my husband wrapped around her little finger. Her surname is Meyer, so can you dig into her background?"

"Yes, we'll do that. We've encountered four different men who have attacked us. The older guy who confronted us near the Ten Bells Pub told us he's Sophia's boss. We suspect they've been tracking us using my phone's location as no-one appeared last night.

I had it switched off."

The conversation paused until she spotted Euan shuffle in his seat before blurting out another question.

"Can we recap who's aware of the letter?" Euan asked.

"Richard, and I think he told Sophia, probably not on purpose," she said, keen to defend her husband, but deep down she had some reservations.

"Would he mention the treasure?"

"Unquestionably, but I don't understand why nothing happened until you started investigating it last week?"

"Can you check with him tonight?"

"He's away tonight, meeting a new artist in Manchester."

"What about Kathy? You mentioned she asked to look at the letter after our meeting a week ago. Did you speak to her about it?" asked Reed.

"I completely forgot," replied Madeleine as she pressed the intercom button. "Kathy, can you come into the office?"

Madeleine studied her PA as she ambled into the office and stood in front of her oak desk.

"Please sit, Kathy," she said with her finger pointed at one of the visitors' chairs. "Last week you asked to examine the letter I had. Remind me again why?"

"I'm a Ripperologist and particularly interested in who Jack the Ripper was."

"What did you do with that information?"

"I posted about it on a Jack the Ripper blog."

"Exactly what did you say?"

Madeleine spotted the change in her PA's face as it went bright red. Something had happened.

"I mentioned the treasure, but the excitement of reading the letter overwhelmed me, and I couldn't remember much else. I've just remembered someone messaged me and asked about the letter. They're probably the ones who broke into the office? Oh

Madeleine, I'm so sorry. What have I done?" babbled Kathy.

Anger bubbled up inside Madeleine, she was at the point of sacking the woman immediately until Reed jumped into the conversation.

"Can you give me the website and your login details? I want to communicate with them. This person is definitely the one behind the recent violence," said Reed.

"Of course," said Kathy, as she jumped up to retrieve her phone from her desk. Madeleine glanced at Reed and gave him a silent thank-you for staying calm. The PA returned with her phone and after her fingers had whizzed over the touch screen, handed it to Reed. She watched silently as he sent a message to BernardJ95.

"I've requested we meet up, so if they agree, we can nail down the antagonists," said Reed.

"Brilliant idea," said Madeleine.

"They probably won't answer straightaway, but screenshot me the response and I'll tell you what to write next," said Reed, and passed the phone back to Kathy.

"Thanks Kathy, we're finished now," said Madeleine and waved her PA out of the office.

The meeting ended soon afterwards, and once Reed and Euan had left, Madeleine wandered over to the window to reflect on what she learnt today. She found it therapeutic, looking out of the window across the rooftops of London. She watched the sliver of blue sky diminish behind dark clouds. Although they had made some progress, finding Jack's treasure remained challenging.

Chapter 28

Ten Bells Pub

Tuesday

Bernie had called a lunchtime meeting of the Rippers Guild after Sophia had updated him on the information she discovered the day before. Early morning frost still lingered outside, whilst in the room the inefficient heater attempted to blow away winter's cold. He sat on one of the worn sofas eating an egg and cress sandwich from the plate he had ordered earlier, after Basil's moans about missing his lunch. Their exploits to discover the contents of Jack's letter had made little progress, and they needed to kick their efforts up a notch. Jakob had appeared just after him as they waited for the other two to arrive, both eating their favourite sandwiches. Bernie was an egg man. He loved them. Fried, boiled, poached, whichever way they were served. The door flew open in a whirlwind of blonde hair and perfume, which interrupted his munching.

"Always first, Jakob," said Sophia. "Sucking up to Bernie? Or getting your mouth round the free sandwiches?"

A grunt from the Polish lad was all he offered in response, which made Bernie smile. The lad had a thick skin and didn't give a shit about anyone. Immediately behind the German girl, Basil blundered into the room with a glass of red wine.

"You've started on the hard stuff early, Basil. Grab a sandwich and let's get started," said Bernie. "A lot has happened since Saturday. Sophia pried information out of Madeleine about the letter....."

Sophia interjected with a sly comment, "The bitch even looks great with blood trickling down her neck!"

Bernie smiled and continued. "Anyway, we know the key element is a hidden access to water where the bells toll. Which matches with the locations that the Sherbet guys have investigated. Whitechapel Foundry and the Ten Bells Pub. Myself and Jakob attempted to stop them Sunday in the alleyway, but the head guy's a fighter. How are your ribs, Jakob?"

Just a grunt from his compatriot.

"I'm convinced there are more clues in the letter. We had been tracking their activity using Hascombe's phone location, but that's now gone dead except for the odd ping. It suggests he's turned it off, so perhaps they were somewhere else yesterday. Do you want to talk about your efforts?" he asked Sophia.

"Sure. Bernie had the idea of me chatting up Hascombe's sidekick. He suggested I go to the New Road Hotel, where they're staying. So yesterday evening, I used my charm to confirm that, but they weren't there. I then created a neat diversion to obtain a master keycard and entered their rooms. Whilst I didn't find out the name of the ginger-haired lad, I found some handwritten notes that suggested Montague John Druitt isn't a viable suspect," she said.

Six eyes turned to the bank manager, who instantly blushed. His membership in the Rippers Guild hinged on the backstory of Druitt.

"Whoa, hang on a minute," Basil said. "That's just one person's opinion. If you search online, there's plenty of evidence that suggests he's a solid suspect."

"It appears they aren't investigating him," said Bernie as he sensed an opportunity to offload the useless bank manager.

"That doesn't mean he's not a viable suspect."

"I've always thought your argument was wafer thin," continued Bernie as he turned the screw.

"But we started the Rippers Guild together, Bernie."

"No, I started the Rippers Guild. You're only part of it because I let you in."

Bernie smiled as the bank manager squirmed in his seat. Should he get rid of him? He continued the verbal assault.

"Let's be honest, Basil. What have you contributed in the past couple of weeks? Nothing. We three do all the work."

"I refused a further bank loan to Madeleine. Without that refusal, she wouldn't have hired the investigation team," said Basil as he twiddled with his purple bowtie.

"Exactly. That's just caused us a load of hassle when we were making significant progress. Without your stupid meddling, we could've continued with our original plan. Instead, she hires a team of investigators, and the letter gets splashed across the internet for everyone to know about."

"But you told me to refuse the loan!" retorted Basil as metaphorical steam blew from his ears and cold sweat gathered across his brow.

"No, I didn't," lied Bernie, now set on his course of ejection for the irritating bank manager. Jakob he could handle, and Sophia was competent, as well as being eye-candy.

"Let's vote," he said. "All those in favour of Basil remaining in the Rippers Guild, raise your hands."

One hand shot up. Basil's. Bernie smiled. Perfect.

"That's it Basil. You're removed from the Rippers Guild. Goodbye."

"You can't, it's not fair," blustered Basil, as Bernie stood and urged him to depart the room. The overweight bank manager struggled to his feet.

"I'll let everyone know about your stupid club, including Madeleine," spat Basil.

"No, you won't Basil, unless you want Jakob to pay a visit to your pretty wife whilst you're at work?"

The bank manager's handlebar moustache twitched rapidly as he cast a forlorn look at each of the members of the guild, but they all stared him down. Bernie waved at the ex-member as he squeezed his bulky figure through the doorway and disappeared.

"Excellent work Sophia," he said as the blonde girl smirked at the events that had unfolded. "I've never enjoyed him being in the guild, the useless lump. Now we can concentrate on understanding the true contents of the letter. Sophia, you carry on with the plan. Oh! I've got something for you."

He reached into his pocket and pulled out a tiny, pill-shaped item. He passed it to Sophia.

"It's a transponder. Place it in the ginger-haired lad's clothing or something, then we can track them without using Hascombe's phone location."

"Of course, I'll work my charm on him. What are you going to do? Look for Jack's hidden location?"

"Let's leave it to them. They are clearly more adept than we are."

"They'll get the treasure," grunted Jakob.

"Yes, and if we know their location, we can steal it. Next time, all of us will be ready to tackle them."

"That sounds like an excellent plan," said Sophia.

"Let's get to work."

Bernie grabbed the remaining ham and mustard sandwich as his thoughts turned to the hidden treasure. They had a coherent plan now, leave the search to the investigation experts and steal the treasure from them if they find it. Stealth was more effective than a full frontal attack, a tactic which hadn't succeeded so far.

Chapter 29

ALL HALLOWS BY THE TOWER
TUESDAY

After their meeting with Madeleine, Reed had treated Euan to a fish and chip lunch in a nearby restaurant, whilst they discussed their next step. Dark clouds had gathered over London as the temperature dropped to almost freezing. A yellow hue tinged the low-lying clouds, a sign of an impending snowstorm. Reed viewed the sky with caution as they observed the Anglican church from the pedestrianised walkway in front of its main entrance. Reputed to be the oldest church in London, built in 675AD, All Hallows by the Tower had a distinctive profile. The turquoise roof tiles would normally sparkle in the sunshine, but not today. The same colour tiles had been applied onto the unique spire that rose majestically from the tower of the traditional church. Ornate features underlined the spires' craftmanship. Reed saw three angels carved into the wall above the entrance as he walked through the heavy wooden doorway.

He looked around the main worship area bereft of people whilst Euan scrolled on his phone. The intricate stained glass windows were so detailed he could imagine on a sunny day they would appear heavenly. The place was empty. Not a soul about. Not even a man of the cloth. It meant they could investigate without being disturbed.

Reed traipsed down the stone steps to the crypt museum, where the stonework was more primitive. Rows of memorials, among them Shackleton's Crow's Nest, were visible through an archway. A wooden relic of his expeditions to the Antarctic. They ambled across the uneven stone floor to view the Undercroft Chapel behind a black wrought-iron gate. A large wooden square embedded in the floor in the corner caught his eye.

"Euan, wait here whilst I check that wooden cover," he said.

"Okay, mate."

Reed clambered over the spiked gate, rushed to the corner, lifted the wooden cover and below was a rusted ladder. The torch from his phone lit the dark pit, and he detected some missing rungs. This would be dangerous. He delved inside his backpack and retrieved his harness, head torch, and a rope before calling out to Euan.

"I'm just searching inside this pit. Keep watch."

"Be careful."

After he had secured the rope to the top rung, Reed climbed down the rusty ladder into the pit of darkness. Thankfully, confined spaces and darkness didn't scare him! Around twenty feet down he listened, water dripped beneath his feet. He edged down with caution until finally one of his feet touched solid ground. An insignificant pool of water had gathered to one side and reflected his head torch beam. He scanned the eight-foot square space, but there was no other exit, just hewn rock on all sides. It appeared to have been a Victorian water-well, but was now relatively dry. Presumably, the primary water source had been blocked. He realised this was another dead-end and peered upwards. The entrance hole was barely visible as the night had drawn in. He heard a shout from above.

"Reed? Are you okay?" asked Euan.

"Yes. I'm now heading back up."

He made swift progress upwards. One section of the ladder climb was difficult with the missing rungs, but nothing a man with his climbing skills couldn't complete with ease. He landed beside his best friend and sat on the cold stone floor, his head torch illuminating the nearby stone plinth memorial to the Knights Templar.

"Someone came into the crypt, so I hid behind that large pillar."

"Well done. That's a dead-end with no off-shoot tunnels."

"Oh, that's disappointing. Let's get out of here."

Reed loaded his backpack, slung it over his shoulder, and they scaled the stone steps back up to the main church area. They still didn't see anyone. This had been a straightforward investigation, although unsuccessful. As they approached the door, they found it locked.

"Why's the door locked?" asked Euan, who then tapped away on his phone as he searched for the church's opening hours. "Oh look, it shuts at five o'clock and it's now gone half five. We're locked in!"

"Oh shit, I didn't think about that."

"What're we going to do?"

"Shout for help."

"HELP," shouted Euan before a punch from his mate landed on his arm.

"I was joking, you idiot. We'll get arrested for trespassing if anyone finds us here. There must be another way out."

Reed wandered off and checked all the external doors, but he found each one locked. He had an idea. A tiny balcony on the spire could provide an opportunity to descend from. He located the narrow stone steps that ascended the tower and wound his way upwards. He reached the pinnacle of the stone staircase, but another locked door barred their exit onto the tiny balcony, however, beside it was an old metal window. Reed tugged out his faithful crowbar and soon prised the window open. As he nudged it outwards, the blizzard, as predicted, sent flakes of snow drifting in.

"This'll be tricky descending in the snow," said Euan.

"Fortunately, we always come prepared."

Both lads donned their balaclavas, and head torches, then ventured out onto the tiny gallery. Reed held the edge of the stone balustrade as he looked downward, identifying the best possible route. He mounted the balustrade and inched his feet over the turquoise tiles that led to the towers ledge. He eased himself over the ledge, extended his arms to their full length before he let go. It was only a two-foot drop onto the main roof of the church, but his feet slipped as the snow gathered on the turquoise tiles made it slippery. He grabbed the corner of the tower to arrest his fall and waited for Euan. His mate hit the church's roof but didn't bend his knees in time and fell over, tumbling down the sloped roof. Snow fell into Reed's eyes as he scrambled to grab Euan's arm.

"Help Reed, I'm falling off!" screamed Euan in a blind panic.

Reed's heart raced as he acted impulsively, grabbing his friend's wrist, but the force pulled him towards the slope. They were on course to slip over the church's roof until he anchored his foot into the stone gulley on the cusp of the roofline. This allowed him to haul Euan back to safety. They sat there like fatigued snowmen as the blizzard continued relentlessly.

"Thanks mate, you saved my life."

Reed clapped his friend on the shoulder and said, "that was close."

His best friend laughed as they crawled along the stone gulley towards another section of roof. They made quick work of that section and paused as Reed heard voices. He peered over the edge through the snowflakes and spotted several lads huddled in the corner, exactly where they needed to drop to the ground. It was difficult to see properly, but the lads appeared to pass a thin object between them. A cigarette or, more likely, drugs. With no other option, he hung precariously over the building's edge and dropped to the ground beside the lads. Startled, they turned and shouted.

"What the fuck are you doing?"

"Sorry, we got stuck in the church."

"Nah, I bet you're robbing it."

"We'll be out of your way in a minute," said Reed as Euan dropped to the ground beside him. This prompted one of the startled lads to flick out a hand with a knife visible amongst the fluttering snowflakes. Why do we always attract trouble? thought Reed. He needed to calm the situation down before it escalated.

"I'm sorry we surprised you, but there was absolutely no other option."

"You'll be sorry when I make you bleed," said the aggressive lad as he flicked the blade towards Reed. With his Jeet Kune Do skills, Reed instinctively dodged the knife and slammed an elbow into the lad's shoulder, knocking him to the floor.

"Hey, take it easy, pal," shouted one of the other lads as they assembled in front of Reed and Euan. One down, three to go, if necessary. Another lad pulled out a knife and brandished it carelessly.

"Put your knife away and we'll be out of your way."

"I don't think so. You've hurt my mate," said the second lad.

Reed didn't waste anymore time talking and drop-kicked the lad who opposed him, landing on top of his mate laid prone on the snow-covered ground. His muscles flexed as he lunged forward with a quick punch to the face of the third adversary. The air crackled with tension as his fists flew, each blow landing with precision. Three aggressors groaned in pain, struggling to get up. But Reed hadn't finished. He triggered his signature move and one leg sweep later, the remaining lad crashed to the floor, leaving the way clear for an exit.

"Let's go," he shouted to Euan. They darted across the pedestrianised walkway as the group of lads and the church disappeared behind a blanket of snow. Reed eased off after five minutes of jogging and entered a nearby pub, keen to relax with a pint of stout. Another dead-end, another suspect crossed off the list, and another fight he had won. They needed a bit of luck soon.

Chapter 30

WHITECHAPEL

TUESDAY

THE BLIZZARD HAD RAGED for several hours, with snow drifts forming against buildings as the wind whipped through central London. The killer hid behind a snow-covered trunk of an oak tree beside the River Thames. They had spent the past hour meandering around the busy tourist areas as they searched for a suitable target. While a secluded, dark alleyway would be perfect, no such chance had presented itself yet. They grasped the handle of the blade as their eyes searched the flurry of snow cascading in front of their eyes. Perhaps tonight wasn't the best choice to indulge in their transgression.

Another group of people wandered along the river's walkway as the murky water lapped higher with the volume of snow. The high stone walls of the Tower of London created dense shadows, which allowed the killer to track the group unseen. Amidst the flurries of snow, the chatter of friends floated on the breeze as the group pulled their coats tighter. The killer watched on as the group paused before some of them trudged over Tower Bridge and a single individual shuffled off towards Tower Bridge Piazza. They followed them, their pulse quickened as a chilly wind blasted flurries of snowflakes into the faces of both parties.

Suddenly, the lone individual stumbled over a tree root on the track amongst the snow-covered trees. The killer emerged from the shadow of a tree trunk, a dark figure highlighted against the snow. A flash of steel glinted in their hand as they lunged forward, aiming for the lone individual. But the lone figure spun their head as they sensed a presence behind them and dodged the initial attack. It proved useless. The killer grabbed their hood and snapped back their head. The snowflakes swirled around them, creating a surreal backdrop to the life-and-death struggle as it unfolded beside the Tower of London. A flick of the knife and the struggle ended. Blood spurted from the swift incision and splashed onto the snow-covered ground. Vivid crimson set against the pristine white.

    The killer laid the body against the closest tree trunk to drain of their vital life fluid. Their chest heaved with the exertion of the effort. They felt another connection with their Victorian family member, who had scarred the lives of Londoners. Now they had repeated the same. A manic chuckle escaped their lips. Their ancestor's silhouette flickered through their mind, like a ghostly apparition. But their actions hadn't gone unnoticed as a Black Cab trundled past, the flurries of snow now diminished, enabling full vision.

Chapter 31

TOWER BRIDGE PIAZZA

WEDNESDAY

THE SNOW CRUNCHED UNDERNEATH her feet as Clara approached the dead body beneath an ancient oak tree in Tower Bridge Piazza. A deep frost overnight had hardened the several inches of snow that fell during the previous day's seven-hour blizzard. Whitechapel was indeed white this morning, she thought. The victim's blood had created a grim crimson tie-dye effect across the snow covered ground. A murder frozen in time. She immediately spotted the clean cut across the throat, flanked by a grey beard. The Detective Chief Inspector re-covered the body and stood to talk with the forensic expert.

"Anderson, what're your thoughts?"

"Asian male, age around fifty-five, heavy build. A sharp blade has slit the throat from behind. Carotid artery severed, which led to the rapid bleed out."

"Estimated time?" asked Clara.

"I would suggest midnight, give or take an hour."

"It looks like a similar MO to the other murder. What do you think?"

"Yes, definitely. No other marks or bruises. I'll have to confirm this after the autopsy," said Anderson.

"Okay, thanks."

Clara searched the murder scene with its many footprints in the snow, deciphering the victim's direction of travel. Eventually, she spotted two different shoe prints that came from the river with just tiny flakes of fresh snow frozen atop the distinct footprints. She tugged out her phone and called DI Charlie Page.

"Page, get over to the murder scene with the footprint kit. We may have a lead at last."

"Yes, ma'am."

Earlier, she had told DI Page to remain at the police station. She didn't want him puking up in the snow on seeing another dead body. He really needed to improve his constitution.

She spoke to the uniform officer close by, who put a police tape boundary around the best set of prints. The snow had led to much less traffic, car and foot, this morning.

Clara ambled over to the Tower of London and pulled out her vape kit as she studied the scene laid out before her. A blast of chocolate mocha refreshed her thoughts this early in the morning. She had run out of salted caramel and this was all the local vape shop stocked that she could stomach. Being so busy with the murder case, she had forgotten to order another bulk pack of her favourite flavour. She gave herself a swift mental rebuke as the mocha taste lingered and caused her slight nausea. Her phone's six o'clock alarm sounded, but she had been awake for hours as a Black Cab driver had phoned in the discovery of the dead body in the early hours.

On the opposite side of the street, a photographer caught Clara's eye. That was the last thing she needed, some eager journalist printing pictures of the murder scene. The media always got updates on major cases, but her superiors had banned the use of corpses' photos. She stormed over to the nearest police officer and almost slipped over in the snow.

"I need a tent around the body immediately. You should have already put a tent around the body," she barked.

She beckoned to another officer.

"Grab that man over there," she pointed. "He's been taking

photos. Confiscate his camera."

"Yes, ma'am."

Both officers rushed off to follow her orders just as DI Page arrived.

"About time Page," Clara said.

"The snow made it difficult."

"You've always got an excuse. Get over here."

Clara dashed across to the footprints and instructed DI Page on what to do. He sprayed the footprints and took suitable photos. Shoe footprints were notoriously difficult to match to individuals, but at least it was a lead. The police officer sent to confiscate the camera returned empty-handed. She wasn't pleased. It could end up splashed across all the newspapers' websites by lunchtime.

Earlier, she noted the victim was taller than the previous one. Another clue. Her evidence was scant, but she hoped the autopsy would yield more. Were the two victims linked? Probably not. If the same person had committed the two murders, she sincerely hoped this wouldn't turn into a serial killer episode.

Chapter 32

Hoxton Car Repair Shop
Wednesday

Their original plans had changed after Madeleine's PA had phoned Euan with the details of where to meet BernardJ95. The elusive character who had grilled her online about the letter. Madeleine's PA gave Euan a Hoxton business address. The pair stood two blocks away in a quiet alleyway as he manoeuvred his drone above the car repair shop. The glare from the sun that bounced off the snow-covered landscape made it difficult to identify anything on the screen of the handheld control unit. He squinted and glimpsed at rooftops concealed under layers of snow. This had become more difficult than expected.

"I can't see anything. What should we do?" he asked his best friend, stood beside him gawping at his phone.

"Sorry, what? I've just read on a news channel there's been another murder."

"Oh really. Where did it happen?"

"Near the Tower of London."

"Oh crikey. I can't see the screen properly," Euan said as he showed the controller to Reed.

"I'll wander round and guide you over the phone."

"Okay doke."

Euan leant against the nearest moss-covered wall whilst he waited for Reed to call him. The cold had penetrated his shoes as he stamped his feet in the snow to keep warm. His phone rang.

"The drone's above the car repair shop. There's a roller-shutter door entrance that's closed halfway, so I can't actually see inside the building properly. There's a green car parked on a ramp. Drop the drone to look into the office window. It's on the top level, to your right," said Reed.

"Can you help me guide it down?"

After some tense manoeuvres to remove the sun's glare from the controller's screen, Euan now had a clear view inside the dirty window of the office. Two men talked animatedly to each other. The older one gestured downwards, but as he zoomed in on their faces, he got a shock. It was one of the assailants that had attacked them in the alleyway close to the Ten Bells Pub. He whispered into his phone.

"I recognise one man."

"Who is it?"

"One of the men who attacked us near the pub on Sunday."

"That makes sense, as they knew who I was. I'll snoop around first," said Reed.

"You should leave now," he said.

"In a minute."

The line went quiet. Euan hoped his friend wouldn't take any unnecessary risks. Things had been tricky enough, and he didn't need Reed being spotted by their antagonists.

Ryan Johnson, fed up with his dad's constant criticism, spun away from him. He didn't want to say anything he would later regret. He gazed out of the compact office window and spotted some movement. Two steps later, he pushed his nose against the murky windowpane as he scanned the outside. His eyes alighted on a drone that hovered a few yards away. What the hell! Someone was watching them.

"Dad, look outside!" He beckoned Bernie over to the window.

"Who's spying on us? Get out there and stop them. Take Mikey," shouted Bernie.

Ryan rushed out of the office, down the metal staircase into the workshop area, and shouted for Mikey to follow him. They crouched underneath the partly drawn roller shutter door, hurtled around the side of the building and slid to a standstill in the snow. He searched frantically for the drone.

"What's going on?" asked Mikey.

"There's a drone outside."

"I can't see it."

"There it is," he said. The drone whisked upwards as he pointed straight at it. "Get the van, we'll track it," Ryan said to Mikey. He kept his eyes locked on the surveillance device whilst Mikey jumped in the works white van. They could barely see the drone as it ascended rapidly away from them before it pivoted south.

"Take the side street," he instructed his friend. He watched the drone slide across the sky and plummet like a hawk after a mouse into a nearby alleyway.

"Quick, down that alleyway. That's where the drone is."

They turned too fast into the narrow alleyway. The van slid in the snow and the front end almost collided with the wall.

"Geez Mikey, get control," Ryan bellowed.

"It's difficult. You drive if you're so good," said his friend, clearly annoyed.

As the van sped down the alley, he spotted a lad hunched over a small silver case. Then he noticed the ginger hair as the lad lifted his head to glance their way.

"It's one of those investigators. Ram him with the van."

He hung onto the dashboard as Mikey floored the accelerator. The van struggled for traction in the snow, swerved, but still headed directly towards their target.

"Get the sneaky git," he urged Mikey. He grinned to himself as panic spread across the ginger-haired lad's face, they had him in their sights. No place for him to run in this narrow alleyway as the wing mirror scraped along the wall. Suddenly, the front wheel hit a hidden object in the snow and caused Mikey to wrestle with the steering wheel erratically. The front bumper caught the offside wall and spun the vehicle around. The frozen snow had created an ice-rink effect as the white van spun a full three-sixty before being lodged against the wall, leaving Ryan unable to get out. Mikey hit his head on the door pillar and was now slumped over the steering wheel; the van had missed the ginger-haired lad.

Ryan shoved his friend, who stirred but could not move. He glanced out of the windscreen to see the ginger-haired lad bounding off down the alleyway. He scrabbled over Mikey's lap and slid out of the white van onto his hands and knees. The coldness of the snow shot through his limbs as he struggled to stand. The ginger-haired lad had exited the alleyway. Ryan scooted as fast as possible to catch up in the treacherous conditions. He was now several hundred yards behind his target. Once he reached the end of the alleyway, he slid onto the main road and straight into a group of pedestrians that blocked his path. He freed himself of the human jumble and scanned the crowds, but couldn't spot the ginger-haired lad.

He trudged back to the van, annoyed with how that incident had ended. Using a drone had given the investigators an advantage over them. He vowed to catch up with the spies and get his revenge. He hated being beaten.

Chapter 33

NEW ROAD HOTEL

WEDNESDAY

EMILY TRAVELLED DOWN TO London to meet Reed and Euan that morning after taking the day off work as a holiday. They required some help and needed to reset their plans, as so far nothing had succeeded. One of her skills was to create visual interpretations of puzzles, akin to the detailed map she had created last year on their treasure hunt in Cornwall. She swept strands of wavy brown hair behind her ears as she honed her thoughts on Whitechapel. Snuggled in Reed's room, against the cold winter snow outside, with her collection of coloured pencils and highlighters, she had put together a map based on the list of suspects they considered being Jack the Ripper. She overlay the 21st century landscape on top of the Victorian schematics. Now they had visual clarity.

"This is amazing, Em. You're extremely skilled at these maps. When you get too old to teach, you could become a cartographer," laughed Euan. He received a playful slap on the arm for his ageist comment.

"You need to mark two further elements on the map. Places visited and locations of fights," she said.

Euan grabbed the blue highlighter that Emily passed him and slapped some colour in distinct locations on the A3 sized map. "The two blokes in the white van earlier today were the same attackers that cornered us in the alleyway Friday," he said.

"We've now seen three men on two occasions, all hellbent on doing damage to us. We've only seen the fourth man once," said Reed.

"They could be the thugs in Madeleine's office, but we haven't seen the blonde girl yet."

"It's highly likely the three attackers are the same guys. It'd be too much of a coincidence if they weren't."

Emily pulled her notes from her handbag and instructed her boyfriend and his best mate on their next steps.

"We need to spend the next few hours researching. I'm going to investigate the owner of the car repair shop in Hoxton, plus you mentioned one lad called themselves Hoxton Hot Rods. That sounds like a gang of sorts. I'll research the Ten Bells pub and the landlord, identify if there's any connection. Euan, you look at Thomas Cutbush and provide a fresh perspective on him. Reed, you investigate Francis Tumblety. Check leads on all Ripper blogs and look for any new information."

Both lads nodded in agreement, and they settled down to focus on their tasks. Emily's next two hours passed in a blur of blogs and articles on her laptop. She checked property ownership records, business accounts, Google satellite pictures of home addresses and as much background information as was available. She had assembled a full picture of both Ron Smythe, the owner of the Ten Bells Pub and Bernard Johnson, the owner of Hoxton car repair shop. Something didn't add up.

Her legs ached after the squashed train journey to London, as well as from squatting with her laptop. She stood up and stretched, peering at the sunset that descended over England's capital. A blur of deep orange interspersed with towers of lights. Both lads had finished before her and rushed out to get an Indian takeaway. The eager babble of their voices increased as they pounded along the corridor, hungry for their food upon their return. The waft of spices assaulted her senses as they entered the hotel room.

"That smells amazing," she said.

"We got your favourite, paneer rogan josh and onion bhajis," said Reed as he placed her food on the hotel's black wooden desk in front of her. His ability to consider her at all times was one of many things she loved about Reed. He always bought her favourite food or splashed out on perfume for birthdays, touches that went a long way to cementing their relationship, developed over the past six years since they met in the Peak District.

"Thanks. Let's eat and discuss our findings afterwards."

Silence descended on the group as they tucked into their food with Indian spices permeating the fabric of the room. After Emily had finished eating, she tidied up the trays before settling on the bed, propped up against the dark faux leather headboard. She would lead the discussion, which was her strength, whilst Reed's was the physical aspect.

"I'll go first. I don't think the landlord of the Ten Bells pub is involved. There's nothing unusual about his business or his home. But Bernard Johnson's house is significantly bigger that you would expect based on the profits of his car repair shop business. His son, Ryan, has to be one of the other two attackers. You said he mentioned a gang name which has the same initials as one mentioned in several Ripper blogs, Hoxton High Rips. It seems too similar to be a coincidence. I'll bet it's linked somehow. You've looked at Thomas Cutbush, what do you think, Euan?"

"People claimed he was part of the Hoxton High Rips, but they expelled him for stealing an extremely valuable object. Perhaps there's some link between Cutbush and Johnson. We need to investigate the car repair shop."

"Reed, what did you find out?"

"Not much more than we knew before. Tumblety worked at the Royal London Hospital during Victorian times when it was a hospital. Now it's the offices for the Tower Hamlet Council. A daylight search would prove difficult." Reed noted this on Emily's map.

Emily reflected on the information. "It makes sense to target the car repair shop next, but it sounds like a night-time activity. Let's plan that for tomorrow evening. We can explore the council offices during working hours."

"That's a perfect plan," responded Reed.

"I'll leave you guys to it," said Euan as he rose to his feet. "I fancy an evening wander and trying the old-world pub we passed yesterday if you wanted to join me."

"We'll have an early night," said Reed with a wink at his mate.

"Of course, I'll catch you in the morning, then."

"Night Euan," said Emily as he left their room. She was pretty tired, but they had made some headway tonight. Time for her and Reed to relax and spend some quality time together. She hoped the car repair shop in Hoxton or the old hospital would prove a positive next step in their quest.

Chapter 34

WHITECHAPEL

WEDNESDAY

WITH THE TEMPERATURE NUDGED slightly above freezing, the recent snow that blanketed the pavements made walking difficult. Sophia had come prepared with her designer trainers, which provided adequate grip as she stalked her target. She had spent the past two hours in a coffee shop opposite the entrance to the New Road Hotel, hoping to catch sight of Reed Hascombe's ginger-haired mate. Awhile ago they had both left the hotel as she followed them to a local Indian takeaway and back. She had been about to finish her surveillance when her target appeared solo at the hotel's front door. Now she had him in her sights. Now she could take decisive action to learn the exact contents of Jack the Ripper's letter. She believed that her ancestor, Walter Sickert, was the infamous killer, and that the hidden treasure belonged to her. She would seduce the ginger-haired lad and plant the transponder on him.

Inside The Castle pub the ginger-haired lad leant against the bar as he sipped on a pint of lager. Sophia made her move. She sidled up close to him and gestured to the barman. A snow-clad winter landscape hadn't stopped patrons from visiting the pub that Wednesday evening. The old-world style decor featured wooden beams, and couples or groups of friends occupied most of the wooden tables. She flicked her long blonde hair, intent on grabbing the lad's attention whilst she waited for her vodka and coke. She swivelled her head to look around the room and completed the three-sixty manoeuvre with a charming smile aimed directly at her target. He reciprocated. The barman brought her drink, and she twirled, pretending to look for a spare seat.

"Gosh, it's busy. There's no free seat," she said to the ginger-haired lad.

"Exactly why I stayed at the bar."

"Probably the best idea. I'm Sophia." She didn't know if he was aware of her existence, but if he did, she would smooth-talk him to achieve her goal.

"I'm Euan. Pleased to meet you."

Sophia waited for him to ply her with chat up lines but he seemed hesitant so she advanced the conversation. She delved into his background, asked lots of questions, pretending she was genuinely interested in him, and found out he was definitely her target. An hour passed, and he had become enthralled with her. Now she had to figure out how to attach Bernie's tiny transponder to him undetected. He wasn't carrying a bag, which meant fewer options. Then she had an idea. Her flat was a few streets away, so if she lured him there, it would give her a better opportunity. With her plan settled, she worked her charm once more on the unsuspecting investigator. The chatter from the pub's customers dwindled as many drifted off home, which gave her the perfect opportunity.

"Did you hear about the murder yesterday?"

"I was almost too scared to come out tonight, but I convinced myself that I would be back home by ten," she said and glanced at her watch.

"How far is home?" asked Euan.

"I'm only a few streets away."

"I could walk you home?"

"Oh, would you? That's so kind," she said with a sensual flick of her hair. He was hooked.

They left the pub and Sophia encouraged Euan with flirty banter, even pretending to slip in the snow to hold on to his arm. A few minutes later, they approached a modern twelve-storey apartment block. Her flat was on the seventh floor.

"Hey, do you fancy coming in for a quick drink?" she asked before Euan stuttered his positive response. He was easy prey for her. She planned to insert the tiny metal transponder inside the sole of his shoe. She entered her flat with Euan close behind, then offered him a seat on the grey leather sofa, after insisting he removed his shoes. Now she had him there, she realised a flaw in the plan. How could she take a shoe without him noticing in the open-plan living area? Also, how could she keep the transponder hidden inside his shoe without it falling out? Could she slip it into the lining or sole? What if he wore different shoes? Then Bernie wouldn't be able to track him.

Annoyed with herself, Sophia nipped to the bathroom to give her space to think. She fiddled with the tiny metal transponder, a quarter of an inch long and the width of an office paperclip, akin to a tiny pill capsule. The answer soon revealed itself. She had to insert the transponder into his body. That meant either knocking him out or drugging him first, then she could use her scalpel to implant the tracking device in his body.

Chapter 35

WHITECHAPEL FLAT
THURSDAY

THE ROOM SPUN AS Euan eased open his eyes. Where the hell was he? He didn't recognise the room or the fragrant vanilla aroma. The clang of metal on metal brought into focus his predicament as he attempted to move his hand to scratch an annoying itch on his nose. He was naked, with one arm handcuffed to the bedframe. His mind whirled with *'What on earth has happened?'* He remembered the attractive blonde woman from last night and replayed the sequence of events that had started inside the pub, culminating in his current situation. The blonde woman had seemed especially interested in him, but why was he now trapped inside her flat? After having a drink, she came on to him and suggested they entered the bedroom. Then everything was hazy. He vaguely remembered her suggesting the handcuffs, which he thought would be fun amid the excitement. Why had she left him tied up?

"Sophia?"

No immediate answer.

"Sophia, are you there?"

Still no answer. He needed to pee, so twisted to a sitting position and shouted this time.

"Sophia!"

Silence met his plea. The closed curtains blocked any view outside, and Euan shivered as his dilemma became clearer. His head pounded as though he had drunk excessive alcohol. He remembered feeling the same last summer when he and Reed had been drugged by gas in Cornwall. She had sedated him. But why? He scanned the bare room, no wardrobe, no bedside table, just a double bed with a yellow mottled blanket thrown to one side. He noticed his clothes on the floor near the door. If he could reach them and grab his phone, he'd escape in no time. He stretched out a leg, attempting to pull his clothes towards him, but he couldn't quite reach. Why hadn't Sophia unlocked the handcuffs last night? Where was she? Panic set in as he realised it had to be deliberate. Was he a prisoner in her flat?

Euan's head slumped forward as he struggled with his plight. What would Reed do? Inspired by thoughts of his best friend in action, he pulled on the handcuffs, but they didn't give. He turned his attention to the bedframe and twisted towards the metal headboard. Unfortunately, it was securely bolted together. He still needed to pee and, unable to hold it any longer, he released a stream of steaming urine onto the carpet, like a torrent of water from an overflow pipe. The release of the bladder pain brought improved clarity to his mind. If he shouted loud enough, someone must hear him, as it was a block of apartments.

"Help."

He listened for any sounds, nothing, no bangs from neighbouring apartments, no scraping of chairs. Were they empty? Or was everyone at work?

"Help me."

"Anyone there? Please help me."

Euan's pleas for help continued for several minutes until he gave up and desperately hoped someone had heard his shouts. He sat in silence and detected a slight pain on his back, but couldn't reach the source. Perhaps he had bumped against something? He twisted back onto the bed, lying flat, and covered himself with the blanket. Time ticked by slowly as he realised he would have to wait until either

Sophia came back to the flat or someone heard his cries for help. He recalled the events of the past week and zoned in on Madeleine's description of the woman who attacked her at the art gallery. Tall with long blonde hair, which seemed to match Sophia perfectly. His quandary became clear as he contemplated Sophia's reason for keeping him prisoner. She had to be part of Bernie's gang, intent on stealing Jack the Ripper's hidden treasure.

His phone suddenly rang as the shrill tone broke his desperate thoughts. He questioned if Reed was calling. If only he could reach it.

Chapter 36

New Road Hotel

Thursday

REED THREW HIS PHONE on the bed and grimaced at Emily. "That's not like Euan. He normally answers the phone straightaway."

"Perhaps he's gone for a walk. Give it a few minutes."

"He never misses breakfast."

"Stay calm Reed, we'll check with reception in ten minutes. Give him time to call you back."

"Okay, fair enough," he said, pacing across the room to scowl at the snow-covered skyline from the large window. Emily usually remained calm in difficult situations, whereas he had a tendency to rush off. She was a supportive girlfriend and he couldn't imagine life without her. But he knew something was amiss. He could feel it. Euan hadn't answered the knock on his hotel room door earlier, nor the phone. Could he still be asleep? His best friend wasn't the earliest of risers in the morning, but eleven o'clock was even late for him. The minutes ticked by at an alarmingly slow rate, then Reed hopped outside to knock on Euan's door again.

"Euan, wake up!"

He shouted whilst banging repetitively. Still no answer. He dashed back into his room, grabbed his phone, and called again. It went to voicemail.

Emily grabbed his hand. "Let's ask the staff to check his room.

Come on," she said.

Together, they hustled downstairs to the reception and explained the situation. The receptionist called Euan's room and then instructed a maid to escort Reed and Emily back upstairs. The maid knocked on the door before using her master keycard to access his room. Euan wasn't in the empty room, and the bed showed no signs of use.

"Something's wrong, Em. It's not like Euan to disappear. Something happened when he visited the pub. We should have gone with him."

"You aren't his keeper, it's not your fault."

"What if those aggressive guys have beaten him and he's laying injured in an alleyway?"

"We'll find him. Let's try asking at the pub."

Reed grabbed his backpack, and as they were about to leave, he had a brainwave. He snatched out his phone and called Jed, a hacker acquaintance from Sheffield he worked with whilst searching for hidden artifacts in the Peak District.

"Hey Jed, it's Reed Hascombe. Can you do me a favour?" he asked.

"Sure Reed, what is it?"

"Euan's disappeared, and I need to locate him. Can you track the whereabouts of his phone?"

"Of course, ping over his number and I'll get back to you shortly," said Jed.

"Thanks."

He messaged Jed with the number and again paced the room whilst he waited, certain that something bad had happened to Euan. He needed to find him immediately. The sun glowed through the hotel window, bringing some optimism to the situation as Reed noticed that some of the snow had melted on the rooftops of nearby buildings. He checked his backpack for weapons and confirmed the crowbar was there, along with his swiss army knife. He would require both if the thugs they had encountered several times had taken Euan captive. His phoned pinged with a message.

Jed: *'Current location is an apartment block on Old Montague Street. Seventh floor on the south side of the building. I'll send a Google maps snapshot with the exact location.'*

Reed: *'Thanks Jed, I owe you'*

Jed: *'No problem'*

Reed downloaded the screenshot from Jed and located the building on Google maps, which suggested an eight-minute walk past Whitechapel Bell Foundry. This area of London was becoming familiar to him. With Emily in tow, he scrambled downstairs, and they rapidly reached their destination. The glass front door to the modern building was keycard entry, which left Reed examining other ways in. He paced the perimeter of the red brick apartment block and identified windows on the south side. That had to be where Euan was. He phoned him again and once more it diverted direct to voicemail. No answer or callback from his mate meant he was badly injured or held against his will.

A glint of something caught his attention. A metal fire escape gleamed in the sunshine and snaked up the side of the building. He could climb the external stairs and access the fire escape door or abseil down from the roof to the window on floor seven. After explaining his plan to Emily, they returned to their hotel to gather his climbing gear and wait for dusk, as he would be highly visible if he descended from the roof in broad daylight. He desperately hoped the postponement wouldn't be too late for Euan.

Chapter 37

WHITECHAPEL FLAT
THURSDAY

SOPHIA TURNED THE KEY in her front door with Jakob close behind. Last night, she had botched her seduction of Euan, the ginger-haired investigator, and he remained handcuffed in her spare bedroom. The sleep-inducing drug worked, letting her insert the metal transponder into Euan's back where he couldn't reach it. She had used her scalpel to make a tiny slit, pushed in the transponder and sealed it with super glue. Then she realised her dilemma. How could she just release him this morning as though nothing had happened? After careful deliberation, she arranged for Jakob to come over after work. The plan was for her fellow Rippers Guild member to exert some physical pressure, then release Euan. That way, her prey would focus solely on the interrogation, unaware of the tiny transponder in his back. There was also a bonus side to her plan; they may learn more about the contents of the letter.

Silence greeted Sophia as she walked into the living area. An orange sunset blossomed through the south-west-facing window. After she had pulled the curtains, her thoughts drifted towards her prisoner, stalking off to the spare bedroom. The acrid stench of stale urine hit her as she entered, observing Euan sprawled on the bed covered by the yellow mottled blanket. He did actually look quite cute, but she caught the essence of Jakob's aftershave as he entered the room, reminding her of their plan.

"Have you pissed on the bed?" she asked.

"No," said Euan. His eyes grew wide when he spotted Jakob standing beside her. He obviously recognised him from their previous encounter. She smiled to herself and reverted to her bad-girl attitude.

"I've brought a friend of mine. I believe you've met before?"

No answer from her prisoner, just a grimace. Let's ramp things up, she thought.

"Let's make this easy, Euan. We know about Jack's treasure letter, but I want the full contents. Tell me now, and Jakob won't hurt you. What do you think? He's a very moody lad who loves to fight. He desperately wants to hurt you, but if you give up the information, I promise he won't. Tell me, what does the letter say?"

She waited for an answer, but nothing was forthcoming.

"Come now, Euan, I don't want Jakob to hurt you."

Then he spoke, "Madeleine told you."

So he had connected her to the events at the art gallery and understood exactly who she was, but it didn't matter.

"But I want to hear it from you," she said.

He hesitated again, so Sophia urged Jakob to move forward, who grabbed the blanket and tore it off Euan. He blabbed straightaway.

"It's from Jack the Ripper and says to search for the hidden ladder access to water where the bells toll."

"That wasn't too difficult. What else does it say? There must be more?"

"Nothing."

She encouraged Jakob to punch Euan, who gleefully smashed a fist into their prisoner's stomach. He would break soon enough.

Five floors above the unfolding brutal scenes, Reed poised on the rooftop, ready to descend. Earlier he had climbed the snake-like metal stairs but couldn't break through the fire escape door, leaving him with only one option. With the weak setting sun behind him, he attached his belay device and began his abseil down the building. Earlier, Jed, his hacker acquaintance, had confirmed that Euan's phone hadn't changed location, time now to rescue his friend. His feet launched off the wall and swung out backwards like a chimpanzee descending from the jungle's canopy. He bounced down, gliding past window after window until he reached the floor he required. He steadied himself and heard a panicked scream from within a room. It sounded like Euan. He had to act fast.

Reed drew out the crowbar strapped to his backpack and smashed the window. Glass rained into the room, crashing against the closed curtains as he wildly eliminated jagged edges protruding from the frame. The curtains suddenly flapped open, and he recognised an assailant from outside the Ten Bells Pub. He pushed off from the building and launched a jack-hammer kick straight at the man's chest. The power of his kick launched the man onto the bed. He fumbled with the belay device and quickly detached himself from the rope. He saw Euan sprawled naked on the bed with blood plastered across his body.

"Jakob, get up," screamed a tall blonde woman stood beside the doorway.

"Euan, are you okay?" he asked.

His friend mumbled some garbled words, clearly under severe duress. The stricken man, Jakob, struggled to his feet and snatched a Bowie knife from the bed. Reed still held his crowbar and waited for the inevitable lunge from his opponent. When it came, he smashed the metal weapon against the man's wrist. A yelp of pain and the bloodied knife skittered across the floor. At that point, the blonde woman darted from the room, the movement distracting his attention, which allowed Jakob to throw a punch. He staggered backwards, another punch connected. He dipped his shoulder out of the way of the third incoming fist but caught his forearm on a stray jagged edge of the window. Blood soaked his jacket sleeve as he swung the crowbar upwards and caught Jakob square on the chin. The lad went straight down, out stone-cold from the impact.

Reed gasped for air as the blonde woman appeared, brandishing a revolver. She noticed Jakob out cold on the floor and immediately aimed the weapon at Reed. In this small space, it could do him severe damage.

"Hands up," she said.

He slowly lifted his hands while his mind whirred, scrabbling with what to do? She was close enough to grab, but that was a risk if she pulled the trigger before he struck. Instead, he executed the only option available, dived to the floor and grabbed her ankle. She went straight over onto her back and fired a bullet into the ceiling. He grabbed her wrist and extracted the revolver from her grasp.

"Listen, it's been a mistake," she said.

"Capturing my friend and inflicting severe harm on him?"

"Jakob got carried away."

"Who the hell is Jakob?"

"My boyfriend, but he got jealous. Take your friend and let's forget about our mistake."

Then Euan spoke up. "That's rubbish. She drugged me. She's Sophia who attacked Madeleine at the art gallery."

Reed stooped to check Jakob's pockets and found his wallet. Inside was a driver's licence in the name of Jakob Kosminski. Everything became clear.

"You're all colluding to beat us to Jack the Ripper's treasure. I assume Aaron Kosminski is Jakob's ancestor?" he asked.

Sophia hesitated, which gave Reed his answer. He reflected on their list of suspects and remembered Madeleine had mentioned the blonde woman was German.

"I'm guessing you're related to Walter Sickert?" he asked.

"So what if I am? The treasure belongs to one of us, not you or my stupid boss's wife!"

"How many individuals are involved?" he asked.

"Too many for you to succeed," she spat.

"Get on the floor next to him. Where's the key to the handcuffs?"

"I've lost it," Sophia laughed.

Reed's anger grew at her arrogance, so he seized Jakob's knife and grabbed a handful of her hair. He leant in close and hissed, "If you don't tell me, I'll cut off your hair."

"On the coffee table in the living area."

He tore a strip off the curtain's linings and bound her hands, then hustled to find the key. Once he had released Euan and his mate had got dressed, he removed Sophia's binding, emptied the revolver of bullets and cast it aside. He helped the woozy Euan down the stairs of the building and they exited into the cool night air.

"What happened in there?" he asked. Euan explained the events of the previous evening and his ordeal at being imprisoned in the apartment.

"I'm so relieved you rescued me, Reed. That Jakob is a complete nutter. He punched me several times and used the knife to make cuts across my torso. Before you arrived, he had threatened to cut off my balls if I didn't tell them everything in the letter."

"He sounds like a nasty piece of work. What did you tell them?"

"I told them about the water source and bells tolling, same as Madeleine, but if you hadn't burst in the window like Spiderman, I would have definitely blabbed about the twentieth brick."

"You did incredibly well to survive what you did. How are you feeling?"

"Groggy and sore, but the cuts are just superficial," said Euan.

"We'll get you fixed up in no time. We've still got some treasure to discover."

"Don't I get any rest?"

"Only tonight Euan," laughed Reed.

Reed held tight to his friend's arm as he guided him through the meandering streets of Whitechapel as they trudged through the thawing snow. Back at their hotel, Emily helped clean Euan up, then listened to his ordeal whilst he smothered antiseptic cream over his cuts. With the names of two antagonists revealed they had increased their knowledge of the group they were battling against. Reed's intuition suggested the challenge had only just begun.

Chapter 38

New Road Hotel

Friday

E MILY SCRUTINISED HER LAPTOP screen, studying the email from Reed's hacker friend, Jed. Reed had asked him to delve into the backgrounds of Jakob Kosminski and Sophia Meyer after Euan's encounter with them the previous day. It didn't make ideal reading. She stood and wandered over to the hotel room's window and gazed outside at the melting snow which had all but disappeared, leaving patches of slush strewn across the pavement. Reed was next door with Euan, so she popped into the corridor and knocked on Euan's hotel room door. He let her inside.

"How're you feeling today?" she asked Euan.

"Much better thanks. The cuts aren't deep and will heal in a few days. My head's cleared of the drugs."

"Ready to get back into action?" interjected Reed.

"Give him a chance, Reed," cut in Emily. "He needs to rest today. I'll come with you to explore the old Royal London Hospital."

"Okay, that's fair."

"I've heard from Jed about Euan's captors."

The two lads' eyes lit up with interest as Emily continued. "Jakob Kosminski has had two prison sentences, albeit short stretches, both for GBH. Jed traced his family tree, and he's definitely related to Aaron Kosminski, a prime suspect in the Jack the Ripper case."

"That's not a surprise. It explains why he's interested in Jack's letter. He must believe that anything valuable we discover should be his. What about Sophia?" said Reed.

"She's lived in England for six months and doesn't have the same profile as Jakob. She doesn't have a criminal record here or in Germany."

"She hesitated when I asked about Walter Sickert. That suggests a relationship between them. They must be working together, planning to steal anything we find. Madeleine also has a claim to anything valuable as the letter is addressed to her ancestor."

Emily readjusted the scrunchy that held her hair back as she contemplated their next steps. If they found Jack's hidden treasure, their opponents could be straight on their tail, so how would they avoid that? They had an advantage with Reed's Jeet Kune Do skills, but if he was fighting all four men, could he manage? Probably not. They needed to be several steps ahead.

"Who's in charge of the group?" she asked.

"The older guy, Bernard Johnson," said Euan.

"Reed and I'll scope out the Tower Hamlets Town Hall today to see if we can find any access to the old Royal London Hospital sections. Do you think you'll be ready if we plan the break-in for Saturday night?" she asked Euan.

"Definitely. Two days' rest and another sleep, then I'll be raring to go."

"Great stuff," said Reed.

Emily wandered back to their room and updated her map with the events of last night, then triangulated the key locations of their opponents. It didn't offer a fresh perspective. Their options had reduced from a week ago, just two sites left to visit, then they would have to reconsider the full list of Jack the Ripper suspects again. None were promising. She hoped the old Royal London Hospital would offer a new opportunity to lead them to Jack's hidden treasure.

Chapter 39

Ten Bells Pub

Friday

THE ATMOSPHERE WAS A tad frosty in the Rippers Guild meeting place in the Ten Bells Pub as Bernie ripped into the other two members.

"Why didn't you tell me? You could've messed up my plan entirely."

"Why is it always your plan we have to follow?" retorted Sophia.

"It's my society and I'm in charge."

Sophia's actions didn't surprise Bernie, but Jakub disappointed him. He had expected more loyalty. The Polish lad had been in the guild for several years and he looked after him with cash for car stealing or other tasks that required extra muscle. Perhaps Sophia's smooth talking and good looks swayed Jakub? Either way, it didn't impress him. He launched into a leader's speech intended to re-motivate both.

"We don't know the full contents of the letter as you knocked Madeleine unconscious," he said, staring at Jakub. "So we need these investigators to lead us to Jack's hidden treasure. There has to be at least one other clue because it's all too vague, yet they're able to pinpoint precise locations to search. We know of three so far. Let's not rile them anymore and track their activity. Mouse has the transponder location on this app." He flicked his phone round to show them a map with a blinking red dot.

"We could've got more of the letter content from Euan, the ginger-haired lad."

"But you didn't."

Bernie waited for her response, but she remained silent, so he continued. "He's still at the New Road Hotel, where they are staying. He's probably resting after your efforts to cut him up," he said, staring at Jakub again.

"I only needed a few more minutes," said Jakub with a slight snarl.

"Let's forget about that. To be fair, it was an excellent idea to insert the transponder into his back," Bernie said as he smiled at Sophia, attempting to pacify the two younger members of the guild. He ran a hand over his bald head and took a sip of his beer.

"We're a team, so let's keep in constant contact. We should aim to intercept the investigators when they discover something. Mouse will track them twenty-four seven and advise me immediately of any change in locale. Between the three of us, plus Ryan and Mikey, we have to be ready to rush straightaway to any location in London."

He sensed Sophia's attitude thaw, so continued.

"The treasure could be just another silver necklace, like that one," he said, pointing to the display cabinet, "but if my gut feeling's right, this is a once-in-a-lifetime opportunity to be incredibly rich."

"How're we splitting the money now?" asked Sophia.

"With Basil no longer in the guild, I suggest half goes to Jack's family member once we find where he hid the treasure, then a quarter each to the remaining two."

"What if it's none of our family members?"

"Then we split it three ways."

That placated her. Bernie reflected on his link to Jack the Ripper, which wasn't family related. His association was with the street gang that Thomas Cutbush had been a part of. He would never disclose that. They didn't need to know. The atmosphere changed as the conversation turned to speculation about the hidden treasure.

Chapter 40

COMMERCIAL STREET POLICE STATION

FRIDAY

DETECTIVE CHIEF INSPECTOR CLARA Loxstone stared into the eyes of her interviewee, searching for a glimpse of guilt. She wasn't seeing any. Her suspect had a flimsy alibi, but it was also important to delve into their heads. Guilty suspects would either unravel or attempt to stare her down. This one did neither, a sign of innocence. At least ten years ago, she had learnt to interpret body language and telltale signs of nervousness. DI Page shuffled in his seat, waiting for her next words, but she liked to play the silent game to unnerve suspects. This was the third potential suspect they had interviewed this morning, with just one more on their list.

Her boss, DS Browne, had marched into her office very early that morning and slapped a copy of a national newspaper on her desk. His face was as red as a ripe tomato. The outrageous headline sparked a heated exchange when he called for an immediate arrest, *'Copy Cat Serial Killer on the Loose'*. This put Clara in a predicament, with only four suspects on her narrow list. They were just possibilities based on the meagre evidence they had complied. She deduced the suspect's height as being over five foot ten with a size ten shoe. Her review of the police database focused on criminals with previous prison sentences for GBH. The system flagged anyone who used knives and lived in Whitechapel or adjoining neighbourhoods. So far, interviewing the three suspects had provided no further leads.

"I'm terminating this interview at one twenty-three pm. Thank you for helping us, Mr Jones. You're free to leave. If we require any further assistance with the case, I'll be in touch." She pressed stop on the recording machine.

"DI Page will escort you out."

Clara strode back to her office and updated the whiteboard with her thoughts on the last interview. Above this was the second victim's details: Hakim Ahmed, male, Asian, fifty-four, five foot ten, lived in Greenwich with his wife and children. The victim had been at a nearby restaurant with friends on Tuesday evening and was a sales manager for a prominent insurance firm. Page had interviewed his friends, and they confirmed he was walking to the nearest tube station to go home. The case troubled her, as the lengthy newspaper coverage contrasted with her sparse evidence.

She needed a blast of nicotine so grabbed her vape kit and wandered into the rear car park. A few blasts of chocolate mocha spurred her body and mind with enough of a buzz to push on with the fourth interview, assuming the uniform police had located her suspect. Back in her office, she sipped another cup of coffee to remove the aftertaste of the vape flavouring. The delivery of her favourite flavour in a couple of days would return things to normal. DI Page bundled into the room.

"Where are we with the last suspect?" she asked.

"Apparently he isn't at home, nor at his workplace."

"We need him in today, Page. We've got nothing so far."

"I know, but we've had no luck locating him."

Her frustration bubbled up, she knew she would have to get involved herself.

"We need Kosminski in today. Come with me. We'll do it if the uniform guys can't even locate one person!"

She stomped out of her office, stopped by the front desk to grab the keys to a patrol car, and jumped in the driver's seat as Page scrambled into the passenger seat.

"Home address?" she asked.

"Flat 19, Batson House, Fairclough Street."

Clara entered the address into the sat nav and drove out of the police station's car park in the general direction of their first destination.

"Where does he work?"

"Frizz Barbers on Whitechapel High Street," said Page.

"Strap yourself in Page. Let's get a result."

Her thoughts drifted off to her argument with DS Browne earlier and wondered if she had overstepped the mark. Yes, the case splashed across the front of the newspapers had put him under extreme pressure, but they couldn't arrest someone based on previous indiscretions. They had to prove the suspect committed the murders. The fundamental problem was the lack of a DNA match, so the perpetrator was clearly wearing gloves. They also needed the murder weapon and a motive. Added to that, no-one had seen either murder happen. The first killing took place in a rarely used street, whilst the second had occurred amid a snow blizzard. Clinical evidence was thin on the ground. She hoped this next suspect might prove to be the answer.

Chapter 41

TOWER HAMLETS TOWN HALL

FRIDAY

REED HAD DECIDED THEY would pretend to be future council tenants as a way of getting inside the Tower Hamlets' Town Hall. Once inside, he hoped to uncover a route into the old Royal London Hospital area. He had asked Emily to draw a map of the building marked with security cameras and exits. The building would be empty tomorrow because of the absence of council workers on Saturdays.

On their afternoon journey, Reed had spotted newsstands proclaiming a copycat killer was on the loose after a second murder. The letter had opened a can of worms and London's inhabitants were being subjected to a re-run of the infamous killings. He stared at the elaborate Georgian front of the eighteenth-century property. How things had changed during the four hundred years it had existed. No roads or cars back then. In 1888, doctors had examined Jack the Ripper's victims there. Their next suspect, Francis Tumblety, had worked there as a senior surgeon and would have detailed knowledge of the layout, as well as access to lots of surgical equipment.

A burly security guard eyed them as they climbed the steps to the vast entrance, his tight brown shirt taut over his bulging muscles. Reed stepped through the glass entrance door and strolled over to the reception desk. Despite the building's old exterior, the council had extensively renovated the interior. Photos of the old building adorned the walls of the reception area. He outlined their request, so the receptionist made a phone call, then engaged with him.

"I'm sorry sir, there's an hour's wait to see Miss Neal. You should really have booked an appointment in advance."

"That's okay. We're happy to wait."

"Take a seat," the receptionist said. She pointed to some blue plastic chairs. "You can help yourself to a water and the toilets are through those double doors, if you require them."

"That's perfect, thanks."

Reed ambled across, and the two of them sat on the uncomfortable chairs. He waited a few minutes until the receptionist dealt with another person before pushing through the double doors towards the toilets with Emily hot on his heels. His hopes had materialised. He scanned the corridor, revamped with a pastel blue shade of paint, which had two doors to the toilets and another set of double doors. Reed ignored the *'Staff Only'* sign and eased them open as he tentatively looked for any council workers. The next corridor was empty. They hustled past several office doors, all wooden with single central panes of glass. He hoped to find remnants of the old hospital, such as a maintenance department. Unsuccessful in their search, they moved on, passing through the next set of double doors into a similar corridor.

"This isn't hopeful," said Emily.

"An entrance into the old hospital facilities must exist somewhere. We know from our research that the Tower Hamlets council offices only use half of the space."

"There's no camera in these corridors," Emily confirmed as she marked up her hand-drawn map.

"Excellent."

The final set of double doors led in to a spacious lobby with traditional wide stairs that ascended. Three other closed doors faced them. One led to a conference room, another was a storage cupboard, and a third locked door. Reed activated the torch on his phone and shone it through a smeary window in the locked door. A grey sign with red letters on the wall attracted his attention. *'Mortuary'*. A smile spread across his face.

"Can you see that, Em?" he asked. Emily peered over his shoulder and immediately marked the sign on her map.

"That's exactly what you wanted. Did you bring your lock picks?"

Reed fished out his equipment from an inside jacket pocket and waved them at her. "Certainly did. Let's get in there." He picked out two tools, stooped, and fiddled with the lock. Nothing happened as he wrenched the levers inside the lock.

"Damn, I bet this is rusted," he muttered.

"Keep going. I'm sure they'll loosen."

His frustration grew as the levers remained stubbornly static. The sounds of footsteps descending the stairs suddenly disrupted his concerted efforts to open the door. He frantically twisted and pushed, eager to open the door before the person caught them in the act. The levers didn't budge. He stood up just in time.

"What're you doing?" asked a chubby man with thick, black-rimmed glasses.

"We're looking for the toilets," said Emily.

"They are back through the corridors. I'll show you," said the chubby man as they followed him back to the toilets.

Reed reflected on the aborted attempt and made a mental note to bring some lubricant oil with him tomorrow that could solve the problem of the rusted lock. They drifted back into the reception area and sat down. He waited until the receptionist busied herself on her computer and then they left the building.

With the evening approaching, Reed called Madeleine and updated her on their lack of progress. They discussed the capture of Euan by Sophia and advised his client to keep well clear of the German woman. He promised to come into her office next week, regardless of finding anything.

Reed had gained useful insight about the building's layout, which would aid their exploration attempt tomorrow morning. The presence of a rusted lock implied that nobody had visited that part of the Georgian building for a long time. He was hopeful it would lead to a positive outcome and push them closer to finding Jack the Ripper's hidden treasure. A minor concern still niggled at the back of his mind regarding the treasure, what if it was a trivial item worth next to nothing?

Chapter 42

WHITECHAPEL

FRIDAY

EARLIER IN THE EVENING, the killer had consumed several shots of vodka and now stood in the shadow of a tall tree. The distinctive towering structures of Tower Bridge dominated the skyline, lights shining in the dark night sky. Snapshots of the hidden scrapbook flashed through their mind as they looked over at Saint Katharine Marina. Fresh press cuttings added to those from the Victorian era. More vile acts alongside their ancestors. Their eyes strayed to a group of people leaving a nearby restaurant. Since the attack a few nights ago, their desire to kill again had grown until it reached a crescendo, buzzing around their head like the dawn chorus. The alcohol had fuelled their thoughts and now they wandered London's streets, flitting between shadows. Their fingers tightened around the blade's handle as they followed the group, waiting for a single person to splinter off.

The killer tracked the group of innocent people along a main road being cautious and patient, waiting for the perfect moment. Several cars and a black cab passed the group, then at the intersection, one person waved goodnight to their friends. The lone individual crossed the main road and disappeared into a side road. The killer waited until there was an obvious opportunity to follow. They didn't want to be seen before having time to carry out their brutal attack.

With their hood pulled tight to obscure their head, the killer hustled down the side road and spotted the lone individual turn into Swan Passage, a small tree-lined park. The perfect area to connect with their Victorian ancestor once again. The killer zipped along the side road, eager to reach the park area. As they reached the entrance bordered by blue railings, they sighted the lone individual smoking beside a tree. Just perfect. With their eyes transfixed on their target, the killer pulled out the knife and strode purposefully across the small park. Their lack of attention clouded by their desire to kill again, as they failed to notice a discarded beer can on the pathway. They clattered the beer can, immediately alerted their target. The sight of a hooded person brandishing a knife caused the individual to burst into action and sprint towards the flats beside the park's exit.

The killer dashed after them but stopped several feet short of the flats as bright streetlamps split the blanket of darkness. They watched the individual disappear into an upper floor flat. A wave of intense disappointment flooded their mind as they spun around to leave the park. Disappointment turned to anger as they trudged from one shadow to another. Ready to flee the area should the person alert the police. The intense fire inside them needed to be satisfied, but tonight wasn't the time to quell that desire.

Chapter 43

TOWER HAMLETS TOWN HALL
SATURDAY

THE CRISP MORNING AIR caused Reed's breath to vaporise into little clouds as he paced the perimeter of the Tower Hamlets Town Hall. Euan had felt much better and joined him as they made their third walk around the distinctive Georgian building. He was reluctant to deploy the drone, at six o'clock in the morning, night-time revellers were returning home with early risers going about their business. Too many people. Whilst the council offices remained closed, the new Royal London Hospital, positioned next to the eighteen-century building, was very much open. How could they gain access to the building?

He had seen only one viable option. At the front, a single storey flat roof extension with a balcony two storeys above offered the only way in he could see. He hoped anyone who spotted them would assume they were activists and not bother reporting them to the police. The grey of twilight would provide sufficient cover once they had reached the rooftop.

"We'll have to try the front," he said to Euan as they hustled towards his preferred access point. "Let's wait until there are fewer pedestrians walking past."

"I agree."

They leant against the gate that barred vehicle entry and waited for the opportune moment, then vaulted the four-foot barrier with ease. Reed sprinted to the corner of the flat roof extension and provided Euan with a boost up. His mate reached down and dragged him onto the flat roof. They lay flat, hidden from passing traffic, whilst he attached a retractable grapple hook to a length of rope before donning their harnesses, gloves, and balaclavas. Close up, the yellowish brickwork had accumulated centuries of dirt, like a garden patio that's never cleaned. Ready for the next stage, Reed threw the grapple and, after three attempts, it snagged on the railings that bordered the balcony. A couple of quick tugs and it was secure to climb. He watched as Euan heaved himself upwards, delivering a quick thumbs up after he had scaled the railings. Reed scooted up, and together they sat on the balcony for a quick breather.

"How's your pains?" Reed asked.

"Okay, thanks. A little sore, but nothing major to worry about."

Reed surveyed their options and decided the easiest way was onto the roof above the main entrance, a simple climb. They quickly ascended the short wall section, making use of a ledge halfway up. Atop the roof, they could wander freely, and he soon discovered a route to access the building. Behind the main entrance, two storeys below them, sat another flat roof. The council had transformed an internal courtyard into additional room space.

"Down there. We could break open a skylight."

"Great idea mate."

The white-painted render on the internal walls of this section contrasted with the original Georgian features of the front facade. A distinct difference to the main building. Installed in the corner, an assortment of air-con and heating pipes offered a quick descent. He checked each of the skylights, probing for a loose lock, there's always a loose lock. Reed tugged out the crowbar from his backpack, broke the lock in no time, and opened it wide. It was a simple drop to the plain white plastered corridor.

"That was easy."

"Where to now? Have you got Em's map?" asked Euan.

"I'm not sure. I don't recognise this corridor. It's different from the style of the ones we walked through yesterday. Let's reach the ground floor and find the reception area. Follow me."

They stepped towards the ornate staircase and descended four connected flights of varnished wooden stairs. Once on the ground level, Reed got his bearings and headed towards the main entrance. The building was both deathly quiet and eerie, with no people in offices or traversing its corridors. After they had advanced through two sets of double doors, they heard a radio playing. He eased open another set of double doors and realised the toilet corridor was on the opposite side of the reception area. Now he knew their exact location.

The security guard from yesterday sat at the reception desk, halting their progress. He glared fiercely at them.

"What're you doing here?" shouted the security guard.

Reed knew they needed to access the other corridor. He sprinted across the reception area, with Euan following. They barged through the double doors with the toilets signage and hid in the men's toilets. The security guard was surprisingly nimble for his bulk and burst through the double doors seconds after them, seeing the toilet door partially open. A complete giveaway. The security guard had cornered them.

"You need to leave," instructed the security guard, his back to the toilet's entrance door.

"We found the tradesmen's entrance open."

"That's bullshit. That entrance's always locked. I can call the police or you can leave. You're trespassing," said the guard.

Reed needed to think. They had reached this point and couldn't just give up. Should he take the bulky security guard on? He spotted the taser on the guard's belt. One jab of that and they would end up in a police cell. There was only one option.

Chapter 44

Hoxton Car Repair Shop
Saturday

B ERNIE STOOPED BESIDE THE sports car, checking that the lads had properly masked off the bumper. Satisfied the car was ready, he strode over to the paint spray machine and jabbed the power button. He loaded a new paint tin, a vivid azure blue, and the machine whirled into action. This was a rush job for an existing customer in Scotland and by painting it today, it would be ready to ship on Monday.

With two hours to kill, Bernie wandered off to his office on the mezzanine floor. His thoughts turned to the letter and Jack the Ripper's missing treasure. Inside the office, he wrote a list of the locations his adversaries had visited. He could definitely link each place to bells that tolled, but he lacked sufficient knowledge of water sources. He quickly concluded that as they were still rushing around London investigating alternative locations that the treasure must remain hidden.

His thoughts drifted back to the Hoxton High Rips and wondered what heist they had carried out. He just didn't know, but remained convinced that Thomas Cutbush was Jack the Ripper. Cutbush's theft from the street gang would have been worth a serious amount of money to warrant his ostracism. Perhaps the eviction from the street gang led Cutbush to commit the murders? Or was he already mentally unstable? Some theories suggested Cutbush had caught a sexually transmitted disease from a prostitute and that he murdered for revenge. His mobile rang, piercing his thoughts. It was Davey Warren.

"Mouse. Have you got some news?" he asked.

"Yes, boss. The tracker's showing the ginger lad at Tower Hamlets Town Hall."

"Hold on," he said. He scrabbled to start his computer and selected the tracking program. The indicator flashed like a beacon.

"How long has he been there?"

"About thirty minutes."

"Why didn't you phone me earlier?"

"I was having a shower," said Davey.

"Okay Mouse, I'll take it from here."

Bernie wondered why they would be inside the council offices on a Saturday? A quick online search soon revealed the Town Hall used to be the Royal London Hospital. Where were the bells that tolled? Confused, he searched Google for the opening hours and that confirmed the council offices were indeed closed. He doubled checked on the Tower Hamlets council website. The building was closed all weekend. Intrigued, he realised he had to get to the Town Hall offices immediately, but on his own he would never apprehend Hascombe. He needed some help and called Jakob. A voicemail message played. He tried again, the same result. Where the hell is he? His next call was to his son.

"Ryan, Hascombe's at Tower Hamlets Town Hall. We need to go there immediately."

"What's he doing there?" asked Ryan.

"The offices are closed. He has to be hunting for treasure."

"I was supposed to be going shopping," whined Ryan.

"You hate shopping. Meet me there in fifteen minutes. I'll call Mikey."

"Okay."

A call to Mikey resulted in more whines, but the lad eventually agreed to meet him there. Bernie called Jakob again and left a voicemail as he wondered where the Polish lad was. He needed some weapons, as the three of them might overcome the two investigators, but after their previous encounters, he wasn't taking any chances. He raced down the stairs to the rear of the workshop area. In the corner sat a huge locked metal cabinet full of expensive tools but also with a false back panel, where he stored multiple weapons.

Bernie unlocked the cabinet door, accessed the secret weapon compartment, and selected a couple of Bowie knives for the two lads. At the bottom lay a hessian wrapped World War Two flare pistol. It resembled a gun and would cause serious harm if fired at a person. This could be enough to give him the advantage when they confronted Hascombe, so slipped it into the side pocket of his combat trousers. After he locked up the cabinet, he spun around and caught his foot on the protruding edge of a broken wooden hatch cover. Damn thing annoyed him. He lifted it and leant the offending item against the back wall and planned to purchase a new one during the week. By removing the hatch cover, it exposed the ladder that descended into the pit below. He had never taken the time to investigate where it led to. Perhaps he should have.

One last call to Jakob went to voicemail again. Damn, he could have done with his help, but the three of them should be enough to corner Hascombe. This time, he would conquer his adversaries, especially with his concealed armoury.

Chapter 45

Tower Hamlets Town Hall

Saturday

The security guard's hand hovered over his taser. Reed motioned to Euan behind his back in the men's toilet of the Tower Hamlets Town Hall. Hopefully, his friend would understand what to do.

"Time to leave, lads," said the security guard.

Reed didn't answer as he felt a tug on his backpack, followed by the coldness of thick metal in the palm of his hand. Euan had understood to give him the crowbar. He whipped it around and threatened the security guard.

"Get down," he said to Euan as the security guard reached for his taser gun and fired it straight at Reed's neck. He had expected the attack and was already ducking when it whizzed past his ear and clattered against a cubicle door. With a swift swing of the crowbar, he smashed the nearest sink tap, creating a plume of water, which sprayed the entire room. The security guard immediately dropped the taser, not wanting to get shocked himself.

With the advantage now on his side, Reed swung the crowbar at the security guard and caught his shoulder. He followed it up with a kick to the guard's leg, who stumbled backwards. He paused his attacks.

"I don't want to hurt you, but won't hesitate unless you back down."

"I'm not paid enough to argue with a man wielding a crowbar."
"Get into the cubicle," said Reed.
Between them, they tied up the security guard. They were now free to investigate the building undisturbed. Reed led the way through two sets of double doors and they reached the lobby with the rusty, locked door. He liberally sprayed the lock with lubricant and waited a minute for it to work. He took two tools from his lock pick set to twist and push the internal levers of the old lock, and eventually he heard the satisfying click as it opened. The pair slipped on head torches, which lit up the old sign declaring the *'Mortuary'* was down the stairs.

They descended the grey stone steps, deep into the old Royal London Hospital to reach the lower level. A dusty corridor stretched out in front of them, with several doorways leading off. They entered the first one, which contained three raised slabs and a bank of drawers that covered one wall. Akin to a barren kitchen with no appliances, this was the mortuary. Reed noticed the lack of equipment, presumably the hospital had transferred it to the new building. Euan wandered over to the drawers and pulled one open, which extended out six feet, and a slight hint of bleach permeated into the room.

"What're you doing?" asked Reed.
"Just checking they didn't leave a body down here!"
The best friends laughed as they exited the room, then Reed popped his head into two more doors. Both were empty offices that contained old filing cabinets and layers of dust. His head torch pierced the gloom as the corridor ended with two more closed doors. The first was a storage cupboard racked with empty shelves, whilst the second opened out into a chapel. In front of them were two worn wooden benches used for prayer, and to one side stood a substantial steel door. Opposite the entrance was a shrine that contained a cross and other items associated with worship.

"This is interesting, but I can't see any association with bells," said

Euan.

"True, but that door might lead somewhere."

Reed strode over to the steel door and tugged on the handle, but it remained shut tight. There was no lock to pick and with it fitted flush with the wall, he couldn't use the crowbar to gain entry. He scratched his head and mused on the puzzle in front of him.

"This door must open somehow," he said.

"Maybe there's a hidden switch."

The faded pictures of Christ that adorned the fourth wall may hide a lever, thought Reed, as he lifted each one. They didn't. He scanned the room, and the shrine refocused his attention. At the back of it, he detected several miniature metal levers draped with dried flowers. Six levers, about half a finger in size, spread across two rows. He pushed one lever; it moved half an inch upward, aligning with two others. Nothing happened. He pushed all six levers upward, so they all lined up. He had half-expected something to happen, but it didn't.

"These levers might open the door," he said, beckoning Euan over.

Their efforts to manipulate the levers for several minutes proved fruitless. Reed's frustration grew. These sorts of puzzles weren't his forte. He could do with Emily's help, but she was back at their hotel. He stepped away and paced the room to let Euan inspect the levers. A triumphant cry alerted him.

"Look Reed, each lever has a name engraved on it."

"Oh really, I didn't see that."

"The letters are tiny and obscured by the dried flowers," said Euan, who promptly discarded them so Reed could see.

Reed peered at the names and identified *'Genesis'*, *'Mark'*, *'Matthew'*, and three others.

"They're bible names," he said.

"Of course. But how do we align them in the correct positions?"

"I don't know. But Em'll know. I'll take a photo and call her."

He shot some photos and pressed send on the message, but he had no signal.

"I'll have to nip upstairs to send the message. You carry on fiddling with the levers," he said to Euan and hustled into the corridor. He ascended the stone steps back to the lobby, got a signal, and waited for the photos to send before calling his girlfriend. After some discussion, she agreed they were books from the bible but had no immediate solution to the puzzle and promised to call back as quick as she could.

Reed paced the lobby as he waited for an answer. Eventually, his phone rang.

"I've cracked it," said Emily. "Two are books from the old testament and four are from the new testament. You need to align Genesis and Joshua, then the other four. That should solve it."

"That's brilliant, thanks Em. We'll see you soon."

"You both take care," said Emily.

"Of course, bye."

He bounded down the stone steps, along the corridor, and into the chapel. After he had explained the solution to Euan, they aligned the levers, as Emily had suggested, and a loud click reverberated around the chapel. Reed rushed to the steel door, tugged the handle, and the hinges groaned as it slowly opened. A smile cracked his face.

"Right, let's go mate," he said. The door provided access to a slope that descended into darkness, the ground a mixture of rock and compacted dirt. Reed sneaked along, careful of any obstacles. Eventually, the tunnel levelled out and several feet later, it opened out into a small chamber. They were deep underneath London, hidden from the millions of people that used the streets daily. The constricted chamber had been roughly hewn and was what looked like another shrine with a decayed wooden cross embedded in the earth. The space was bare except for the cross, but then at the base, he spotted a metal casket.

"Geez, this is creepy," said Euan.

"Certainly is. What's that down there?"

Reed bent to pick up the casket and peered at it. Is this what they were searching for? But where was the water source? It didn't seem to fit with the letter's wording. The rusted lid resisted, so he grabbed a screwdriver from his backpack and pried it open. Disappointment flushed his face as he stared at the single finger bone that lay on matted velvet inside the casket. He showed it to Euan.

"That's disappointing."

"Let's get out of here. Another dead-end," said Reed.

"We need to re-evaluate our suspects," said Euan.

"We definitely need to re-assess our options. I feel we've not moved forward."

"Agreed. Let's return to the hotel."

He closed the casket lid and placed it back on the ground before the lads swung around and began their short trek back to the chapel. Once there, they closed the steel door and unaligned the levers to lock it. Before long, they had reached the toilets and checked the tied up security guard. Reed removed the ties from the guard's hand and feet before they rushed to the reception area. He tried the front door of the council offices, but found it locked. They had no choice but to retrace their steps. Reed led the way up through the skylight, climbed the air-con pipework back onto the outside balcony.

He drew a breath of fresh air, the pavement below thronged with people as lunchtime approached. Police sirens sounded in the distance, the guard must have reported their trespassing. Hunting for treasure was always a time-consuming exercise, but the three investigators would need to reassess their progress. He relaxed a bit and clambered over the railings, unaware of a pair of eyes that tracked his movements.

Bernie leant against the wall of the new Royal London Hospital as he watched two sides of the Tower Hamlets Town Hall building. Between the three of them, they had all four sides covered. His stomach rumbled, it needed some food. He had waited for four hours and was bored. He called Davey again, and he confirmed the ginger-haired lad was still inside the building. This had become tiresome. He wandered across the entrance to the hospital to stretch his legs when his phoned rang.

"Anything happening, Mikey?"

"They've just climbed down onto a balcony and are now descending near the front entrance."

"Brilliant, I'll get round there now. Call Ryan."

He ended the call and strode away from the hospital, eager to arrive quickly. The flare gun bounced in his side pocket as he hustled down the side street. Within a minute, the three of them had assembled by the front entrance and eagerly watched Reed and his mate drop from a single storey extension. Bernie hid behind a parked van whilst the other two stood either side of the entrance gate. They waited until their opponents clambered over the main entrance gate and surrounded them.

"We meet again, Hascombe," Bernie said, pleased with the concern etched across Reed's face. Ryan and Mikey appeared behind them and prodded Bowie knives into their backs whilst grasping their arms.

"Nice and slow. Let's not make a scene. We'll find a quiet alleyway to have a proper chat."

"We have nothing," said Reed.

"I'll be the judge of that once we've searched you."

Bernie led the assembly of five men through the Saturday

lunchtime crowds, swiftly through a side street, and into a narrow alleyway. Ryan and Mikey held on tightly to their opponents, eager to ensure they didn't break free. The wind whistled down the alleyway. The brick walls on either side lacked any doors or windows, a perfect spot for a mugging or a beating.

"We can make this easy. Give me what you've found!" he said, staring straight at Reed.

"I told you, we found nothing."

"Okay, the hard way it is. You first Hascombe. Bring him here, Mikey."

Mikey pushed Reed towards Bernie, but got caught out with the speed of his opponent's actions, who twisted and flicked away Mikey's hand that gripped his wrist. Bernie leapt towards Euan, snatched out his flare gun and put it against the lad's head.

"I thought you might try something, so I came prepared." Bernie laughed out loud. "Comply, or your mate dies!"

"I told you earlier, we found nothing," said Reed.

"Hands against the wall, legs spread. Ryan search him and his backpack."

His son moved forward and kicked Reed's legs wider for sheer pleasure. He frisked him and emptied the contents of the backpack on the floor. Rope, head torch, carabiners and more, but no treasure.

"There's nothing," Ryan said.

"Told you."

"This one now, against the wall, legs spread," said Bernie as he shoved Euan against the wall and then aimed the flare gun at Reed.

Same result, no treasure! Bernie took his disappointment out on Euan, punching him in the stomach.

"When you find Jack's treasure, it's mine. Remember that Hascombe. We know this city better than you, and we'll be following you. There are more of us, so we'll win this battle," vented Bernie. "Let's go."

Bernie, Ryan and Mikey trooped off, disappointed with the outcome. Did these investigators actually know what they were doing? Should he be thinking about probable locations? He would assign that task to Davey. The obvious location had to be a church on a river where the bells would toll above a water source, he thought.

Chapter 46

Hungarian Restaurant

Sunday

AFTER THE PREVIOUS DAY'S efforts at the Tower Hamlets Town Hall, Euan was exhausted. Instead of another busy day, the team chose a relaxing lunch. He sat with Reed and Emily at a table in the corner of a Hungarian restaurant in Whitechapel. He had beef goulash followed by chimney cake. A sweet, crunchy dough wound onto a thick wooden spit and rolled in powdered cinnamon. The restaurant was quiet after the lunchtime buzz, allowing them to talk freely about their challenging case. Pictures of old Hungary graced the white walls, complemented by dark wooden furniture. Sunlight filtered through the lace curtains as Euan scanned the room before turning his attention back to the task at hand.

"I still don't understand how they knew our location," he said.

"Was your phone on?" asked Reed.

"Yes. But yours was off?"

"It was. Perhaps they've tracked your number by linking mine?"

"That sounds feasible. I'll turn mine off. Unless there's a way to block location tracking?"

"Good shout Euan. I'll call Jed."

Euan sipped his pint of lager while Emily bashed away on her laptop and Reed phoned Jed, his hacker mate. His pains had diminished from the cuts that Jakob Kosminski had given him on Thursday, but the ordeal still flashed through his mind on random occasions. This was certainly a memorable quest, quite different from their investigations in the Peak District and Cornwall. Their lack of progress confused him. Five suspects and no leads to the hidden treasure. Reed plonked his phone on the table.

"Jed's sending me a link to a location blocking app. If we all install it, then no-one can track us."

"Excellent," said Euan. He took a large gulp of lager and expressed his confusion. "It seems bizarre that we've identified five prime suspects, and not one of them has led to discovering anything."

"Exactly. That's why we need to approach it from a different angle," interjected Emily. "I've got a list of churches in the Whitechapel area. The problem is knowing which ones can access underground water."

"Don't we need to link the churches to a suspect?" asked Reed.

"That'll be difficult as we lack pertinent information on each suspect."

"Remind me, what does Jack's letter say about the water access?" asked Euan.

He waited for Reed to pull up the photo on his phone. "Go beneath where the bells toll, find the hidden access to the water."

"Mmmm, that's very generic, not specific. It might mean a sewer, a river or even a water-well."

"It can't be a water-well," said Emily. "You can't walk inside a water-well nor a river. The only river nearby is the River Thames, and that's huge. It has to be a storm drain or sewer."

"There's no prospect of matching churches to storm drains or sewers, as they'll all be near one," said Euan.

The three investigators sat in silence as they realised the enormity of their task. They had started their investigation using a short list of prime Jack the Ripper suspects, but maybe they should reassess the entire suspect list again. Euan pondered on the dilemma and didn't relish the idea of breaking into churches for the next week. They needed more people to help them. Then he had a lightbulb moment.

"I've had an idea. Let's get Bernie Johnson and his team to help. There are several of them. They can check churches in Hoxton whilst we do Whitechapel. Agree with them to halve the sale proceeds of anything discovered," he blurted out.

He received a strange look from Reed.

"Have you gone bonkers, mate?"

"Don't you think it's a good idea?"

"Not at all. They absolutely won't tell us if they discovered any treasure."

"I suppose."

"You were thinking outside the box. Just not the right box," laughed Reed and received a punch for his taunt. "To be honest, Euan, I'd rather remove them than be involved."

"How do we do that?"

Euan waited for Reed to launch into his grand idea.

"Bernie Johnson and his Hoxton Hot Rod gang are looking for the treasure the same as us. Several of them consider Jack the Ripper suspects to be ancestors and believe the hidden treasure should be theirs. Thomas Cutbush was in the Hoxton High Rips and we know the gang performed a heist, but we don't know what they stole. The initials match Johnson's gang name, so his link to Cutbush is clear. We need to get inside his car repair shop, where there may be more something to help us. He isn't averse to beating people up, so my guess is there'll be something illegal going on inside the car repair shop which we can use to leverage action by the police."

Reed drank some beer and continued. "Another idea is to pin the copy-cat murders on Kosminski. He would be a credible suspect, so if I phoned the lead detective, we could also remove him from the action, at least for a while."

"Wow, that's amazing mate," gushed Euan.

"Brilliant," said Emily, giving Reed a peck on the cheek.

It didn't take long to get Detective Chief Inspector Clara

Loxstone's contact number, so Reed called her with his thoughts on the suspect for the murders.

"What did she say?" asked Euan.

"I've got to go into the police station on Commercial Road at eight tomorrow morning. Afterwards, we'll pay Bernie Johnson a visit at his car repair shop."

Euan smiled. His friend always found a way through problematic circumstances. He had wondered if this case was actually beyond them, but Reed had rescued it and now they were rolling again. Positivity surged through him, looking forward to tomorrow.

Chapter 47

REFLECTIONS ART GALLERY
SUNDAY

MADELEINE STROLLED TOWARDS HER husband's art gallery as she mulled over her motives for the visit. He had left earlier this morning after explaining the cleanup process from last week's exhibition needed to be completed today. She suspected it was an excuse to see the blonde girl. Did he honestly think she was that gullible? He could attempt to hide it better. However, she knew Sophia did not reciprocate the feelings unless she was lying. Either way, she had to find out and confront him to resolve the discord between them. Her phone rang with Reed Hascombe's name displayed.

"Hi Reed."

"Hi Madeleine. I wanted to give you an update on our progress since we spoke on Friday."

"Did you discover anything in the hospital?"

"Unfortunately not. We've re-appraised the letter and concluded there's some merit in visiting the local churches, which is an enormous task. We're hampered by Bernie Johnson and his thugs, so I've spoken to the DCI on the copy-cat murder case and suggested Kosminski as a possible suspect. The police want me to pop in tomorrow morning. After that, we plan to visit Johnson's car repair shop. I'm convinced he's doing something dodgy, so if I can get some heat on him, then we'll be free to investigate the churches unhindered," said Reed.

"That's proactive of you, but I had hoped you'd discover something valuable from the letter by now."

"So did we. Hopefully, you're happy for us to continue?"

"Yes, for now. If you don't find any treasure in the next week, I might need to rethink the situation," she said.

"Okay, that's fair, as we've had virtually two weeks already."

"Come into the office during the week for another catch up please."

"Will do, bye."

She pushed her phone back in the handbag slung over her shoulder and entered the gallery with some apprehension. She had avoided all conversations with her husband about what had transpired at the art gallery last weekend, but today it needed to happen. Richard had removed the Smirks' *'Future'* display, leaving the exhibition area empty. She edged towards the smaller room, which still contained the water-colour paintings from the previous weekend's exhibition. Her heart rate increased as she neared the office door, concerned with what she would find. She eased the handle down and nudged the door slowly, creating a tiny gap. She listened for any noise. Nothing. She stepped inside and spotted the sofa in the back room with its door stood open. She half-expected to see blonde hair dash through the open doorway. Richard was on his own at the workbench, a relief to her. Her shoulders, previously hunched with tension, visibly relaxed, slumping slightly as the muscles uncoiled. A deep breath escaped her lips, her chest expanding fully for the first time in what felt like days.

"Hey Rich, I was passing so dropped in to see if I can help?"

Her husband shuffled a book into a drawer, then turned, surprised to see his wife standing there.

"Oh hi love, that's okay, you don't have to help me. I'll get it done and be home soon."

"Honestly, it's no problem. Is Sophia here?" she asked. This was it, the key moment.

"No, she doesn't enjoy working weekends and has said she may leave the gallery."

Madeleine's heart jumped for joy as something had clearly caused a change in the situation between her husband and the blonde girl. She desperately wanted to probe him further, after all, that was why she had gone there today.

"Oh, really, what's happened? I thought she was very good?"

"On Friday she said she wasn't enjoying working here, which took me by surprise."

"You sound disappointed?" said Madeleine.

"She was very good at her job."

"Nothing else then?"

"What do you mean by that?" enquired her husband, his voice laced with annoyance.

"I'm going to be honest with you, Richard. I thought you fancied her, and she appeared to like you with all the touching that happened at the art exhibition. You had often worked late over the past few months, ever since she started working here. Plus, there's been a couple of nights you've slept here and not come home."

A sheepish look on his face revealed her words had hit home and there was an element of truth to what she had said. He didn't answer, so she changed tact.

"Actually, I know the truth. I didn't tell you this before, but at the art exhibition, she accosted me. She persuaded me to come into the back office and admitted she had played you, then threatened me with a scalpel. She even broke skin on my throat and shoulder with it."

The directness of Madeleine's words surprised her husband as he scrunched up his face.

"Oh, shit Maddy, so that's where you got those marks from? I didn't realise I'm so sorry. I'll sack her tomorrow, I promise."

That's all she needed to hear and embraced him, holding her

husband tight as he whispered his apologies again. Richard then ushered her from the premises so he could finish the clear-up. Madeleine was pleased to have resolved the situation with him that afternoon. Now she could focus on the hidden treasure mentioned in the letter and hoped it would bring about a revival in her company's fortunes.

Chapter 48

WHITECHAPEL

SUNDAY

THEY HAD WOKEN FOR the third time during the night, the uncomfortable sleeping place enveloped by darkness. Their mind raced with disappointment at the failed attempt two nights ago. Earlier that evening, they had stalked the streets of Whitechapel, searching for a lone victim, but without success. Their smartwatch light illuminated its face, 3:18am, still time to satisfy their desire for blood undercover of darkness. The killer dressed rapidly and fed their desires with a cursory scan of the accumulating scrapbook. They picked up their weapon of choice and slipped into the street, their hair tucked underneath the hood of the coat. Winter's chilly wind blasted around every corner as they trudged to their favourite hunting ground. Outside a nightclub.

A cackle of laughter drifted across the street as a group of girls stepped from the doorway underneath the flashing neon banner, *'The Vault'*, an apt name for a nightclub. The killer established the group was a hen party, identified by the 'L' plates plastered across the chest of one individual. The laughing group of girls wobbled from the influence of alcohol, unaware of the piercing eyes that tracked their movements. At the next road junction, the group split into two. Which group to follow? They chose the larger group of five, as it offered a better chance of success.

The hen party turned left and headed into Aldgate East

underground station, which gave the killer another decision to make. Although the risk was higher, their intense desire pushed them to ignore the warning in their mind. What about the cameras? They hustled to the end of the platform, hood pulled tight, eyes still on the hen party. Deep rumbles signalled the approaching train, the hen party jumped on board, the killer one carriage away. They edged closer to the group, keen to observe anyone departing the train. Four stops later, one girl stood away from the group by the exit door, pressing the door's open button as the train stopped at Blackfriars station.

The killer hopped off the train and tracked the girl through the station, swerving as a group of lads burst past. The lack of security in the early hours of the morning meant they could leap the ticket barriers without being stopped. Several feet ahead, the target walked towards St Paul's Cathedral. The iconic domed building was prominent across the night-time skyline with its strategically placed lighting. Nine minutes later the girl entered the tree-covered grounds of the cathedral, wobbling on her heels, the effects of alcohol undiminished. The killer gripped the handle of their blade, ready to pounce. The adrenaline flooded their veins; they quickened their pace and closed the gap rapidly. Suddenly, the girl turned, spotted the knife and swung her handbag, crashing it into the killer's face, who grabbed the victim's blonde hair and jerked it hard. The girl staggered backwards. A quick slash and blood oozed from the wound on the victim's throat.

With their desire sated, the killer dragged the body into a bush beside the cathedral, leaving it to drain of life fluid. Another offering to their Victorian ancestor. A smile flickered across their lips. Only two more to go, they thought.

Chapter 49

COMMERCIAL STREET POLICE STATION

MONDAY

REED HAD CONSIDERED IF he was doing the right thing of implicating Jakob Kosminski in the copy-cat murders, but he needed to get Bernie Johnson's gang off their tails. The hard plastic seat in the bland reception area of the police station had been his waiting point for over ten minutes. His appointment time had come and gone. Whilst he pondered the approach to his next step in their case, visiting the car repair shop owner, the door opened. In walked a medium-height woman, mid-forties, he guessed, with wavy black hair dragged back into a ponytail. She wore a plain black trouser suit and unlabelled black trainers, quite nondescript.

"Mr Hascombe, DCI Loxstone," she said, her arm extended, ready for a handshake. Reed obliged.

"Pleased to meet you."

"Follow me."

The detective strode off down a corridor; the walls were strewn with information posters. She opened a door and ushered him into the confines of a simple room containing a stainless steel desk and four chairs. He glanced at a recording unit sat on the corner of the desk.

"Don't worry about that, Mr Hascombe. We won't be recording anything today. It's just an informal chat after your phone call yesterday."

"Call me Reed."

"Okay, Reed. I obviously checked your criminal record, of which there isn't one. I researched you on the internet and it's fair to say, you are mildly famous. If that's such a thing. Your activities in the Peak District and Cornwall certainly attracted some favourable press coverage over the past two years. So tell me again. Why are you here?"

"You asked me to come in?"

"Nobody likes a clever-dick! Obviously, I want to know why you consider Kosminski has anything to do with the copy-cat murders? Let's start simply. How do you know him?"

"I'm on an investigative case and he captured and tortured my friend," Reed said, not wanting to impart too much information.

"Come on Reed. I need more details than that. You know how this works. You've been inside a police station before."

Within a minute, Reed had remembered why he hated police stations. He would bite his tongue and comply for now.

"My client found a Victorian letter and we're searching for some hidden treasure. As you know, that's my area of expertise. Anyway, Kosminski has popped up twice during our investigation and then Thursday he was involved in taking my friend hostage. Kosminski cut my friend several times with a knife. So I thought you might be interested in investigating him. Didn't the copy-cat murderer use a knife?"

"I'll ask the questions," came the abrupt answer. "A few knife cuts don't make a murderer. But I'll make a note," said DCI Loxstone as she scribbled on her pad.

"Another thing to consider. Kosminski works for Bernie Johnson, who owns a car repair shop in Hoxton. I'm sure something dodgy happens there."

"You really are full of accusations!"

Then the conversation halted as a young plain-clothes officer opened the door, strode over to DCI Loxstone and whispered in her ear. Reed watched her face turn ashen grey.

"We need to finish our conversation now. I'll be in touch if I need anything further. Show Mr Hascombe out Page and grab a car," she said and hustled from the room. The young plain-clothes officer escorted Reed out of the police station and wondered what had brought about a swift end to their discussion.

Clara grabbed her coat and phone from her office before dashing to the car park. Another bloody murder. She wasn't having much luck. She was no closer to a resolution, and now a third one. Her boss would call once he had heard and demand immediate answers. She needed to get to the crime scene quickly. Page was already inside a police vehicle as she deposited herself in the passenger seat.

"Lights on," she instructed her junior officer. "Put your foot down."

"Yes, boss."

They hurtled out of the car park, blue lights flashing, swinging left as vehicles pulled over to allow them to pass. Her thoughts drifted back to earlier and whilst she felt Reed Hascombe had an ulterior motive for mentioning Kosminski, her instinct suggested he might be right. They still hadn't located the Polish man, either at his flat or the barbershop where he worked. He was clearly keeping a low profile. That usually signified guilt of some form. Page's forceful driving ensured they reached the murder location in eleven minutes. Clara jumped out as Page bumped up the curb and headed towards the yellow cordon tape that flapped in the wind. The serene stone cathedral stood sentry over the gardens, offered a stark contrast to the dead body lain at its feet. She jogged over and spotted Anderson, the forensics guy, pleased he was there already. The body lay on the concrete pathway beside shrubbery with bloodstains on the soil.

"Anderson, what have you got?" she asked.

"We have to stop meeting like this, Loxstone. People will talk."

"Shut up, you goof, just give me the lowdown and make it snappy." Clara didn't dislike Anderson, but he could be a tad annoying.

"White female, age around twenty-five, inebriated. Again, a sharp blade that slit her throat. Carotid artery severed, exactly as before. I suggest it's the same perpetrator with the identical MO. Time of death about four am."

"Geez, this is getting out of hand. My boss will jump up and down. Anything else?"

"I can't see anything obvious, but I'll carry out a full autopsy back at the ranch."

Clara's disappointment washed over her. Still no substantial evidence to work with. Her phone rang and, as expected, DS Browne.

"I've just heard Clara. Why haven't you phoned me?"

She didn't want another argument with her boss, so diffused the comment with a simple statement of facts. "I'm at the crime scene now. Caucasian female this time, same MO, according to Anderson."

"You realise the newspapers will publish it in the next hour?"

"Yes, and we're doing everything we can to find the culprit."

"The MCC wants an update before this latest development hits the papers. Get back here and prime me on your suspects."

"I should analyse the area around the victim before I come to your office, sir."

"Fine. One hour Loxstone!"

No thanks or a goodbye. Being a DCI was a tough gig, but mostly Clara enjoyed it. This was an exceptional time, where the murders fitted a pattern set in Victorian times by a character dubbed Jack the Ripper. What she couldn't understand was what event had triggered a murderer to replicate those killings from a century ago? She didn't have time to digest that fully and wandered around the grounds of St Paul's Cathedral, searching for any clues. The only thing of interest was the girl's discarded handbag, so she slipped on blue latex gloves to handle it. Inside was a purse, a mobile phone and some makeup items. As Clara turned over the handbag, she spotted a slight indentation in one corner of the gold glittery bag. She snapped a quick photo and called over to Anderson.

"Have you seen this?" she asked.

"What?"

"I've found a slight mark on the victim's handbag."

Anderson wandered over and peered at the mark that Clara had pointed out.

"Bag it up and I'll carry out some tests. It might be nothing but definitely worth a check."

"Let's hope so Anderson. We need a break on this case."

Clara looked around for her DI and sighted him talking to the police officer assigned to stop the public from contaminating the crime scene. She strode over to grab his attention, they jumped into the police vehicle, and he switched the blue lights on again. Clara imparted her instructions to DI Page to get straight on with when they reached the station.

"I want all the local camera footage trawled over today. Anderson has the victim's handbag to analyse alongside the body. That could take two days. I noticed an indentation in one corner. Hopefully, she hit the perpetrator with it. We might get a DNA match."

Page hurtled around a tight corner, causing Clara to bump her shoulder against the passenger door.

"I said quick Page, but not so quick that you injure me!"

"Sorry, boss."

Clara had given up telling him to stop calling her boss, she just rode with it now.

"Contact the victim's family, arrange a meeting with them for two hours' time and get outline details of her activities last night. I'll be in with the Super for the next hour. Got that?"

"Yes, boss."

As Page swung the vehicle into the police station car park, Clara jumped out and sprinted to her office. She quickly updated the whiteboard and grabbed her original list of suspects before rushing off to meet DS Browne. If the Metropolitan Chief Constable was involved, she needed a result soon, otherwise the heat would be on. She crossed her fingers as she recalled the handbag, hoping it would be a crucial piece of evidence.

Chapter 50

Hoxton Car Repair Shop
Monday

THE ROLLER SHUTTER DOORS of the car repair shop in Hoxton were fully open as Reed marched towards it. He had come alone whilst Euan waited around the corner, their phones on an open conversation. They had agreed on a trigger word in case things got difficult for Reed, *'Legacy'*, but he expected nothing untoward to occur as he was unarmed and had nothing of value with him. He slipped inside the entrance and remained motionless, allowing him time to observe the inside of the car repair shop. It had two bays with vehicle inspection pits and a third without, all occupied with cars. A radio blasted out music across the space, littered with tools and bottles of car lubricants. A set of stairs rose at the far end up, leading to a mezzanine floor, which had an office above one bay. In the far corner stood a huge metal cabinet beside a stained wooden workbench. An open tattered door in the back wall banged as the wind blew it, presumably that led to a rear yard.

Reed crept along the wall to look around before he announced his arrival, wary of the two lads working inside the vehicle inspection pits. He avoided a stack of old tyres as he neared the metal cabinet. Leant against the wall was a broken wooden hatch cover beside a hole in the floor, the rungs of a ladder just visible in the darkness. That looked of interest. Worthy of investigation, he thought. He pushed the handle on the tattered rear door and moved outside. The back yard contained waste disposal bins and a smaller single-story building opposite. He smiled to himself as he wedged the back door ajar. Six quick steps later, he eased down the handle of the door into the smaller building. He spotted a pristine, vivid blue sports car parked inside, unattended. An immense machine stood in front of him with a robotic arm, labelled *'Spraybot'*. A simple desk beside the machine contained paperwork, which he grabbed and skimmed. He had found Bernie's dodgy dealings. Shipping paperwork and an email from an individual in Scotland that specified a particular model and colour of car they required. That suggested a stolen car.

"Euan, are you there?" he whispered.

"Yes."

"I've found a resprayed sports car that's possibly stolen."

"Really, take some photos."

"Will do. We need to alert the police to this immediately," said Reed.

"Let me phone them. You wait there until I call you back. Put your phone on silent."

"Make it an anonymous tip-off. We need to come back here tonight. I've also found a ladder that seems to lead underneath the car repair shop. It maybe nothing, but it's worth investigating further."

He hung up the call to Euan and snapped a few photos whilst he waited. His mate called him back, and now he was ready to confront Bernie Johnson.

Reed left the paint spray building and eased open the rear door to the car repair shop. He slipped inside and noticed only one lad was in a vehicle inspection pit. He scanned the car repair shop and heard footsteps on the metal stairway. Time to move, so he hustled back along the wall and stood close to the roller shutter doors at the front of the workshop. He came face to face with Ryan Johnson, who stepped out of a vehicle inspection pit.

"What the fuck are you doing here?" asked Ryan.

"To see the organ grinder."

His adversary stared at him, wary of Reed's ability to attack him.

"Screw you."

"Where is he?"

"Upstairs, I'll call him."

Reed waited until Bernie Johnson appeared downstairs, backed up by Ryan and Mikey on either side of him, brandishing heavy implements.

"That's brave of you coming here, Hascombe," said Bernie.

"I'm unarmed and have nothing on me," he said, spreading his arms wide. "Search me?"

"Do it Mikey."

Mikey stepped forward and warily frisked Reed, confirming he was unarmed.

"What do you want?" asked Bernie.

"Shall we go upstairs for a chat?"

"No. We talk here."

Reed's calculated pause created a palpable tension, clearly meant to enrage his opponent.

"We want the same result, to locate the treasure. We should join forces and agree to split the proceeds fifty-fifty."

Bernie laughed. "You really expect me to fall for the oldest trick in the book? I thought you worked for Madeleine Robinson-Smith?"

"She's agreed," said Reed, a blatant lie.

"How can I trust you?"

"You have my word. Can I trust you?"

"Humph, I'll consider it," snorted Bernie.

Both men stared at each other intensely before Reed announced his departure.

"I'll leave it with you, call me if you're interested."

At that, Reed spun on his heels and exited the building via the roller shutter doors. He strode purposely towards the alleyway where Euan waited. As he approached the alleyway's entrance, he heard police sirens and hoped they intended to raid Bernie's car repair shop.

Chapter 51

HOXTON CAR REPAIR SHOP
MONDAY

BERNIE HAD SCAMPERED UP to his office after Hascombe's visit, and was now discussing with Davey the list of churches they could search. His tech guy had worked diligently on this for the past few hours, identifying fourteen possibilities. He considered how to approach the task when he heard police sirens wailing nearby. The churches stood in several neighbourhoods, including Hoxton and Whitechapel. His plan was to visit one each day whilst the lads managed the vehicle repair business. He had pinpointed the one for today, the nearest church, St. Monica's, which was just around the corner. The sound of police sirens intensified and broke his concentration as suddenly blue lights flickered around the room. He sprang up immediately to peer through the window.

Startled by a police car outside, Bernie rushed down the metal stairway and shouted at Ryan.

"Get the car out now!"

His son knew immediately what he meant and hurtled through the rear door just as a police officer entered the car repair shop. He needed to stall the police officer.

"Hello officer, how may I help you?"

"Are you Bernard Johnson?" asked the policeman.

"Yes, how can I help?"

"It's come to our attention you may have a stolen vehicle on the premises."

"I don't think so, unless one of our customers has been naughty," he said as cold sweat trickled down his back. How did they know?

The officer in charge spoke to his colleague and pointed at the vehicles in the car repair shop.

"Run these plates through the computer back at base."

"Will do," said the junior officer.

"I'm sure they'll be fine," said Bernie.

"We'll be the judge of that. I'll just wander around, okay?"

"Of course, I've got nothing to hide." Bernie identified the muffled engine of the sports car from behind him. The police officer didn't appear to hear it as he wandered around, scanning the car repair shop.

"What's in here?" asked the police officer in charge, stood in front of the metal cabinet. "Can you open it?"

Oh no, thought Bernie, if he finds my weapons, I'm done for.

"The key's upstairs, let me fetch it."

Bernie scooted off up the stairs, worry now etched across his face. He grabbed the key from his desk drawer and descended the stairs just as the police officer opened the rear door. He had to avert the officer's attention, so jumped down the remaining steps.

"Officer, I've got the cupboard key."

As luck would have it, the police officer turned to watch Bernie open the cabinet. The police officer scanned the tools stored inside but missed the false panel that hid Bernie's weapons.

"Sir, I've got the results," said the junior officer to his superior as he strode into the workshop.

"Anything stolen, Jenkins?"

"No boss, they're all clean."

"It seems we've received some misinformation, Mr Johnson."

"Oh, no problem. Let me show you out."

Bernie ushered the police officers towards the roller shutter doors. He breathed a sigh of relief; he'd escaped being arrested.

"Wait a minute, I want to look outside," said the police officer. The officer spun rapidly on his heels and crashed through the back door. Bernie hustled to catch up as the officer entered the single-story building. His heart raced until he glimpsed daylight at the end of the spray booth, as the blue sports car wasn't there. Phew, Ryan had driven it out in time. The police officer glanced at the machine and asked,

"What's this equipment for?"

"It resprays sections of vehicles after accident damage, which is quicker than hand spraying," he said.

"So you wouldn't be involved in repainting stolen cars?"

"Of course not officer, I repair cars, not steal them." Bernie felt the glare of the police officer bore into him. A few seconds passed before the officer answered.

"We've got our eyes on you Johnson, if we receive any further information about stolen vehicles, I'll be getting a warrant."

The police officer returned to his vehicle and left the premises. Bernie plonked down at his desk with a deep sigh, that was stressful, but they hadn't caught him. He wondered who tipped off the police and his immediate thought was Hascombe. It couldn't have been a coincidence that his adversary had left the car repair shop a mere five minutes before the police arrived. Had Hascombe wandered into the spray booth building? He vowed there wouldn't be a pact; the game was on. After all, they could still track Hascombe's mate.

Chapter 52

HOXTON CAR REPAIR SHOP
MONDAY

REED PAUSED IN THE shadows beside the rear door to the car repair shop, lock picks ready in his gloved hands. After the earlier confrontation with Bernie Johnson, Reed had waited until they saw the four men leave the Hoxton car repair shop, although the office light remained on amidst the darkness of the building. No sounds, so he bent and twiddled his two picks until the locked clicked open. He crept inside, with Euan close behind him. They had come prepared with backpacks containing equipment for every eventuality. The whiff of oil lingered in the workshop's air with the roller shutter doors down and locked. Only one car remained parked above a vehicle inspection pit. Reed was interested in three items: the huge locked metal cabinet, the office, and the ladder that descended into a pit. Both lads stood beside the door, waiting a moment until their eyes grew accustomed to the dark.

"Can you spot any cameras?" he asked Euan.

"There's one fixed to the metal beam close to the office."

"Right, let's search the office, but first I'll block the camera. Balaclavas on just in case."

He padded across the concrete floor, avoiding the stack of car tyres, and ascended the metal stairway. He clambered on top of the railing, grasped the beam to his right, then edged along towards the corner. The camera was inches away now. He grabbed the black spray can of paint from his backpack's outer pocket, removed the cap, and sprayed the lens. Camera disabled!

Reed leapt back onto the mezzanine floor and, several seconds later, he had unlocked the office door. The door creaked as it opened to reveal a vacant room with an overhead fluorescent tube that generated a stone-cold glare. He flicked the switch to plunge them into darkness and fumbled for his head torch, Euan followed suit.

"You take the desk, I'll search the cabinets and floor safe," he whispered.

Euan gave him a thumbs up and opened the desk drawers as Reed crouched to look at the safe. It wasn't a simple lock, unfortunately. With a numerical combination-dial, he concluded there was no way to access the floor safe's contents without blowing the steel door off its hinges. He had no reason to resort to explosions yet. The metal filing cabinets held paperwork, filed by month, that stretched back almost five years. He was about to close the bottom drawer when he spotted one folder with no label. Curious, he pulled it out and rifled through the paperwork. A shrewd smile lit his face as he had stumbled upon Johnson's shipping information for stolen cars. He counted sixteen records. Quickly, he spread them atop the desk and photographed the newest ones. If necessary, he could provide the DCI he had met earlier that morning with the information.

"What've you found?" asked Euan.

"Lot's of stolen car information. Exactly like the paperwork I saw in the paint spray building out the back."

He presented Euan with the paperwork for the vivid blue sports car he had seen earlier that day.

"The bloke has his fingers in lots of dodgy dealings. There's nothing of interest in the desk drawers, just stationary."

"Let's check out that huge cabinet downstairs."

They returned the paperwork before Reed switched the light back on and locked the office door. He slipped down the metal stairway and grasped the padlock that held the clasps together on the cabinet doors. It didn't take long to pick the chunky lock, allowing him access to the cabinet. Inside sat a myriad of power tools, carefully hung and labelled. He saw nothing out of the ordinary.

"Just tools. Now for the ladder," he said.

Reed bent over the hole, about a two-foot square, and shone the beam of his head torch inside. The ladder, surrounded by old brickwork, disappeared out of sight. He put on his harness, tied a rope to the leg of a heavy wooden workbench and attached it to his harness with a belay device, swung a leg over and began his descent.

"I'll give you an update," he said to Euan as he waved his two-way radio at his mate.

His feet eased down one rung at a time, ensuring the ladder was secure at each step. After several minutes of descent, the entrance to the hole was a mere pinprick of light above his head. Then his foot hit solid ground. He managed a three-sixty degree turn and realised he was at the end of a storm drain. He pressed the button on the two-way radio.

"I'm down Euan. It's a storm drain. We should investigate it further. I've unhooked the rope, your turn mate."

"Okay, I'll be there shortly."

A few minutes later, Reed stood to one side as his mate joined him and they headed into the storm drain.

"I prefer the caves in the Peak District to these tunnels," said Euan.

"Me too. They're a tad claustrophobic."

They plodded on, careful with their footing on the slippery brick surface, as the storm drain swept into a corner. Around the bend, a crude brick wall became visible. It was a slapdash mix of bricks and concrete, uneven with many cracks. Intrigued, Reed pulled out his crowbar and wedged the end into a crack around waist height. He wrenched hard, and the bricks crashed to the ground, pursued by a wave of dirty rainwater that swept Euan off his feet unexpectedly.

The water sloshed past as it raced around the corner, diminishing in depth.

"Are you okay, mate?" asked Reed when he spotted Euan lying in a torrent of dirty water like a beetle stuck on its back, legs flapping rapidly.

As the water eased to ankle depth, Euan stood. "Geez, you could have warned me!"

"I didn't realise there was water behind the wall."

"I'm bloody freezing now."

"Put your spare trousers and waterproof on. That'll warm you up. Then do some star jumps."

"Funny," said Euan, never happy when wet.

Reed waited until Euan had changed before they clambered through the broken wall. He scrolled through the widgets on his smartwatch and checked their direction of travel. It was southwest towards Shoreditch. Seventy feet later, the storm drain plunged down a slippery slope. He had taken several steps when his foot slipped on a patch of wet moss, tumbling backwards, he slid on his side down the rest of the slope section to level ground. His hip grumbled in pain as he rose from the uneven Victorian brickwork. He had landed at an intersection. A storm drain similar to the one they had just traversed opened up directly in front, heading eastwards. North and south of his position was a much grander tunnel with what appeared to be a modest river flowing through the middle southwards, presumably towards the Thames. Euan landed beside him.

"Oh wow, this is impressive."

"But which way?"

"Not sure. I think this is the underground river I read about whilst researching our suspects. It's called Walbrook River," explained Euan.

"Is this the hidden water access?"

"Possibly."

Above his head, Reed identified the end of a ladder that disappeared into the ceiling of the intersection chamber. Moss clung to cracks in the brickwork across the entire ceiling, fungi lined the point between the walls and the river. He spun round several times and wondered which way to go? South definitely went towards the river Thames. East was another storm drain and might lead them to a place where the bells tolled. Was this a real crossroads in the search for Jack the Ripper's missing treasure? Or yet another dead-end?

Chapter 53

HOXTON CAR REPAIR SHOP
MONDAY

B ERNIE HAD BEEN HALFWAY through his steak and chips dinner when Davey Warren called to advise him that the investigators were at the car repair shop. In a blind panic, he had raced there, ignoring the speed limits, and was now sitting outside the building in his car. Everything seemed normal. The roller shutter doors remained locked and the upstairs office light was on, as he had left it. He had skirted the building, there were no signs of forced entry. Perhaps Davey had got it wrong? Better check to be sure.

"Are they still at the car repair shop, Mouse?"

"Let me look. They've moved, they're now three streets away."

"Where exactly?"

"Next to the Courthouse Hotel in Shoreditch."

"Why would they be there?"

"I don't know, boss."

"Okay, thanks Mouse," said Bernie as he hung up.

His next step was to call Ryan and Mikey, directing them to the hotel. With that sorted, he opened the roller shutter door, moved inside, and climbed the stairway to the office. His stomach growled, which reminded him of his half eaten meal. The office was undisturbed, so after turning on his desktop computer, he used the microwave to heat the steak and chips his wife had stuffed into a plastic container. He clicked on the CCTV program and tucked into his food whilst it loaded. A few more clicks and he scanned the recordings whilst shovelling chips into his mouth. As he chewed on a succulent piece of meat, a shadowy hand appeared on the CCTV footage before the camera went blank. Someone had covered it up. Bernie fumed and opened the tracking app. It still showed the investigators at the hotel, so called Ryan.

"Have you found them?"

"They aren't here, Mouse must be mistaken."

"They broke into the repair shop and covered up the security camera with spray paint. The tracking app still shows they are there. Find them and give them a beating."

He slammed his phone on the desk and consumed the last piece of steak. Damn those investigators; they had ruined his evening meal. His mind worked overtime as he checked every drawer and cabinet in the office to ensure nothing was missing. Everything seemed in order. He went downstairs, opened the cupboard, checked his hidden stash of weapons, and found them safely stored. As he spun around, he noticed a length of rope attached to the workbench leading into the pit with the ladder. A wicked grin spread across his face as he realised they were underground. He grabbed a nearby light used for working underneath vehicles and shone it down the pit, but the beam disappeared into a blanket of darkness. He called his son again.

"Ryan, get back here. They're underground. I've found a rope in the pit, so we need to corner them when they return."

"That explains why we couldn't find them."

Bernie checked the spray paint building before returning to the office. They might need reinforcements, so he called Jakob Kosminski again. It clicked to voicemail once more. Was he deliberately avoiding him? He then typed a meeting message on the Rippers Guild WhatsApp group, as the lad never missed a meeting. Sophia answered immediately, but Jakob didn't. He called the German girl.

"Have you seen or heard from Jakob in the past couple of days?"

"No, not since Friday's meeting. He seemed preoccupied that day, almost as if the events at my flat had affected him."

"His ego would've taken a battering, but it's unlike him not to answer my calls."

"I'll call him and let you know."

"Okay, thanks."

He checked the tracker app again whilst he waited for Ryan and Mikey to arrive. The investigator's location was unchanged. He mulled over his capture plans and decided the lads could wait downstairs in the dark whilst he monitored the tracker app on the computer in the office. If Hascombe has found anything worthwhile, this could be the perfect opportunity to steal it from him. His phone beeped with a message from Sophia, which confirmed Jakob would call Bernie shortly. That was ideal, as he would need Jakob to help conquer the investigators when the time arrived.

Chapter 54

WALBROOK RIVER

MONDAY

AT THE INTERSECTION WITH Walbrook river, Reed chose east along a storm drain akin to the one they had passed through from the car repair shop in Hoxton. He always preferred to move forward rather than backwards, unless it became impossible. This storm drain had a steady slope as he and Euan edged their way upwards. A gleam of white caught the beam from his head torch as they neared a bend in the tunnel. Part of the Victorian tunnel had broken away above their heads as a stack of bricks partially blocked their passageway. He stooped to view the gleaming white object and realised it was a pile of bones. He estimated the longest one to be around eighteen inches, so based on that, he concluded the bones had to be human. Rats had gnawed the bones clean, presumably scavenging for food.

"These are pretty old bones," he said to Euan.
"No smell or sinews."
"The roof must have collapsed on them."
"Not a nice way to die."

They clambered over the unusual pile of bricks and bones. Reed trudged along the uneven brick surface until his head torch beam glinted on a metallic object in the distance. A few steps later and he identified the bottom rungs of a ladder, giving them a route out, although the tunnel carried on around another bend.

"Let's look up here."

"Good plan mate," said Euan.

Reed climbed the old ladder, its rungs slightly rusty, and after several minutes he reached the top, but a wooden panel blocked the exit. He shoved the partially rotted panel upward, but it barely moved. Taking out his crowbar, and with one hand grasping the rung of the ladder, he levered the wooden panel. It nudged a fraction, so had to be obstructed by an object on top of it. Several more shoves, and with no further movement, Reed's frustration grew, so he smashed the corner, which caused the rotted wood to crumble as the crowbar clanged against metal. He carried on smashing the wood and eventually had a gap to work with. He shoved the crowbar into the gap and levered the metal object aside, now they could climb free of the pit.

The beam of Reed's head torch flickered as he scanned the space they found themselves in. He delved into his backpack, found new batteries and replaced them in his failing head torch. The metal object that blocked the wooden panel was a locked cast iron trunk about the size of a modern-day microwave. Various bottles, stacks of crates, and a few tools were visible in the space, like a handyman's storeroom. He wondered where they were? The door opened with a creak as he peered through the gap and instantly recognised the rows of pews and an altar. They were inside a church. Reed's mind whirred as he connected the clues, then turned to Euan.

"It's a church and we've climbed up from a hidden water access."

Euan's eyes sparkled in his head torch beam. "Geez, it fits. What exactly did the letter say?" asked Euan.

Reed whizzed through his photos and enlarged the one of Jack's letter. "Behind the twentieth brick from the ladder, you will find a key to my treasure," he recited. He closed the storeroom's door and climbed back into the pit, eager to search the storm drain. He landed on the worn brickwork floor and counted twenty bricks west, whilst Euan went east, underneath the church. His scrutinisation of the wall and ceiling revealed no loose bricks and then, as he turned, Euan let out a triumphant yelp.

"Over here Reed."

"Coming, mate," he said, hustling as fast as possible across the uneven ground. Euan pointed to a loose brick about knee height, so Reed squatted and eased it out carefully with his crowbar. Behind the brick was a tiny hessian bundle. He tugged it free and unwrapped the cloth, exposing a piece of paper with a weighty object inside. Beneath the light of both of their head torches, he unfolded the old piece of paper to reveal an iron key.

"It is literally a key. I assumed the letter meant there would be another clue."

"So did I, or at least a map of Jack's treasure location."

"Hang on, what's on the paper?" asked Euan.

Reed flipped over the piece of paper so they could both analyse it. Unfortunately, it contained mainly black splotches with a few identifiable handwritten letters. The years sat in a damp environment had caused the ink to run. He activated his phone once more and compared the writing on the piece of paper to Jack's letter. It matched. Now they had to locate the lock that the key fitted.

"Let's analyse the letter in daylight. We might decipher some whole words if there are slight indentations on the paper," he said.

"We can also research the size and style of the key to fathom out whether it fits a door, a trunk or something else," said Euan.

An idea flashed through Reed's mind. "That box in the storeroom is a storage trunk. Could it be that?"

Euan slapped his mate on the back and proclaimed., "You're a genius. We might have found Jack's treasure."

"You're the genius, you said trunk."

"Enough trunks. A herd of elephants might fly by next," said Euan.

"Mate, your jokes are shite!"

They raced back to the ladder and climbed up into the storeroom. Reed stood next to the metal trunk, the key poised in his hand.

With a bit of jiggling, it fitted inside the lock, but wouldn't turn. He tried several times, but it wasn't the correct key for the lock. Disappointed, he deposited it safely in the secure pocket of his backpack. He didn't want to lose it.

"Never mind, we'll find the correct lock. Even if we have to search the whole of London hunting for it, like Prince Charming did with the glass slipper." Euan laughed. His mate's jokes were flowing, but Reed still punched him affectionately.

"Let's return to the hotel and phone Emily. Tell her the good news."

"We should call Madeleine as well. She'll be happy."

"Let's wait until tomorrow, after we've looked online at locks that could match the key," said Reed. He moved the cast iron metal trunk over the pit entrance, then eased out of the handyman's storeroom into the church. Now they had to get outside.

It wasn't a big church, although a large arch-shaped stained glass window above the altar let in some light from a nearby streetlamp. Above the main worship area were two balconies shrouded in darkness, accessed by wooden stairs. He tried the heavy wooden main entrance door, but found it securely locked. There was no escape that way.

Reed skipped up the stairs and spotted a window at the end of one balcony. It had an old-style metal handle with a latch at the base. He moved the handle upwards, lifted the latch, and pushed, but it wouldn't open until he applied some force. A blast of chilly night air hit his face, a refreshing relief to the stale underground air he had breathed for the past two hours.

With Euan close behind, he clambered out of the window, used his parkour skills to slide down the ornate walls of the church, and jumped the last two feet to the ground. An information board in the minuscule garden, which was barely more than a patch of grass, declared it was St Leonard's Church, Shoreditch. They vaulted the railings that surrounded the church onto the pedestrian walkway.

Reed immediately spotted a car's headlights; the car had jumped the kerb and was heading straight for them.

"Euan, look out," he shouted, then rolled to one side as the car ploughed towards him. It stopped, the doors flung open, and out jumped Ryan Johnson with his boxer mate. They needed an escape route quick, Reed scanned the area and noticed an e-scooter station about fifty feet away.

"Euan, grab a scooter whilst I keep them at bay."

He adopted a defensive position in front of his adversaries, avoiding the punches thrown, whilst Euan scanned the QR code and paid for the e-scooter hire.

"Ready," shouted Euan. Reed sprinted over to his mate, jumped on the back of the e-scooter, and they whizzed away from danger. Another close call, but they had the key, safe inside his backpack.

Earlier, Ryan had received a call from his dad to reach St Leonards Church in Shoreditch. The tracker app had shown the investigators to have been there for at least ten minutes. He and Mikey had driven there as quick as possible, circling the church in his car. He saw two men jump the railings and had hoped to stop them with his off-road driving skills, but they had now sped away on an e-scooter through a pedestrianised area where he couldn't follow. As his car was quicker, they could catch up using the roads, but only if he knew which direction to go.

"Call Mouse," he said to Mikey. "He needs to instruct us on their exact location."

Ryan reversed his car out onto the main road and turned right to chase the investigators. Mikey connected with Davey, using the speaker on his phone.

"They're on Boundary Street, headed south. Where are you?"

"At the north end of it," said Mikey.

Keen to catch the investigators, Ryan pressed the accelerator hard as they flew past parked cars on both sides, hoping no vehicles pulled out of the side streets. Ahead, he spotted his targets on the e-scooter as they neared a junction before spinning left so he braked hard. The tyres squealed as he flung his car around the corner, just in time to see them turn right down a narrow street. He was hard on their tail as the ginger-haired lad spun his head around before the e-scooter jumped up onto the pavement as it hurtled towards another junction. He wanted to flip his car onto the pavement to knock them off, but a series of concrete bollards prevented it. The chase led onto Bethnal Green Road, but being a major traffic route, he had to stop at the give way sign.

Ryan watched in annoyance as the investigators gained a lead over him, their e-scooter now following a bus whilst he was two cars behind them. He noticed the ginger-haired lad on the back wave one arm as they passed a side road. He spotted an opportunity and slammed the accelerator to the floor, overtaking the two vehicles and with laser-focus zoned in on his target. The bus indicated to pull in as Ryan drew level with the rear of the e-scooter. A quick flick of the steering wheel and he clipped the rear-end of the e-scooter, which shunted his target. Reed smashed the e-scooter's handlebars against the rear-end of the bus, then tumbled on to the road. The other lad bounced into the back of Reed but remained upright.

"Let's get them," he shouted to Mikey.

They flung open both car doors as Reed got to his feet, blood smeared across his face. His opponent took two steps forward and positioned himself, ready for a fight. Behind his adversary, the ginger-haired lad fumbled with the stricken e-scooter as people hooted their horns in passing vehicles. Ryan threw the first punch, but Reed ducked and avoided it. Mikey attacked with jabs to Reed's ribs, but only one connected. They needed to finish this quickly as a crowd of people gathered underneath the streetlight, staring at the ruckus as jeers and shouts punctuated the traffic noise. He advanced and seconds later landed on his backside as Reed triggered a leg sweep move that caught him unaware. As Mikey launched another punch, Reed swiftly flipped Mikey's wrist behind his back, which sent his friend tumbling to the floor. Next thing, their two opponents had jumped on the e-scooter and raced across the main road into a darkened alleyway.

"Shit Mikey, we need some help. He's too good for us."

Ryan called his father and explained the situation, but got short shrift from Bernie. Shaking his head, he jumped into his car and gave chase once more. Mikey connected with Davey again.

"Where are there Mouse?" asked Mikey.

"They've just gone through a green space and are on Hunton Street. I think they're headed for their hotel."

"Right, let's head directly there," Ryan said and navigated the main roads to the hotel, hoping to catch them outside.

Seven minutes later, he parked outside the entrance to the New Road Hotel with the engine still running, and seconds later, the two investigators appeared from an alleyway beside the hotel. As Ryan was about to drive into them, a white van passed his car and instead he caught the rear end of the van and smashed a tail-light. Out jumped a burly man, arms waving as expletives exploded from the man's mouth, aimed at him. His day couldn't get any worse. He offered his apologies and promised to fix the man's van.

Ryan sighed as he drove slowly back to the car repair shop, expecting to incur his father's wrath. That hadn't gone to plan. If the investigators had discovered some treasure, then they had little hope of stealing it from inside their hotel. If another opportunity arose, they would need all four of them to defeat the investigators.

Chapter 55

New Road Hotel

Tuesday

The early morning sun streamed into Euan's window as Reed sat in a hotel's plain chair, scrolling on his phone.

"How's your face?" Euan asked Reed.

"Sore."

"I'm not surprised. You took a hefty bang against that bus."

"We've both had some injuries on this quest!"

"Very true."

Reed pulled out the iron key and placed it on the desk, but kept the piece of paper to decipher. Euan picked up the key and estimated it to be about two inches long. He sprayed the rusted key with a lubricant and cleaned it up to scrutinise it closely for any markings and codes, nothing obvious. A quick photo and use of Google's identification software, LENS, revealed nothing helpful either. He typed associated words on his phone into a Google internet search bar to find out what type of lock the key might fit. Eventually, he came across a website that listed Victorian locks. It suggested the key would fit a small cupboard door lock or carry case, like the trunk they had found in the church.

"The key only fits a cupboard or trunk, according to my research. It'll be impossible to find the lock unless the piece of paper can offer us any clues," he said.

"I've identified some words on the paper. There's a '*ch*' and if you slant the paper towards the light, you can see the next letters are *'ur'* with the faintest amount of ink remaining. That has to be church," said Reed.

"Spot on. That makes sense, considering the location we found the key. Anything else?"

"I can see the words *'rice'*, *'pray'*, *'the'* and *'pipe'*. Rice must be part of Beatrice. It's near the top of the page. Pray links with the church location, the others I'm not sure about. There are other isolated letters, but nothing that I can piece together," explained Reed.

"Do you think the treasure is inside the church?"

"It seems the most likely explanation. Jack could have locked it somewhere and then hidden the key in the storm drain."

"I agree. It would be strange to hide the key in a completely different place to the treasure," said Euan.

Euan pondered the information they had discovered, convincing himself the treasure had to be inside St Leonard's Church as another thought flashed through his mind.

"How'd they know we were at the church?"

"I've been mulling that over. There must be a transponder somewhere. Perhaps they placed a tracker in your backpack or shoes when they captured you?" asked Reed.

"That's possible, let me check."

Euan leapt up from the bed, grabbed his backpack, and frantically tugged everything out, then ran his fingers over every item. He checked the inner linings, the corners of all the pockets, and the outer shell, but he found nothing. He scrutinised his three pairs of shoes and still found nothing.

Dismayed, he said, "That's disappointing."

"I'll check my stuff in a bit," said Reed.

"Are we searching the church later?"

"Of course, mate, let's go late afternoon after it's locked up for the day. We can climb in through that upper floor window again. I doubt anyone would have noticed the latch wasn't properly closed."

Happy with their plan, Euan insisted they went out for some pizza as it had been several days since he had last eaten his favourite food. He felt they had made significant progress in the past twenty-four hours and were close to discovering the treasure. It still niggled him how the Hoxton Hot Rod gang always appeared where they were.

Chapter 56

St Leonard's Church

Tuesday

REED PEERED THROUGH THE black railings outside St Leonards Church as he watched the vicar lock the huge wooden entrance door. The winter evenings stretched out as February progressed into March, with the sun disappearing behind the myriad of London's skyscrapers. Rain clouds spread across the sky, created a contrast of purple and oranges as the sun closed out another day in England's busy capital. Black cabs raced past and pedestrians hustled home from work. Reed drew a calm breath as the vicar locked the spiked gate that led into the gardens of the church. A few bare trees stood guard over the centuries old building which hid an important secret, or at least that's what he hoped.

"Ready?" he asked Euan.

"Yes, boss."

"Geez, mate, cut out the boss thing!" He turned to face his best friend, who grinned like a cheshire cat at him. Once a joker, always a joker.

Pedestrians ambled past frequently, but a lull in people on the walkway allowed Reed the opportunity to jump over the railings. A quick leap followed by scrambled legs over the top before he jumped down and sprinted into cover beside the entrance door. With Euan close behind, they hustled around the Palladian-style church to the rear, below the unlatched window. He fumbled in his backpack to retrieve his climbing gloves and shoes, then leapt on to the nearby drainpipe for a quick climb up. He manoeuvred across to the window ledge and stood upright to open it. It wouldn't open. The vicar must have noticed and locked it properly. He pulled the crowbar from his backpack and levered the window open, breaking the old lock easily. Once inside, Euan followed him and they began their exploration of the church, searching for the lock that the key they had found could open.

Reed found a pair of storage trunks on the upper floor, but neither had the correct lock. On the ground floor, they checked the side rooms and main church area with no luck. He sat on a pew, retrieved his head torch and mounted it on his forehead, with the beam of light cutting through the gloom.

"The lock must be here somewhere."

"It wouldn't make sense if not. Should we check the floor? What about in the tower?"

"How do we get into the tower?" asked Reed.

"I saw a roof hatch on the top level."

Both lads darted upstairs and, with no ladder, Reed gave Euan a boost into the roof space. His mate clambered inside and searched the tower, but seconds later, Euan dropped back down.

"Nothing in there. It's tiny."

"Let's check the floors."

Reed paced one side of the upper balcony, whilst Euan checked the other. He scooted around the huge static organ that dominated the third side of the upper balcony and, whilst staring at the floor, noticed it had a crawl space at the back. He paused and squatted to look inside. Directly in front of him was a small cupboard door, presumably an access point for the internal workings of the pipe organ. He slipped off his backpack and retrieved the iron key from the zipped inner pocket. It slipped nicely into the lock. A flick of his wrist and it opened.

The space allowed his head and shoulders to fit inside, enough room to shine the head torch on some lubrication points for the organ's pipes. He flipped onto his back and shone the light upwards. Illuminated about two feet above his head was a ledge. He reached up with his fingers and touched a hessian cloth-wrapped bundle. He grasped it with glee, bringing it down in his gloved hands, and squirmed back out of the crawl space.

"I've found it, Euan!" he proclaimed after locking the small door.

His best mate appeared, and they squatted on the floor as Reed unwrapped the mysterious bundle. The beams of the head torches shone on the bundle as darkness had now enveloped the whole church. A surreal scene as a chunk of red reflected their lights. It was a magnificent ruby, about the size of an egg. They gazed at its beauty with many facets cut to create an awe-inspiring jewel that could be worth millions. Reed exploded with joy as they high-fived each other. They had found Jack the Ripper's hidden treasure, and it was absolutely incredible.

"Oh mate, we've done it!"

"It's amazing. I've never seen something this big."

"Do you think it's a famous jewel?" asked Euan.

"I hope so, then it'll be worth a massive amount of money."

Reed pulled out his phone and snapped photos of their discovery. He would call Madeleine once they reached the hotel and arrange a meeting for tomorrow. He re-wrapped the jewel in the hessian cloth and packed it securely inside his backpack. They swiftly left the church via their entry route and, wary of what happened yesterday, he scanned the area before leaping over the black railings. In his haste, Reed caught his combat trouser pocket on a spiked end and ripped it open. A couple of carabiners spilled out onto the floor, which he quickly recovered. With none of the Hoxton Hot Rod gang in sight, they hustled south towards the hotel, keeping to side streets and alleyways.

As they entered Plumbers Row close to the hotel, Reed heard an engine roar behind them as two headlights appeared out of the darkness, headed straight towards them.

"Run Euan," he shouted and sprinted south towards an alleyway, away from the car and the safety of their hotel. He plunged into the mouth of the alleyway, grabbing Euan's jacket to drag him clear of the marauding vehicle.

"That was close."

"They'll wait for us."

"That'll block us from getting back to the hotel."

"What're we going to do?" Euan said, as his voice faltered.

Reed considered their options, but the rumble of an engine at the mouth of the alleyway decided his next course of action.

"Let's get to The Shard and call Madeleine. They have security guards, plus she can put the jewel in her wall safe."

"Brilliant idea."

Reed dashed off with Euan in tow as they weaved their way amongst back streets, leapt gates and vaulted walls. The car followed them as they spied it frequently, racing along the wider streets. He recognised it as Ryan Johnson's car, the one that had chased them last night. Eventually they reached the outskirts of St Katherine Docks Marina beside the river Thames. Moonlight shimmered across the rippling river that wound through the heart of London as water taxis buzzed across its open waters. He stared at Tower Bridge, its security lights glowed bright in the darkness, their only opportunity to cross the river.

In the distance stood The Shard, majestically dominating the south-bank skyline, which burst into life, the tip of the building transformed by a brilliant burst of coloured lights that celebrated eight o'clock. A regular display every hour, generated by LED lights embedded in the walls. Reed knew they had to outwit the Hoxton Hot Rod gang and sprang into action. He jumped on to the marina's border wall and jogged along it towards Tower Bridge, reaching its access road. There was no sign of the chasing vehicle as they sprinted along the pavement. He glanced over his shoulder and then saw his adversary's vehicle speeding straight at them, albeit fifty yards away.

"Push harder Euan," he gasped between the gulps of chilly night air required to fuel his lungs. They bolted beneath the entrance archway and dashed towards the first tower on the pedestrianised walkway.

The engine roar increased and the car quickly raced past them, spinning to a stop underneath the first tower, as tyres squealed dramatically. Ryan and Mikey hopped out of the vehicle and jumped the blue railings on to the walkway. Reed stopped, then spun around, ready to race away. To his dismay, another vehicle stopped behind them, out jumped Bernie and Jakob, who clambered onto the walkway. The latest arrivals had cornered them.

"We meet again, Hascombe," said Bernie. "I'm taking a guess that you've discovered something after you've visited the church twice?"

Reed's heart still pumped from the exertion of sprinting as he realised their predicament. Four against two wasn't great odds. Two he could handle, three possibly, but not all four, plus they had the aggressive Polish lad with them again. Instead of answering the question, he scanned the area for an escape route.

Chapter 57

Tower Bridge

Tuesday

REED REMAINED SILENT AND considered their options. The four men surrounded them, two faced him and two behind, with very little chance of escaping. They could probably leap the blue railings that separated vehicles from pedestrians, but his adversaries had cars to chase them down. He felt sure he could battle past the two lads that blocked their progress to cross Tower Bridge, but without a doubt, they would capture Euan. If they remained stationary, the members of the Hoxton Hot Rod's gang would overpower them. With the jewel in his backpack, could he throw it into the river? He immediately discarded that thought as reckless. There was only one option left. They had to go up. He leant close to his mate and whispered.

"We're going up over the Tower. They can't leave their cars blocking traffic on the bridge for long without some angry driver calling the police. There's a ridge beside the entrance door, above the steps. Climb that. I'll keep these two occupied, then join you."

"Got that."

They fist bumped as Reed leapt into action. He swung out a dropkick to make Ryan and Mikey move, whilst Euan dived to the floor between their two opponents and scampered to the first tower. Shouts from behind reminded him that Bernie and Jakob were closing in fast. He flung a couple of punches, then a heavy fist landed on his shoulder from behind. He had seconds to get past before the four men overwhelmed him. Euan was already atop the ornamental stone ridge assembling a retractable grapple hook with a rope.

Reed went all in with his next attack and focussed on Ryan, the weak link, with a leg sweep. His opponent slammed to the ground, allowing Reed to gain a few feet of advantage. Just enough to reach the first tower and grab the cornice above his head. His climbing gloves gripped the cold stone as he hauled himself upwards until he felt a hand grab his trailing leg, threatening to tear him from the building. A swift kick on to the wrist put paid to that as he clambered onto the ornamental stone ridge. Euan had vacated the space and clambered up the face of the tower, reaching the first set of Victorian leaded windows. He waited until his friend let go of the rope as loud instructions from below broke his focus.

"Get up there Mikey," shouted Bernie.

The rope dangled in front of Reed and he grabbed it, ready for his ascent as Mikey struggled to scale the stone building below him. He rapidly climbed the rope and joined Euan on the window ledge before tugging up the rope. Though safe from the attack, it left them stranded on Tower Bridge. Whilst balanced precariously, he flung the rope up the next level, hooking the grapple over a balcony. The honk of horns attracted his attention, and he sighted a few passer-bys watching their climb from below as traffic accumulated on the road. He scaled the rope and with Euan beside him on the stone balcony; he glanced back down and spotted Bernie and his gang drive away. Southwards.

"They've driven south. Should we go back down now? Get to the hotel?" asked Euan.

"I'd like to finish climbing up. Add that to our list of achievements. We climbed Tower Bridge."

"Brilliant idea. The view will be amazing up there."

"I think we should continue with our plan and reach The Shard.

The jewel will only be secure inside a safe."

"Good point. Plus, they may have someone stationed at the hotel."

"Exactly. They won't know we're heading towards The Shard," said Reed.

"But they still located us. Somehow, they're still tracking us."

"I can't figure that out. We need some expert advice to help us. I'll phone Jed or Brian Morgan later and see what suggestions they have," said Reed.

Reed strained his neck to scan upwards, and another balcony loomed out of the dark. They swiftly repeated the exercise with the grapple hook and rope. The final section to the top of the tower was shorter, which they comfortably climbed and alighted on the parapet.

In each corner of the tower stood a short spire topped with a stone cross. A parapet encircled a bigger central spire. Majestically adorning the top of the central tower was a gilded gold crest representing the City of London. He pulled out his phone to grab some photos of an impossible angle of the crests, fully aware that no-one would normally see them this close up. They then edged around the parapet and reached the covered walkways that joined the other tower. He clambered on top and surveyed London, illuminated for miles in all directions. The river below twinkled from the many lights that reflected off the water's surface. Such an amazing view, but fraught with danger as one slip on the wet roof would mean instant death.

Reed noticed each walkway had a narrow access platform that ran alongside the structures. He dropped to it and waited for Euan before they scuttled across to the other tower. The towers were mirror images, constructed exactly alike back in the nineteenth century. He clambered on to the stone parapet, edged around to the opposite side, and scanned the road leading away from Tower Bridge. No sign of the two vehicles that contained the rogue gang.

Satisfied this was the right course of action, he pulled two climbing ropes from his bag and knotted them together to abseil down the face of the tower rather than climb. It would be quicker and safer. He tied one end to a sturdy stone section of the parapet before both lads donned their harnesses. Reed connected with the rope using a belay device and shuffled over the edge, feet pressed against the wall, leaning horizontally. He scrambled down the building, past two balconies and a pair of lead glass windows before landing safe on the ground. Euan stood beside him within minutes.

"Did you enjoy that?" Reed asked his best friend.

"That was fantastic, a real lifetime experience."

"Proper urban exploration."

"The Shard's over there. Are you going to call Madeleine now?"

"Let me sort the route first," responded Reed. He opened Google maps and plotted the route. "Through Potter's Field Park, then the graveyard, Druid Street, Crucifix Lane and finally St Thomas's Street."

"It's like a horror movie route!"

"Yeah, weird."

Reed bounced down some stone steps and, with the river on their right-hand side, they entered Potters Field Park. A large green space dimly light with isolated trees and rows of bushes. He pulled out his phone, ready to call Madeleine, but a shout from some nearby bushes distracted him.

"NOW!".

After the earlier encounter on Tower Bridge, Bernie had gathered the four of them together and devised his plan. The investigators had sprinted from the hotel and not once had they attempted to backtrack, so it seemed obvious their planned destination had changed. Once clear of Tower Bridge, he had phoned Davey Warren to get regular updates on their position. Their crossing of Tower Bridge confirmed their southward direction. Their new destination had to be The Shard, where Madeleine Robinson-Smith's office was situated. He put himself in their shoes and guessed they would avoid major routes, so crossing Potters Field Park was the more likely path to take.

The four of them had squatted inside a row of bushes, away from the immediate glare of riverside streetlights, ready to attack. Bernie jumped out, followed swiftly by the other three, just a few feet from his opponents, and caught them unaware. Jakob and Mikey tackled Reed whilst Bernie lunged at Euan, crashing to the floor on top of the ginger-haired lad. Ryan held a Bowie knife against the lad's throat, leaving Bernie to leap up and assist the other two, who were struggling to contain Reed.

"Give up Hascombe. Otherwise your mate dies."

Bernie pulled the flare gun out of his pocket and aimed it at Euan's head. Reed's hands dropped to his side in defeat.

"Okay, you win this one. What do you want?"

"On the floor," instructed Bernie. "Take the backpack off. Search him Jakob."

Jakob didn't need any further encouragement and punched Reed in the stomach, then removed the backpack. Bernie snatched up the backpack as Jakob knelt on Reed's back, frisking him. He spilled the contents on the grass and checked in the backpack, his hand brushed over a package inside a zipped pocket, which he removed. Under the dim light of the closest streetlight, he unwrapped the hessian cloth and gasped when he saw the contents. He dropped to his knees, overwhelmed by thirty years of effort that had crystallised in this poignant moment. It was Jack's hidden treasure. He used the light from his phone to inspect the jewel and gawped at the redness that gleamed intensely.

"Oh wow. This is incredible. Look," he said, raising the stunning red jewel for the other members of his gang to see. Whistles and words of exclamation greeted him. "I said they would lead us to Jack's treasure."

"A third is mine," said Jakob.

"Not now, Jakob. We'll talk about that tomorrow with Sophia."

Bernie stashed the hessian-wrapped jewel inside his jacket pocket, then stooped to speak to Reed.

"I'm going to take your mate with us, any trouble from you, and he ends up in the Thames. Clear?"

"Crystal."

"Right lads, let's roll. Ryan, bring the ginger one with us. Let's get back to the cars."

Whilst Reed remained in the park, Bernie led the way back to their parked cars two streets away, using Euan as his protection. He released Euan and manoeuvred his car to head back across the river via Tower Bridge. He felt pretty smug having outwitted the two investigators. Finally, he had achieved his lifelong ambition. Now to reap the rewards.

After Bernie and his gang had left the park, Reed sprang into action. He refilled his backpack and sprinted through the park towards Tower Bridge, confident that Bernie would drive back across the bridge to Hoxton. The ambush had annoyed him, as he should have anticipated it. Nevertheless, he had uncovered two key facts. They were still being tracked and there was definitely an agreement between Bernie, Jakob, and Sophia regarding Jack the Ripper's treasure.

Reed reached the bridge and scanned the passing vehicles. He waited for the black BMW with the personalised number plate: BJ95. Traffic was light when he spotted it following behind Ryan's car. He crouched down behind the blue railings and waited for his opportunity. He only had one shot at this.

As Bernie's car drew level with Reed, he leapt up and swung his crowbar at the windscreen. It slammed into it and caused a spiderweb of cracks to emanate. The brake lights lit up, providing Reed with the chance to leap the barrier and retrieve the weapon. With it, he smashed the passenger window and slammed Jakob's head into the dashboard before leaping across the bonnet. As he swung the crowbar again, a panicked Bernie floored the accelerator and the metal weapon smashed the rear passenger window instead.

Reed sprinted after the speeding vehicle as it raced across the bridge, intent on reclaiming the jewel. It slowed as the traffic in front hindered its exit on the constricted driving lanes. He got close enough to jump onto the moving vehicle and swung the crowbar at the rear window, taking it out instantly. As he tried to enter the vehicle, it sped up again and unbalanced him. Reed landed in a heap on the road, in front of an oncoming car. He leapt to his feet and chased after Bernie's car, but now it was clear of Tower Bridge, he had no prospect of catching it. Despondent, he trudged back across Tower Bridge to locate Euan. He found his mate sat on a bench overlooking the Thames and joined him.

"You okay?" he asked.

"Yes, I'm fine, no damage done."

"I'm so annoyed with myself for not expecting an ambush."

"They've been tracking us all the time. That's obvious from the comments. We have to find out how."

"And reclaim the jewel."

"Any plans Reed?"

"There's only one option. We need some expert help. I'll call Brian Morgan tomorrow."

Reed recalled their previous encounter with Brian Morgan, another of his professional contacts that could help him with their quest. The ex-SAS soldier had a wide range of skills, including the use of explosives. He would also need to contact Madeleine but made a quick phone call to Emily first, who agreed to travel to London tomorrow morning. They needed her help as well.

Chapter 58

Whitechapel Coffee Shop
Wednesday

THE COFFEE MACHINE BEHIND the counter hissed for the umpteenth time that day as Emily sat with Reed and Euan, discussing their exploits over the past two days. She had arrived earlier and as time was tight, they grabbed some coffees ahead of a scheduled meeting with Madeleine in two hours' time. Her laptop was open as she searched for information about prominent red jewels and realised Reed had stumbled upon an extremely famous one. She waited whilst he finished his excessively long call with Brian Morgan. The coffee shop buzzed with a constant turnover of clients whizzing in for a hit of caffeine. She finished her pastry and washed it down with the dregs of her coffee. Reed eventually finished his call and jumped straight in to relay the conversation.

"Brian's agreed to come tomorrow and help us retrieve the jewel. I'll have to persuade Madeleine to cover his costs, but we all know he's worth every penny. He suggested a solution for the tracking problem after I relayed the sequence of events. We need a metal detector to scan your body, Euan. He thinks you may have had something inserted whilst being drugged. Apparently, it's a common technique: make a tiny slit in a person's skin, insert a transponder and seal it with glue."

Emily laid her hand on Euan's arm when his face screwed up with revulsion.

"That's disgusting," said Euan.

"Mate, you're like a cyborg," laughed Reed.

"I need to remove it now."

"We'll nip back to the hotel before going to the meeting. The underwater scanner we used in Cornwall is in my room."

"Okay, thanks."

Emily brushed her wavy hair behind her ears and said, "I'm pleased that's sorted. Let's talk about the jewel." Before she could start, Reed rose and took orders for another round of coffees. She consoled Euan whilst her boyfriend sauntered over to the counter and returned laden with more caffeine. Now to discuss her research.

"What you've found is the real Black Prince's Ruby."

"Whoa, what do you mean by real?" asked Reed.

"The imperial state crown of England contains a Maltese Cross. Embedded in the cross is the Black Prince's Ruby. However, that's actually a red spinel, which isn't a true gem. I found information on the dark web suggesting that thieves stole the real ruby in a heist during Victorian times. This happened before it was due to be mounted on the Maltese Cross. The royal family then replaced it with the red spinel, pretending it was the real ruby."

"That ties up with our information about Thomas Cutbush. The Hoxton High Rips exiled him after he stole something from the gains of a heist."

"That makes Cutbush Jack the Ripper," said Euan.

"We said he was the most likely suspect. Anything else Em?"

"Yes, give me a second. I need a toilet break first."

She wandered off to the cloakroom, pleased with her research, and returned to deliver the next key piece of information.

"According to the history of the Black Prince's Ruby, someone stole it from a sultan in the fourteenth century. It passed between kings during the next two centuries. Coincidentally, they all suffered obscure illnesses or died in battle. This pattern ceased when the Tudors inherited it and Queen Elizabeth I owned the ruby. It passed down through the royal line to Queen Victoria. There's talk of a curse that affects only male kings."

"Oh wow, that's interesting."

The two lads absorbed Emily's readings, fascinated by the curse. With her part completed, Emily shut down her laptop, sat back, and sipped her fresh latte. One thing still bothered her.

"Where do you think Bernie will hide the jewel?" she asked.

"The obvious places to me are his floor safe at the car repair shop or in the locked Ripper room at the Ten Bells Pub," said Reed.

"Is that your plan? To target both those?"

"Unless anyone can think of another location?"

Euan shook his head before Emily added, "he might take it home."

"Good point Em. We should visit the most likely locations first."

"Agreed."

Emily noticed Euan jump up, eager to return to the hotel and find out if someone had bugged him, as his normal smile had disappeared. She rose and packed her laptop, encouraging Reed to hurry. They needed to resolve the tracking issue before their meeting with Madeleine, which began in an hour.

Chapter 59

TEN BELLS PUB

WEDNESDAY

THE LUNCHTIME RUSH WAS in full swing at the Ten Bells Pub as the babble of conversation greeted Bernie. It wasn't so busy that he couldn't spot Jakob and Sophia sat together. Their heads were down in conversation as he strolled past. The two of them sitting together annoyed him; it broke Rippers Guild rules, he would have to reiterate them to the two younger members. He was also concerned they had grown close since the episode at Sophia's flat with the ginger-haired investigator. Earlier he had purchased a new lock and after opening the door to the Ripper Guild's meeting space, he discarded the old, worn padlock. Security needed to be increased until he could sell the jewel.

The other two members joined him, so he plucked out the precious jewel, still wrapped in the hessian cloth. He had even slept with it grasped in his hand. He intended to keep possession of the valuable artifact, even though he didn't know its true worth yet.

"Let me see the jewel," said Sophia, her hands outstretched.

Bernie passed her the red jewel and stationed himself by the door, just in case she planned a quick exit. He really didn't trust her, and his confidence in Jakob had diminished after his disappearing act.

"Oh wow Bernie, this is amazing! Jakob outlined last night's events. You guys are such warriors."

"It's pretty impressive."

"What's it worth?"

"I don't know yet. It looks like a ruby, so Davey is researching famous rubies. Then we need to find an unscrupulous artifact dealer to give us a valuation."

"I can help with that. My uncle back in Germany trades artifacts."

His caution kicked in, "the jewel stays with me. I'll find someone suitable."

He spotted Sophia's face tighten with a slight grimace, followed by a flick of the long blonde hair before she spoke. "Why does the jewel stay with you? We should put it somewhere safe where we can all have access to it."

Bernie expected the conversation would take this track. He expected to get half of the proceeds from the sale because Thomas Cutbush had stolen the jewel from the Hoxton High Rip gang. His great-great-grandfather had been a member of the gang, not Cutbush himself. He had falsely claimed that Cutbush was his relation, which the other two believed. Plus, the Rippers Guild was his secret society, not either of theirs.

"I'm entitled to half of the sale," he said.

"Why's that?" asked Sophia, her hands aggressively positioned on her hips, whilst Jakob gazed at the jewel.

"With the jewel discovered inside the church, it clearly shows Thomas Cutbush hid it."

"I disagree. Walter Sickert may have hidden it there. So could Aaron Kosminski."

He had to admit she knew her Jack the Ripper history pretty well.

"I've been looking for this for thirty years, not six months!"

"You always said it should be obvious who the treasure belonged to. In my mind, it's not clear. So we should split it three ways. What do you think, Jakob?"

Sophia spun to stare at Jakob, who was clearly under her influence.

"I agree," he grunted.

The atmosphere had turned frosty as Bernie glared at Sophia. She nudged Jakob casually, which he noticed and sensed something would happen. Fortunately, he had the forethought to come prepared. He slipped his hand into his jacket pocket and clutched the handle of the Bowie knife inside. Jakob made his move, but was too slow.

Bernie avoided the half-hearted punch and grasped Jakob's wrist, then pulled out the knife, holding it to the lad's throat.

"Seriously, Jakob, I can't believe you've switched your allegiance?"

"I didn't want to. It was her idea," Jakob growled.

"After everything I've done for you."

"Leave him alone Bernie. We're entitled to a third each after everything we've done to help," said Sophia.

"Another thing," he said, "I told you not to sit together in the pub."

"Yeah, yeah, another one of your stupid rules," she said.

"It's for a reason!"

"The investigators are aware we're associated, so it doesn't matter anymore."

"What about the police? For a clever woman, you aren't that bright sometimes."

Her faced clouded over with anger, Bernie had gained the upper hand now. Sophia plonked herself down on a battered sofa, allowing him to release Jakob. He knew a compromise was required to keep them from rising against him again. He took the jewel off Jakob, re-wrapped it in the hessian cloth, and slipped it into his jacket pocket.

"Okay, I understand your argument, so as a compromise, I'll take forty per cent, you both get thirty per cent. That's a pretty fair split, but we have to function together as a united team to sell the jewel. I want no more disputes from either of you. Agreed?"

Sophia sat with her arms crossed, but Jakob agreed immediately with his usual grunt.

"Okay, I agree," she muttered.

"Great, we're all in agreement. Here's the plan," Bernie said. "I'll keep hold of the jewel and contact some artifact dealers. We'll chose the best offer and the buyer can pay each of us our shares directly. Happy with that?"

Both of the younger members of the Rippers Guild nodded in agreement.

Sophia fired yet another question at him. "How do we stop the investigators from stealing the jewel back?"

"Hascombe's the only one who can beat us, so I'll store the jewel securely. Don't forget, we have the tracker on the ginger one."

"Are you going to tell us where you're storing the jewel?"

"No, the investigators can't extract the location from you if you're unaware of where it's kept."

"I'm still not happy with you holding the jewel, Bernie," she said.

"If you want thirty per cent, then get used to it, Sophia."

Bernie detected her pursed lips, showing she wasn't happy, but the thought of mega money should be enough to keep her in line. With his plan in place, he had to find a suitable artifact dealer to appraise the jewel and hopefully agree to purchase it for several million.

Chapter 60

THE SHARD

WEDNESDAY

MADELEINE CHECKED HER MAKE-UP using a compact mirror ahead of the scheduled meeting with Reed Hascombe and his team. She looked tired. The dark circles around her eyes had increased in size, as stress had cluttered every aspect of her life. The failing business, marriage difficulties with her husband, and the tribulations of the treasure search. Something else had bothered her for the past two weeks. Was she related to Jack the Ripper? The love letter was addressed to her great-great-grandmother, Beatrice, but did that mean her great-grandmother was his child? Confusion had spun around her mind for days.

The intercom buzzed. She stopped gazing through the window at London's skyline. An activity that calmed her jumbled thoughts.

"Yes, Kathy?"

"Mr Hascombe is here for your meeting."

"Send him in, please."

In walked Reed with Euan and an unknown woman, followed by her PA.

"Hi Madeleine, this is Emily. My girlfriend and the third member of our team," Reed said.

"Pleased to meet you," she said as they shook hands and everyone ordered their drinks. Kathy filed off to fulfil their requests.

"It's been a few days since we've spoken, Reed. Hopefully, you've got some good news for me?"

"Good and bad, unfortunately. We found Jack the Ripper's hidden treasure. I discovered it hidden inside the pipe maintenance nook of the organ in St Leonard's church in Shoreditch. But Bernie Johnson and his gang ambushed us. They stole it from us," explained Reed.

Her thoughts were in turmoil, so close, but annoyingly, now out of reach.

"What's the treasure?" she asked.

At this point, Emily jumped in. "We believe it's the Black Prince's Ruby." Madeleine listened to her detailed theory before Reed passed over his phone with a photo of the jewel.

"It's impressive. How big is it?"

"About the size of an egg."

"That's abnormally large for a ruby. It must be worth millions?"

"I expect so, but we haven't verified it yet. I know a trusted artifact dealer who could advise us once we reclaim the jewel."

Madeleine's heart leapt as she sensed Reed's resolute determination, a quality she had admired from the offset.

"How did you find the ruby?"

Reed opened his mouth to answer when Kathy bustled into the office with a tray of drinks. Madeleine had softened her stance on her PA's previous gaffe and allowed her to listen to Reed's explanation.

"It was sheer luck to be fair. We discovered a ladder in Bernie Johnson's car repair shop, then travelled through a storm drain. This led to an underground river with another storm drain leading to the church. We found an iron key in the brickwork underneath the building, exactly as the letter detailed. With it was another piece of paper, which was virtually washed out. In the end, we searched the church and established the key fitted in the maintenance door lock of the pipe organ. The ruby was inside the nook on a ledge."

"That's pretty impressive. Well done. You can go now, Kathy."

Once her PA had left the office, she continued with the

conversation.

"How did you get ambushed?"

"They've been tracking us. Unfortunately, Sophia secretly inserted a tiny transponder into Euan's back during his time as her hostage. We only found it an hour ago. The gang followed us from the church, planning on intercepting us before we got back to the hotel. We escaped initially and were making our way here last night. I literally had my phone out to call you when they ambushed us in Potters Field Park. I thought the jewel would be secure in your safe."

"You wouldn't have reached me, anyway. I went to bed early with a nasty headache and turn off my phone at night. I dined out with my husband, as I hadn't seen him properly for two days. Sunday, he cleared away the art exhibition displays and stayed late at the art gallery, falling asleep on his sofa there, again!" she explained.

She noticed a puzzled look on Reed's face. Perhaps that was too much personal information. She had let her worries encroach on her words.

"Does he do that regularly?" he asked.

Without thinking, she replied.

"Once before, when he set up the art exhibition."

She then rebuked herself for discussing her marriage, but Reed had a way of calmly extracting information.

"That's actually irrelevant," she said.

"Okay, fair enough. I had tried to put the police on to the gang's trail by suggesting Jakob Kosminski was the copy-cat killer after the third murder happened on Sunday night. I also called in a stolen car at Johnson's car repair shop, but neither had any impact," said Reed.

"At least you tried. How do you plan to reclaim the jewel?" she asked.

Reed shuffled in his seat as though something troubled him. "It'll be difficult because it's me and Euan against four men, so I phoned a contact who can help us. He's an ex-SAS soldier with access to weapons and explosives. His skills are perfect for this situation, he helped us last summer in Cornwall, but he's very expensive."

Madeleine twirled her hair and now saw why Reed looked uncomfortable.

"I assume you expect me to pay him?"

"I can't afford to pay him from our fees," said Reed.

"How much will he cost?"

"Fifty grand, but there's no time limit, plus he brings all the equipment we need. He wants fifty per cent today, then he'll travel here tonight."

"Crikey Reed, that's extremely expensive. I've already forked out twenty thousand for you." Her business brain kicked in and she mentally allowed another five thousand for Reed's remaining days. What if they didn't retrieve the ruby, or it was worthless? There was also the ten per cent of the ruby's value to pay to Reed, meaning she could be light by several hundred thousand if the valuation of the jewel was more than a million.

"I need assurance on the potential value of the ruby before I commit to this extra expenditure," she said.

Reed appeared prepared for this eventuality and pulled out his phone. "I'll call Alistair Edgeworth. He's a dealer I've done business with before." He pressed call and put the phone on speaker, laying it on her desk.

"Hi Reed, how're you?" asked Alistair.

"Good, thanks Alistair."

"What can I help you with?"

"We've discovered the real Black Prince's Ruby and wanted to know what sort of valuation you would put on it?" asked Reed.

"I thought that was part of the state crown?"

The conversation continued as she sat back and absorbed the details. Then the artifact dealer concluded his thoughts.

"Obviously subject to seeing the ruby, my estimate would be between ten and fifteen million on the black market."

Reed wrapped up the conversation as Madeleine sat back in awe.

This would solve all of her company's money worries. The jewel had to be recovered, and spending another fifty grand was insignificant compared to the immense value of the prize.

"It's a straightforward decision, so call Brian Morgan now and get me his bank details," she said.

Within minutes, she transferred the funds and the ex-SAS solider confirmed he would arrive in London that evening. The meeting had been a resounding success as they all said their goodbyes, and Reed promised to keep her abreast of any developments.

Madeleine's mind filled with positive thoughts. She could clear the company's debts and find another lithium mine to supply the metal. There would be plenty of money leftover for her personal use. Amazing what one old letter could lead to. With total confidence in Reed, she hoped he would successfully recover the ruby.

Chapter 61

TOWER BRIDGE

WEDNESDAY

THE LATE AFTERNOON SUN shone into Reed's eyes as he left The Shard following the meeting. Although still officially winter, spring was around the corner and the warmth from the sun encouraged flowers to bloom early. He always enjoyed this time of year, when nature stirred from its slumber, providing a really positive vibe. It usually gave him clear thoughts, but something niggled at the back of his mind. The bustle of people jostling for position as they neared the entrance to London Bridge underground station interrupted his thoughts.

"Let's walk instead of cramming into the underground. We can take a leisurely stroll across Tower Bridge," he said to Emily and Euan.

"You can show me where they ambushed you," said Emily.

That embarrassing event from last night still cut to his core. He had been lax, but he would rectify it.

"I wanted to talk with you about something that's bothering me."

"From the meeting?"

"Yes. Nothing to do with the ruby. Euan, did you link the dates of her husband not being home?"

"Don't know what you mean? What dates?"

"Okay, hear me out. Madeleine said he crashed at the art gallery on Sunday night when the third murder happened. I also remember her saying he was in Manchester on the night of the second murder."

Euan's face lit up. "I remember that. I suggested she checked with Richard when we were discussing who had leaked the details of the letter."

"Exactly, mate," Reed said as he turned into Potters Field Park. "Let's grab an empty bench by the river."

Mothers guided young children to the play area, with the park much busier than the previous evening. They found an empty bench that overlooked the river Thames and gave them a fantastic view of Tower Bridge.

"You climbed to the top and across?" said Emily, open-mouthed, as she pointed at the impressive bridge.

"We certainly did. It was difficult, but how many people can say they've scaled Tower Bridge?"

"Very few, I'm sure. Anyway, back to Richard. Em, can you check the date of the first murder because Madeleine also said he crashed at the art gallery the night before the exhibition?"

Reed stared across the river towards Whitechapel as tourist boats glided past. He spotted a pair of jet skis that buzzed close to the opposite shoreline, creating sprays of white-topped foam.

"The first murder happened on the Friday night before the art exhibition, when he stayed at the art gallery."

"I knew it. Something clicked when Madeleine mentioned he slept there a second time and then I remembered Euan's comment about questioning Richard, but he was supposedly away."

"Hang on Reed, you're jumping to a conclusion, but with zero evidence."

"Possibly."

"He could've been working on both occasions and genuinely travelled to Manchester."

"Or he's having an affair with Sophia?" interjected Euan.

"Exactly," said Emily. "You can't just assume he's the murderer."

Reed grasped his long black hair and bunched it up into a bun on the top of his head. "Let's check the art gallery. Come on, Euan," he said as he leapt to his feet, ready for action. "What else can you find out about him?" he asked Emily.

"Hang on, you need to focus on getting the ruby back."

"That's tomorrow with Brian. I need to check our hunch first."

He strode off towards Tower Bridge with his girlfriend and best mate struggling to keep up. Once he had an idea in his head, it ploughed on relentlessly. After he had shuffled through the crowds strolling across the bridge, he paused for them to catch up at a cafe near the Tower of London.

"Richard's American and moved to London eight years ago when his art business went bust in New York. He was previously married in the United States. He and Madeleine got married six years ago," explained Emily. "The art gallery opened three years ago. The accounts filed at Companies House show two years of losses. That must put a strain on their marriage, along with Madeleine's cash-flow issues."

"So he might have spent those nights with Sophia?"

"It's much more likely than him being the murderer and there's probably no connection between the dates."

"Okay, I get it. But I want to check the art gallery."

"Fine. I'll go back to the hotel whilst you two search the art gallery," said Emily. "First, I'm going to enjoy a cup of tea at this cafe."

"Okay, Em, see you back there in an hour."

Reed always carried his backpack, as it contained many useful items, including his lock pick set. He checked it was inside and strode off towards Reflections Art Gallery in Whitechapel.

Fifteen minutes later, Reed strolled to the main entrance of the art gallery and noticed it was closed for the day. With traffic, pedestrians and cameras, he didn't want to break in at the front. He beckoned Euan to follow him as he searched for a rear entrance in the alleyway parallel to the main road. Rubbish littered the alleyway edges as he sought the rear door, eventually finding a small plaque which identified the art gallery. He slipped on his climbing gloves, as there was no point in leaving any evidence of their presence. There were no obvious CCTV cameras in place to record him fiddle with the lock and open the door. They entered quietly, and he scanned the room, which contained a workbench, one cabinet and racks stacked with water-colour paintings. Atop the untidy workbench laid art preservation tools and an empty coffee mug.

"There's no sofa here?" said Euan.

"Check that door," Reed said, pointing to one positioned next to the racks.

"It leads into the gallery."

"It must be through here."

A different door led to the back room with a navy-blue sofa, its seats sagging, sat against the far wall. Scrunched behind the sofa was a bag that contained a pillow and quilt. On the opposite wall was a sink inset into a small section of worktop, crammed with a kettle, coffee jar, dirty mugs and sugar sachets. A fridge underneath the worktop and a cabinet above completed the mini kitchen setup.

"You check the kitchen, I'll search the sofa."

Reed flipped the sofa's seats, rustled through the bedding bag and peered underneath Richard's temporary bed, whilst Euan rooted through the mini kitchen area. They found nothing. He wandered into the untidy work area that doubled as the art gallery's office and rifled through the paperwork in the filing cabinet. Still nothing. He waited whilst Euan completed his search of the racked area, ready to leave, now convinced by Emily's argument that Richard had either genuinely worked or was having an affair with Sophia. As he turned towards the back door, he spotted a pair of drawers underneath the workbench, slightly set back. He pulled the first one open. It contained wire, string and other assorted artwork accessories. He grasped the second handle and pulled. It was locked.

"A locked drawer," he said to Euan. "They always contain secrets."

He tugged out his lock pick set, selected a different tool, and promptly had the drawer opened within seconds. More artwork accessories, but underneath the paraphernalia was a large but thin book. He eased it out and placed it on the workbench. As they turned the pages, their mouths dropped open.

"Geez, look at this Euan. What have we discovered?"

Chapter 62

COMMERCIAL STREET POLICE STATION

WEDNESDAY

SIXTY HOURS HAD PASSED since the third murder occurred, but DCI Clara Loxstone was still no closer to making an arrest. The DNA results from the handbag discovered at the scene of the third murder had arrived earlier, but with no match on the police database of criminals. Coupled with this, they had extensive CCTV footage of the suspect at the scene of the crime. DI Page had compiled the victim's journey from *'The Vault'* nightclub, through two London underground stations, to St Paul's Cathedral. This provided additional footage of the suspect, but without a clear image of their face at any point. Technical experts had determined it was most likely a man from the gait, standing around five foot ten. The suspect had worn a black puffer jacket with the hood pulled tight over their face, hiding their hair.

Clara studied the list of suspects on her whiteboard, all of which were crossed through with a red line. The DNA didn't match any of them, including Jakob Kosminski. The lack of evidence meant she couldn't pinpoint the perpetrator and concluded they were searching for a first-time offender. That made the case extremely challenging, plus her boss, DS Browne, had requested another update the following morning. Currently, she had no fresh information to impart. She rose from her desk and ambled outside to enjoy a blast of salted caramel on her vape kit as the bulk order for her favourite flavour had finally arrived on Monday.

As Clara wandered back into her office, her mobile rang from an unknown number.

"DCI Clara Loxstone," she said.

"It's Reed Hascombe, we met on Monday."

"Ah, Mr Hascombe, for your information, we have removed Kosminski from our list of suspects."

"That wasn't why I'm calling."

"What have you got, another accusation?" she said sarcastically.

"Actually, yes."

"Listen, I've already wasted enough time on your last offering."

Her aggressive stance caused Hascombe to pause, and for a second, she thought he had hung up.

"Check out Richard Smith at the Reflections Art Gallery."

"What are you playing at, Mr Hascombe? You can't keep throwing names at me of people you don't like!"

"I've seen evidence. Check the art gallery and his whereabouts at the time of the murders."

The guy was persistent, she thought, as she made a quick scribbled note of the name.

"Okay, leave it with me," she concluded before ending the call.

With no other leads or concrete evidence, Clara felt she should follow up on Hascombe's suggestion. She reviewed the list of suspects yet again as the red lines jumped out at her. DI Page still sat at his desk in the detective pool, so she called him in.

"Page, get everything you can on Richard Smith, who owns the Reflections Art Gallery. Answers in ten minutes."

"Yes, ma'am, I'm on it now."

Clara used her time to look up the art gallery online, but other than reported losses, there was nothing untoward. Page bundled into the office with seconds to spare.

"Fire away," she instructed.

"He's American and moved to the UK eight years ago. His wife is Madeleine Robinson-Smith. She is CEO and shareholder of Robinson's Mining Supplies. There's no criminal record in the UK, not even a parking ticket. I've put an urgent request into our American friends for their records on him. Should be an hour."

"Okay, I thought it was a long shot, but worth a try."

"Where did you get the name, ma'am?" asked Page.

"That Hascombe guy again, but I think he's pulling my chain."

Page didn't answer, as he knew better than to contradict her or agree with the flippant comment. She sauntered over to the coffee station and grabbed a fresh cup before returning to deal with her trivial emails. The clock ticked by as thirty minutes extended into an hour with no response from their American counterparts. After ninety minutes, she decided that was enough for today, picked up her handbag and mobile, then bid goodnight to Page as she slipped off to the car park. She turned the key in the ignition, reversed and drove towards the exit. Suddenly Page flew out of the main entrance waving a piece of paper akin to a heron with a fresh fish catch. She wound down the window.

"What is it Page?"

"He's got previous in New York. GBH."

That was enough to spark Clara into action as she quickly parked her car, slammed the door, and raced over to an empty police vehicle. Page returned with the keys and they hurtled off, blue lights flashing.

Across the table from Clara sat a grey-haired man in his fifties and his solicitor. His downcast face implied guilt. Earlier, she had visited Richard Smith at his home and requested he came to the police station for an interview. His initial refusal prompted her to make an impromptu arrest. Upon arrival at the station, she had organised an urgent DNA test for him, with a two-hour turnaround. She had sent Page to the art gallery to search for any evidence, whilst a tech guy trawled the camera footage from the gallery's main entrance.

"Mr Smith, I'm DCI Clara Loxstone and this interview is being recorded. For the purposes of the recording, can you state your name please?"

"Richard Smith."

"I'd like to know your whereabouts on Sunday evening?" she asked.

"Working in my art gallery."

"What time did you leave?"

"I can't remember exactly because I was very busy taking down the exhibition displays."

The interview continued as Clara delved into his whereabouts at the times of the previous two murders. His solicitor advised him not to answer some questions, but she persisted and her instincts told her the man was hiding something. She concluded the interview after an hour and left him to stew, then chased up the DNA test. It still hadn't arrived. Her phone rang, shattering the silence in her office.

"Yes, boss?"

"Is he the murderer?" asked DS Browne.

"I'm still waiting on the DNA test and for Page to return from the art gallery."

"Call me when you know as the MCC is hassling me."

"Will do," she said.

Clara immediately called Page, but it went straight to voicemail. She closed her eyes and remembered her yoga breathing techniques to calm her thoughts. Hurried footsteps interrupted her mindfulness time as Page burst into her office and slapped an evidence bag on to her desk.

"Look at this ma'am."

She slipped on some latex gloves and pulled a large, thin book from the evidence bag. Her mouth dropped open as she turned the pages. Excerpts from old Jack the Ripper newspaper cuttings. Then a list of suspects for the serial killer with one name underlined at the top. Francis Tumblety. A quick internet search revealed him to be an American doctor. Newspaper excerpts from the past two weeks that reported the recent murders completed the scrapbook.

"Where did you find this book?" she asked Page.

"In a locked drawer at the art gallery."

"Are forensics there? We need fingerprints, DNA, the works."

"Already on it, ma'am," said Page.

"Brilliant Page, you'll make a fine detective one day."

Then an email received notification pinged on her computer. It was the DNA results. She clicked on the email as the key words jumped out at her, *'it matches the DNA discovered on the corner of the victim's handbag, recovered at the scene of the murder on Sunday ....'*. The DNA evidence revealed the murderer's identity, providing ample evidence for the CPS to build a strong case to prosecute him. A confession would expedite the process. She bounded back into the interview room and laid the scrapbook on the table, directly in front of Richard Smith.

"Do you recognise this scrapbook?" she asked.

His expression gave away his guilt immediately. After she mentioned the DNA match to the handbag, the suspect blurted out a full confession. Clara had caught the copy-cat murderer, but only with some help. London residents could sleep safely at night again.

Chapter 63

HOXTON CAR REPAIR SHOP
THURSDAY

B ERNIE GAZED OUT OF the tarnished office window of his car repair shop at the clouds massing in the distance. He sensed a heavy storm developing. His thoughts turned to the ruby stored safely as he fiddled with the metal key which held the secret to his future. The past thirty-six hours had been fraught with internal conflict as he struggled with his next course of action. Over the years, he had amassed a small collection of items linked to Jack the Ripper and, whilst he wasn't a direct descendant of the infamous killer, he felt a connection. He displayed those items in a cabinet in the Ripper's Guild meeting room, although none were valuable. Unlike the ruby. He knew Sophia and Jakob only wanted their share of the precious jewel's worth, once sold. Initially he had considered keeping it, but after meeting with a discrete jeweller earlier, he had changed his mind. The substantial amount of money from the sale meant he could achieve everything he ever wanted in life. The jeweller had suggested the value to be around ten million pounds. Although he did stress, there wouldn't be many buyers because of the high price point and only marketing it on the black market. The jeweller had offered to act as broker for a ten per-cent fee, but Bernie had baulked at this and began his own sale process.

That's where Davey came in. Bernie's tech lad had spent the past hour searching the dark web for artifact dealers. The limited list included three dealers based in the UK, with others in Europe and America. He contacted the UK dealers first, as it would be easier to complete a deal with one of them. He had left a voicemail with all three: Alistair Edgeworth in Cornwall, Rory McDuff in Scotland and Eric Coulson in Nottingham.

"Who else can I contact Mouse?" he asked Davey.

"There's Xavier Boucher in Paris, but if you want English speaking, then Robert Eisenberg in New York or Alice Boone in Jacksonville."

"Give me their numbers and I'll see if there's any interest. Where are the investigators?"

Davey scribbled out more numbers on the list and checked the tracking app. "Still at the hotel."

Bernie laughed, "They must be so distraught at losing the ruby they're sulking in their rooms!" He picked up his phone to call Robert Eisenberg when it rang with an unsaved number.

"Bernie Johnson speaking."

"It's Eric Coulson. You left me a voice message. You mentioned a jewel being available for purchase?"

"Thanks for calling back, Eric. I have in my possession a large ruby that Jack the Ripper stole from a heist of the Royal family's jewels back in eighteen eighty-eight. Would you be interested in it?"

"Possibly. I only deal with genuine artifacts, so I'll have to check the backstory and have it analysed. First, I need some photos. I have a secure data system on the dark web. I'll get my tech guy to set you up. Text me your email address," said Coulson.

"Thanks. I've been told it's worth circa ten million."

"I'll be the judge of that. Everyone thinks their artifacts are worth more than someone is prepared to pay."

Bernie didn't warm to the guy. His forceful nature raised a red flag. As no-one else had replied yet, he would send over photos and arrange a meeting.

"Fair enough. When can we meet?"

"Depends on the photos," said Coulson.

"Okay, I'll text you my email address."

"Fine," came the abrupt reply as Coulson ended the call, leaving Bernie slightly annoyed with the dealer's attitude.

He promptly text the dealer his email address and waited for confirmation of a login. In the meantime, he called the American dealers, but because of time differences, both flipped to voicemail. He had several options to sell the ruby now, but realised it wouldn't be a swift conclusion. To deflect from his impatience, he wandered downstairs to tackle one job planned in for today. He dropped into the vehicle inspection pit underneath a blue VW car to start an oil change.

Bernie didn't have to wait long as the login details arrived within the hour. The photo uploads triggered a rapid text from the artifact dealer. Coulson arranged a meeting for the following day at nine am in Nottingham at the dealer's home. Clearly impressed with the photos, Coulson wanted to analyse Jack's ruby himself. He arranged for Jakob to travel with him as security. They would set off at six in the morning, so he would take the ruby home with him tonight. The situation had moved quicker than expected, so presumably the ruby was worth what the jeweller suggested.

Chapter 64

TEN BELLS PUB

THURSDAY

EUAN, REED AND BRIAN Morgan had spent the past couple of hours planning the retrieval of the Black Prince's Ruby. Euan now sat opposite Brian in the Ten Bells Pub sipping an orange juice, as the ex-SAS soldier had been quite clear about no consumption of alcohol until completion of the mission. He felt slightly nervous around Brian with his calm but forthright way of issuing instructions. The soldier had changed little since last year. His shaved bald head, empathic muscles and icy stare gave a formidable impression. With Reed, they had discussed where they thought Bernie Johnson would hide the ruby and settled on the Rippers Guild's secret meeting place as first choice. They had arrived shortly after opening time and with a few customers present; it seemed a straightforward exercise. Brian had picked a table close to the corridor that led to the toilets and the basement room, which provided a perfect surveillance point. He had offered to search the room once Reed opened the padlock.

"Are you ready, Euan?" asked Brian.

"Born ready," he said as cold sweat trickled down his back.

"We don't need jokes, focus."

A nod of his head confirmed he understood Brian's comment as Reed appeared from the corridor and sat down. Then muttered a simple phrase.

"It's open."

Euan rose to his feet, ambled towards the corridor, and descended the stone steps to the secret room. The lock hung loosely, so Euan whipped it off, entered the room, and closed the door. Brian said he had five minutes to search what was a relatively small space. He'd imagined this several times on the walk over here, and each time he had started with the display cabinet. He eased open the glass doors of the dark-wooden cabinet, looked inside a vase and underneath a dirty black handkerchief without success. The small drawer underneath the narrow ledge yielded only cuttings of newspapers. He squatted and prised open the remaining wooden door to access more storage space. Inside were two Bowie knives, some empty glass bottles and a can of lighter fluid. Tools and implements probably used for Bernie's illegal gains, he thought.

The ruby wasn't in the cabinet, so Euan moved over to one of the tattered brown sofas. He patted each cushion, checking for the jewel, once convinced it wasn't inside, he threw it on the floor. He knelt down to search through the base of the sofa, plunging his arms into the lining, without success. A spark of an idea flashed through his mind and he laid flat on the floor, peering underneath the sofa like a racoon searching for discarded breadcrumbs. The scratched sofa legs provided a four-inch gap to the floor, but unfortunately, no objects underneath. He repeated the exercise for the second sofa with no luck.

Euan scanned the room for other hiding places, but still nothing, so he checked behind the display cabinet. That was empty, as well. Disappointed, he left the room, locked the door and returned to his friends empty-handed.

"Nothing there."

"Did you check underneath the sofa?" asked Reed.

"Yes, everywhere."

"Okay, where next?"

"The car repair shop is the next logical place. He has a floor safe in his office."

"No problem," said Brian as he patted his holdall on the floor. "Have you got the drone?"

"It's here," Euan said, lifting the silver case up for Brian to see.

Brian downed the remnants of his drink. "When we reach the car repair shop, I want the drone in the sky with thermal imaging activated to determine how many people we're dealing with. We'll need the contents of my bag to assist our assault."

Euan trusted Brian's skills, recalling his effective handling of the drug gang last summer. Would they find the Black Prince's Ruby at the car repair shop?

Chapter 65

Hoxton Car Repair Shop

Thursday

Reed stood out of sight of the car repair shop and reflected on his call with Alistair Edgeworth earlier. His artifact dealer friend had advised him that Bernie was looking to sell a precious jewel. Reclaiming the Black Prince's Ruby had just become critical as his rival sought to sell it quickly. He glanced at the drone in the sky above the car repair shop as Euan activated the thermal imaging. The screen displayed a few hotspots as Euan manoeuvred the drone above the car repair shop.

"How many have we got?" asked Brian.

"It looks like three, one on the top floor, in the office."

"That'll be Bernie up there. The others will be in the workshop below working on vehicles," said Reed.

He watched whilst Brian pulled out some binoculars and zoomed in on the car repair shop. The three of them could overwhelm their opponents and get the code for the floor-safe easily, but Brian was meticulous in his planning. Brian tucked away his binoculars and outlined his idea.

"Here's the plan, lads. I'll go in the front, you two take the rear. I'm using a flashbang so sunglasses on and turn away with eyes shut when I shout 'Go'."

He dug into his bag and flung a black balaclava at Reed, then one to Euan.

"No point getting caught on camera. Pack the drone Euan and let's prepare for the action."

Reed helped Euan pack away the drone whilst Brian slipped on his tactical belt, complete with flashbangs. He and Euan wound their way around to the rear of the car repair shop beside the open back door and waited. The radio blasted out a rap song, but he still heard Brian walk in and start talking.

"Go," shouted Brian. Reed averted his eyes as the flashbang exploded, their earplugs blocked the bulk of the noise.

Bernie overheard Ryan talking with a customer, then someone shouted before an explosion and something incredibly bright lit up the workshop area. They were under attack. He was underneath the car, finishing the oil change, but now was stunned, deaf and blind. He struggled to find the steps to climb out of the inspection pit.

"Ryan, what's going on?"

"I don't know."

A mechanical whirr above his head caused Bernie to panic. He found the first step and climbed swiftly until he smacked his head on the engine block of the car. He realised the noise was the vehicle lift descending. The force of hitting his head caused him to stumble backwards, promptly lost his footing, and he crashed backwards down the steps. His arms flailed, searching to grab hold of the pit wall to stop his fall. The next few seconds slipped by in slow-motion as his head smashed into the hard concrete floor of the vehicle inspection pit. Pain erupted in his head that absorbed his entire thoughts. His hand touched his head and felt something warm and sticky, blood. Everything then went black.

As Reed leapt into the car repair shop, he saw Brian overwhelm Ryan, pinning him to the floor. He scanned for the others and eventually saw Bernie on the floor of a vehicle inspection pit, out cold.

"Tie him up. I stopped him getting out whilst I dealt with this one," said Brian as he fiddled with some buttons on the control panel of the vehicle lift. Eventually, it raised enough for Reed to get underneath, where he spotted a pool of blood beside Bernie's head.

"There's blood."

"Let's get the ruby, then we'll call an ambulance when we leave. Search him."

Reed tied Bernie's hands and quickly frisked the unconscious man. He felt uncomfortable with the man lying in a pool of blood and engine oil, but he needed the ruby. It wasn't in Bernie's pockets or anywhere else on his body. As he climbed the steps, he heard a shout from above.

"Is everything alright Bernie?"

He didn't recognise the voice, but Brian had already responded, footsteps echoing as he bounced up the metal stairway. Reed climbed out of the vehicle inspection pit and spotted Brian slam a skinny guy against the wall of the office. The ex-SAS soldier had the guy bound within seconds, but he didn't recognise them. Where was the boxer? He received the answer as Euan let out a yell.

"Reed, help."

Reed spun to see Mikey holding Euan with a knife to his throat beside the tool cabinet, its doors wide open. Where had he come from? He approached cautiously.

"Take it easy, let him go and you won't get hurt," said Reed.

"Ginger will get hurt if you don't release the others."

"Where's the ruby?"

"Bernie has it," said Mikey.

Reed sensed Brian behind him and, buoyed by this, he activated his trademark move. Straight out of the Jeet Kune Do instruction manual, he launched a leg sweep, slamming Mikey to the floor, which allowed Euan to roll away to safety. He flashed a roundhouse kick, but the boxer recovered quickly to catch his ankle and spun him into the blue VW car on the vehicle lift. His shoulder banged into the passenger's door as Mikey advanced. The boxer flung punches at Reed, but he dodged them all, bar the last one. Reed stumbled backwards to the edge of the inspection pit, one foot hanging over the side. He couldn't fall in there, it could be fatal, so remained on one knee pretending to be dazed, to draw Mikey in. As the boxer came within range, Reed fired a rising uppercut into Mikey's jaw that swept the boxer into the air and against the workbench. He pounced on the stunned boxer, twisted his arm behind his back, and asked Brian to assist. Between them, they bound Mikey and shoved him to the floor alongside Ryan, two trussed turkeys ready for Thanksgiving.

"That's four people. Your drone was one short," said Brian, staring at Euan.

"He grabbed me from behind, so must have been inside the paint shop. I didn't think to check there," said Euan sheepishly.

"He could have killed you. Let's locate the jewel before the police arrive."

With the tool cabinet already open, Reed peered inside. A rear compartment was open and contained knives and a flare gun. He rooted around, checking for the ruby, but it wasn't in there. He searched around the workbench, in tool boxes and under oily rags, but no red jewel.

"The safe is upstairs," he said.

The three of them raced upstairs and Brian knelt to look at the floor-safe, with its combination dial. Reed scrabbled through the desk drawers, looking for a scrap of paper that might contain the access code. With nothing visible, he hustled outside to speak to the skinny lad whilst the other two searched the rest of the office space.

"What's the combination?"

"Only Bernie knows it."

This caused Reed some consternation, with Bernie still unconscious. He approached Ryan and then Mikey, asking the same question. Both provided the same answer. He returned to the office empty-handed and wondered how they would get inside the floor-safe.

"Bernie's the only one with the combination code," he said to Brian.

"No problem."

Reed's eyes lit up as Brian pulled some TNT from his tactical belt and slapped it against the hinges of the safe. The ex-SAS soldier pushed a slim metal stick into each block of TNT and attached a length of fuse to each before rolling it outside of the office.

"Get down the stairs whilst I light the fuses."

They rushed downstairs, quickly followed by Brian after he lit the fuses. They covered their ears and waited. Seconds later, a massive explosion rocked the entire building as the metal stairway wobbled from the impact. Dust and debris floated out of the open office doorway as they ascended the stairs. Reed entered first and surveyed the damage with the metal door of the floor-safe several feet away from its original position.

"I used too much TNT," Brian laughed.

Reed knelt beside the floor-safe and examined the contents. The thin film of dust that lingered in the air caused him to cough. Only paperwork for illegal car deals, cash, some torn from the explosion, a couple of keys, but no ruby.

"It's not here," he said.

Disappointment washed over him, now concerned that Bernie had hidden it somewhere difficult to access.

"What about the paint shop?" asked Euan.

"Good point. Let's check there."

Police sirens sounded in the distance as Reed rushed out of the office, downstairs, through the workshop area and into the paint shop. The three of them frantically rustled through empty paint tins, desk drawers and searched underneath piles of used, multi-coloured masking tape. All the while, the police sirens zoned in on their location. Their search didn't reveal the stolen ruby.

"It must be at his home," said Euan.

"It's the only logical location left to search."

"We need to hustle. Keep that discussion for later," said Brian.

As they dashed back through the workshop, Reed pulled out his phone and called an ambulance. He couldn't leave Bernie to die with no help, even if he had stolen the ruby from them. With one other location to check, he was worried that Bernie had stored the ruby in a safe deposit box somewhere they would never find. He pondered the situation and wondered if Sophia or Jakob knew the ruby's hiding place? That would be his backup plan if they didn't locate the ruby at Bernie's house.

Chapter 66

*W*HITECHAPEL

THURSDAY

H EAVY RAIN CLOUDS DRIFTED in from the east as the late afternoon sun cast long shadows. The dark layers looked laden with moisture, ready to burst. Reed sheltered underneath a nearby bus stop as he finished his call with Emily. After searching the internet, she had confirmed Bernie's home address, which she found linked to his business. They were several streets away and with Brian and Euan in tow; he hustled towards the address as tiny raindrops struck his head. Several minutes later, he eyed the three-storey Georgian townhouse with close neighbours on either side. No lights were on and the curtains gaped open. Presumably Bernie's wife had been called regarding the accident and was at the local hospital. He considered how to enter the house and, with CCTV cameras along the road plus a video doorbell, the front wasn't an option. Brian pulled him to one side.

"You're making it too obvious standing in front of the house. Let's reconvene down that alleyway."

Reed realised that his impatience to reclaim the stolen ruby had clouded his judgement, and he needed to remain calm. Bernie's injuries would delay the car thief's plans to sell the jewel, which gave them a longer window of opportunity to locate it. Nestled inside the mouth of the alleyway, they leant against the wall whilst Euan unpacked the drone. Brian insisted they do a quick surveillance of the building before the rain took hold.

Using the drone's thermal camera, the men gathered around the screen. They established the house was empty and that they could access the rear garden from an alleyway running parallel to the road. After a few minutes of discussion, they set off to implement their plan.

One by one, minutes apart, they entered the alleyway at the rear of Bernie's garden, each quickly and quietly clambering over the gate. Brian and Euan stood underneath a large willow tree, concealed from nosy neighbours, whilst Reed approached the back door. He had donned his balaclava, harness, climbing gloves and with a black spray paint can in hand to black out the camera above the rear door. A few quick sprays obscured any recording. He whipped out the lock picks and swiftly opened the back door. He turned the handle and pushed to enter the property, but bounced off the double-glazed window panel. Someone had bolted the door from inside, annoyed, he returned to the willow tree.

"The damn door's bolted. We can't enter that way without smashing the glass."

Brian pointed to the third floor.

"There's a window ajar, probably a bathroom. Could you squeeze through there?" he asked.

"Yes, I think so. I'll shimmy up the drainpipe and then let you both in."

Reed shuffled to the drainpipe beside the kitchen window, keeping an eye out for neighbours. The sun had set now, but with the impending storm, interested people might decide to monitor its progress from the nearby homes. He gripped the drainpipe and easily made it to the second level when a flash of lightning momentarily lit up the sky. He counted before the thunder boomed. It was nine miles away. Another scurry up the wall whilst clutching the black plastic drainpipe brought him to the third-floor window ledge. He drew on his extensive rock climbing experience and pulled a rope from his backpack, along with a belay device. Safety first, was his motto. He tied the rope around a drainpipe anchor point before attaching himself via the belay device and harness.

Raindrops splattered the window ledge as Reed pushed the window fully open. He peered inside. It was the bathroom, but entering it would be a tight squeeze. He launched himself head first. When halfway through the gap, the rope snagged on the window ledge's corner. Hard tugs didn't dislodge the rope, and in the end, he had to release the belay device. He dropped head first on to the bathroom floor, scattering bottles and cans from the windowsill like a bowling ball smashing into a stack of pins. He avoided hitting his head on the bathtub but smashed glass bottles as he fell and a waft of expensive perfume enveloped the bathroom. After he reached the kitchen, Reed threw back the bolts, opened the back door, and ushered his accomplices inside.

Brian looked concerned.

"The alarm's flashing outside."

"Oh shit, I didn't realise. Can we stop it?"

"Unlikely," said Brian as he strode off to find the control panel. Reed and Euan caught up with him as the ex-SAS soldier turned and said, "We can't stop it. If it's linked to the police, we have five minutes maximum. Search quickly, take a floor each. I'll do downstairs, Reed second floor, Euan top floor. Go."

Reed started a five-minute timer on his smart watch, raced up the stairs and entered the first room of five. It was a home office with a desk and a filing cabinet. He quickly rifled through the cabinet and, with no other places to hide a jewel he dashed to the next bedroom. 4:12 said his watch. This contained workout equipment, including a rower and exercise bike. It didn't take long to search this with no obvious hiding places. 3:35 left. The next room had an empty wardrobe and a chest of drawers. He yanked out each drawer, chucking the contents onto the bed. Stealth was futile with the alarm triggered. He rummaged through the bedcovers and checked underneath the bed, but no hidden ruby. Time ebbed away, only 2:45 left. The fourth door lead to a bathroom, so he poked through the cabinets, which only contained health and vanity products. He was about to leave when he remembered the toilet cistern, a perfect hiding place he learned from their exploits in Cornwall last year. The ruby wasn't in there either. With ninety seconds remaining, he had to hurry.

The final door led into the master bedroom, where a quick search of the humongous glossy wardrobe yielded nothing. Bedside cabinets and a dressing table held perfumes, make-up, and more vanity products. Reed checked his smart watch as 0:48 ticked over to 0:47 in the blink of an eye. A lightning flash outside diverted his attention before he burst into the ensuite and searched the solitary wall cabinet. A quick look inside the toilet cistern and he had completed his search. He bounded out to the staircase and shouted,

"Twenty seconds left."

Euan hurtled down the staircase from the floor above and they joined Brian in the kitchen.

"Anything?" asked Brian.

Both lads shook their heads in disappointment.

"We need to get out now."

The three men shot out of the kitchen door as big raindrops splotched onto the garden path. Reed turned and remembered the rope anchored to the drainpipe. Brian must have read his mind.

"Leave it Reed. We've caused enough carnage. One rope with no DNA traces won't change anything."

They jumped the garden gate and bolted from the scene of their crime from one alleyway to another. Eventually, they came to a stop close to their hotel and considered their next course of action.

"Where else could it be?" asked Brian.

"I've two other ideas," said Reed. "He might have stored it in a safe deposit box? Or either Sophia or Jakob have it? Or they know where it is?"

"If it's in a safe deposit box, you can say goodbye to reclaiming it. Who're the other two?"

"They're other members of his little cliche that meet at the pub."

Brian stared at Euan and asked, "Did you fully search that room?"

"Yes. I looked under the sofas, searched the cabinet and the cushions."

"What about anything on the wall? Pictures that might hide a wall-safe?"

"Now you mention it, there were a couple of pictures."

Brian shook his head. "Anything else? Maybe a loose floorboard?"

"I don't remember seeing one, but the floorboard creaked beside the cabinet."

Reed sensed Brian's annoyance and jumped in.

"We should search the pub room again. I'll go this time," he said.

"You should have done it correctly the first time, Euan. I hope you searched the house properly."

"Yes," said Euan indignantly.

"No point arguing about it now," Reed said, protecting his best mate from the wrath of the ex-SAS soldier.

"If we don't find the ruby there, then we progress to Sophia's flat and interrogate her."

With the course of action firmly agreed, Reed strode towards the Ten Bells Pub as the intermittent rain continued to fall. The thunder roll was only four miles apart from the lightning flash. It wouldn't be long before a full-blown storm raged across Whitechapel. He hoped Euan had missed the ruby stashed in the pub's room, but he also relished the thought of exacting revenge on Sophia for her part in Euan's abduction.

Chapter 67

ROYAL LONDON HOSPITAL

THURSDAY

As Bernie awoke, the darkness surrounding him slowly faded. Light filtered through the slit in his eyelids as faint voices stirred his brain into action, with words of encouragement from two different voices.

"Dad."

"Bernie."

Someone clasped his hand, squeezing it. The regular beep of a machine added another layer of sound. His eyes eased open before shutting again as the stark artificial light hurt. Suddenly, he noticed the pounding in his head. He slowly recalled the events at the car repair shop. Where was his son?

"Ryan?"

"I'm here, dad," said Ryan.

"I'm here too Bernie, take it easy love," said his wife.

Bernie edged open his eyes and absorbed the scene before him. He was in the hospital with his son and wife at his bedside, worried looks on their faces. He remembered the loud bang and bright light at the car repair shop, followed by his fall. His next thought was that someone had stolen the ruby. He faced Ryan.

"What happened at the car repair shop?"

"Those damn investigators broke in, threw a grenade that exploded and blinded us all. A bulky guy overpowered me. You hit your head on the car in the vehicle inspection pit and fell backwards. They easily captured Davey before Mikey burst in from the paint shop, putting up a good fight until Hascombe knocked him over. They wanted the floor-safe combination and when we didn't give them the access code, they blew it up."

"Did you tell the police?"

"I gave them Hascombe's name, but because they wore balaclavas, I couldn't definitely confirm he was one of them."

"Bernie, you need to rest," interjected his wife.

"Soon. I need to discuss something with Ryan."

"Who are these investigators? Are you in trouble?" she asked.

Bernie had shared none of his dodgy business dealings with his wife. The less she knew, the less hassle he would get. He didn't intend changing that stance now.

"Nothing for you to worry about love, Ryan will sort it."

"Ryan?" she asked her son.

"As dad said, I'll sort it mum."

"I'm fetching the doctor. He needs to check you over," she said, rising and wandered off in search of a doctor.

Whilst his wife was out of earshot, this was his chance to bring Ryan into the loop to deputise for him. He beckoned his son close.

"I've arranged a meeting for tomorrow morning in Nottingham to sell the jewel, but there's zero chance of me going now. You'll have to represent me. Jakob is also going, plus he knows where I've hidden the jewel. Take these keys, phone Jakob and get the jewel tonight. Keep it safe and do the deal tomorrow. I'm expecting at least five million for it. I'll text you the address shortly. Go now before your mother comes back. I'll make up an excuse. Make me proud, son."

"Of course, always. Take the doctor's advice and rest. With Jakob's help, we'll get it done."

Bernie waved off his son, grabbed his phone, and forwarded the text that contained Coulson's address. He also sent Jakob a message that explained the situation. It was important to sell the jewel quickly, as he didn't want the investigators stealing it back. He could trust his son, and also Jakob, when Sophia didn't wield influence over him. The burst of brain activity had caused him more pain. A flash of lightning from outside lit up the room, made him close his eyes. He hoped Ryan could seal the deal and bring home the millions. Rain battered the window as he drifted into sleep, his thoughts centred on his son's mission.

Chapter 68

Ten Bells Pub

Thursday

Reed burst into the Ten Bell's Pub, dripping wet from the deluge of rain that accompanied the thunderstorm over central London. Lightning flashed and thunder boomed directly overhead. He hustled through the throng of pub revellers and reached the bar. Once they had their drinks, they settled on the only free table on the second floor beside the staircase that overlooked the entrance to the corridor leading to the toilets. Brian sat opposite the staircase with Euan beside him, which left Reed to sit with his back to the stairs, but that didn't matter, as he was ready to move.

"You go down now Reed, we'll keep watch. Check absolutely everywhere. I don't intend coming back a third time!" said Brian.

"Other than behind wall hangings and under floorboards, anywhere else specifically?"

"Check there's no false panel in the cabinet. Check for flaps on the sofas. Literally check everywhere."

"Okay will do. Let's hope I'm successful," he said.

He left his wet jacket and backpack strewn across the arms of the wooden chair and hustled down the staircase with his lock pick set, turning into the corridor behind an older man. Reed lingered whilst the man entered the toilet; he checked behind himself before slipping down the stone steps to the secret cult's room. Several seconds later, he disappeared into the room, clasping the padlock. He lifted two framed newspaper cuttings about Jack the Ripper from the wall and, with no hidden safe, he checked the sofas. He upturned the cushions, listening for movement inside, before casting them aside. Dust and debris covered the exposed floorboards underneath the sofas. He rammed his arms into the base of the sofas as he searched for hidden objects, but there was nothing inside. He knelt to scrutinise the floorboards, but with no loose boards or visible screw fixings, he reassembled the sofas back into their original positions.

With just the display cabinet to search, Reed's earlier positivity had waned. It sickened him to look at the ornaments and artifacts that Bernie had assembled as homage to the infamous serial killer. Like Euan several hours earlier, he searched the contents of the cabinet without success. He dragged the heavy cabinet slightly away from the wall, knocked on all sides, searching for any hidden compartments. Again, nothing. He glanced down at the floorboards and noticed a slight scuff mark. He dropped to his knees and saw the scuff mark led under the cabinet, as though someone had recently moved it. His positivity increased as he dragged the heavy cabinet further away from the wall into the centre of the room. In front of him was a short section of floorboard with a worn edge.

Reed tried to get his finger into the gap between the short section, but the gap wasn't big enough. He used the handle of a flipped lock pick tool and levered the floorboard up, grasping its worn edge. Underneath the floorboard sat a small locked cash tin. He lifted the metal tin out of its hiding place and used lock pick levers to open it. Inside lay the hessian cloth-wrapped ruby on top of a bundle of cash in fifty-pound notes. Not only had he reclaimed the Black Prince's Ruby, he had also discovered Bernie's little nest-egg stash. He pondered whether to relieve Bernie of his cash when he felt his phone buzzing in his pocket. Euan flashed on the display.

"I've found it, mate," he said.

"You need to get out of there. Ryan Johnson has just entered the pub, and he's on his way down."

He ended the call and slipped the ruby into his trousers pocket, leaving the cash. As Bernie's son would be inside within seconds, he left the cabinet in the centre of the room and darted behind the door just as it opened. In stalked Ryan, brandishing a Bowie knife. Reed didn't have the space for an effective kick, so punched Ryan's shoulder. His opponent stumbled forward and crashed into the cabinet before quickly regaining his stance.

"I knew it would be you!" he spat.

"Glad I didn't disappoint you."

"My dad's in hospital because of you," said Ryan as he waved the knife at Reed.

"He shouldn't take something that isn't his."

"It actually belongs to him as Jack the Ripper was his great-great-grandfather."

"Is that what he told you? A pack of lies," said Reed.

This sparked further anger from Ryan, who lunged vengefully at Reed. He stepped sideways, but the sofa restricted him, and the knife caught his upper arm. It sliced through his fleece and t-shirt and split his skin as blood bloomed into his clothes. He brought his Jeet Kune Do training to the fore, focussed and considered his best option. He leapt onto the top edge of one sofa and spun with a swift roundhouse kick to Ryan's head. His opponent stumbled into the wall but still held the knife tightly gripped in his fist. As Ryan stumbled, Reed had leapt to the floor and followed up with several chest punches as wild knife swipes headed his way. Fixed to the spot, he avoided them with dips and swerves of his body, and finished with a solid throat punch, just as someone entered the doorway.

Fortunately, it was Brian Morgan to assist him, but he didn't need it, as Ryan was now out cold on the floor.

"Neat work. You didn't need my help."

"Thanks though."

"You're bleeding."

"It's not too bad. Let's get the ruby to The Shard where Madeleine can store it safely."

"Shouldn't you treat that cut first?" asked Brian.

"It'll be fine. Come on, let's go. I'll call Madeleine on the way."

He grabbed his jacket and backpack on the way out, transferring the ruby into his jacket pocket. With Euan in tow, the three of them left the Ten Bells Pub and headed south towards Tower Bridge again. They had barely taken five steps in the teeming rain when Euan gasped.

"Over there Reed, that's Sophia and the nutter, Jakob," Euan said, pointing at a couple in the middle of the road, directly in front of them

"They must be planning to meet Ryan."

"What should we do?"

"Just keep walking. They might not have seen us," said Brian.

Heads down, they sauntered off. Reed hoped they could flee without being seen. He didn't fancy another encounter with his arm still bleeding badly. As the adrenaline diminished, the pain increased and his arm throbbed. They crept away and kept to the shadows as another burst of lightning lit up the nearby buildings.

Chapter 69

TOWER BRIDGE

THURSDAY

SOPHIA TUGGED HER NAVY baseball cap tighter to her head, her long blonde hair swirled in the wind as the rain hammered down. Jakob had called her earlier, explained that Bernie was in the hospital injured and she agreed to come with Jakob to meet Ryan, as apparently Bernie was meeting an artifact dealer the next day. Unless Ryan disagreed, she planned to travel with the two lads the following morning. As they crossed the road to the Ten Bells Pub, home to the Ripper Guild meetings, she recognised two men walk out of the entrance door and head south. It was the ginger-haired investigator she had abducted and his mate. Panic set in as she considered the implications of seeing them.

"Jakob, did you see them?"

"Who?"

"Hascombe and ginger boy," she said and pointed at the group walking away from them.

"I didn't see their faces. Who's the third one?"

"I didn't recognise him. You follow them. I'll meet Ryan and call you. I have a bad feeling about this."

"Okay," Jakob grunted.

"Avoid being seen."

"I won't!"

A lightning flash followed rapidly by a boom of thunder greeted her arrival at the pub entrance. Sophia pushed through the busy bar and scuttled down the stone steps. The Ripper Guild's door was wide open, she cautiously entered, immediately spotting Ryan laid prone on the floor amongst the disarray, the cabinet moved and a floorboard loose. She knelt beside him and checked his pulse. He was alive, but unconscious. She snatched out her phone and called Jakob.

"Ryan's unconscious in our meeting room and someones moved the cabinet."

"Bernie hid the ruby under the floorboards. Has Ryan got it?"

Sophia put the phone on the floor as she searched Ryan's clothes. "It's not here Jakob!"

"What about under the floorboards?"

"Empty, just an open metal tin beside the gap."

"They've taken the ruby."

"Where are you?" she asked.

"Nearly at Aldgate East tube station. They're walking towards Tower Bridge. Tuesday night, Bernie said they were heading to The Shard, and that's how we ambushed them in the park."

"Okay, I'll get there as quick as I can. We need to stop them. Have you got a weapon on you?"

"My Bowie knife."

"Not good enough. We need a gun. I'll collect my revolver from the flat and get there as soon as possible."

"Don't be long," said Jakob.

The thunderstorm continued unabated, although Sophia hardly noticed the heavy rain as adrenaline kicked in. They had to retrieve the ruby tonight. She jogged across the road, but running wasn't her strong point and it would be impossible to reach to Jakob in time. She needed a taxi, so whipped out her phone and checked the wait times in the Uber app. Over thirty minutes, which wasn't a surprise as it approached pub's closing time. She turned another corner and spotted a discarded e-scooter, the perfect solution. Seconds later, she whizzed away and reached her flat.

Sophia leapt up the stairs, burst into her flat and grabbed her revolver from its hiding place inside a cushion. Now she had a proper weapon, they stood a better chance, but she needed to hurry. She bounded down the stairs two at a time, jumped on board the e-scooter, and headed south. She cranked up the speed to twenty-five miles per hour, flipped from the road onto the pavement as traffic lights approached. The rain still hammered down as her long blonde hair trailed in the wind like a crazy banshee. Pedestrians avoided, cars swerved and corners slid past as she approached Tower Bridge. The lights twinkled amongst the raindrops as she spotted Jakob trailing the group of three men. She whizzed past her friend and the group before sliding to a stop fifty yards from the iconic bridge.

The e-scooter fell on the floor as Sophia reached into her pocket for the revolver. Her ancestor flashed through her mind as she drew the revolver up level. Everything slipped into slow-motion as thoughts of the unique ruby nestled in her hands spurred her into action. Hascombe had disarmed her at the flat, but it wouldn't happen this time. Thunder reverberated overhead as she fired a shot at the group. One man dropped to his knees.

Reed saw the flash of blonde hair hurtle past them but didn't react quick enough as Sophia drew out a gun and fired at them. Unfortunately, the bullet punctured Brian in the stomach, dropping him to his knees. He dragged Euan to the floor as Sophia's finger squeezed the trigger again. He expected to hear the whoosh of a bullet and the crack of the gun, but it had clearly jammed. Sophia's long blonde hair flapped in the wind as she fiddled with the gun, giving them an opportunity to escape. He jerked Euan to his feet and spun around to run away, only to be faced by Jakob, brandishing a knife. Jakob had cornered them. Another crack of lightning averted his gaze momentarily and highlighted an escape route.

"Climb down the bridge to the shoreline," he said to Euan.

"Right behind you."

They sprinted to the edge of the bridge and swung over, clambering down the metal framework until they reached a ledge. Reed peered up as his opponents stared over before they rushed along the river embankment towards some stone steps in the distance. The drop to the stoney shoreline was too dangerous. They could break their legs, so he removed a rope attached to his backpack and tied it against the bridge's frame. It unfurled and slapped against the ground as he ushered Euan to go first, who slid down quickly. His shoulder screamed in pain as he descended. He glanced up at the shoreline and spotted Sophia and Jakob leaping down the stone steps a hundred feet away. They would be in trouble if their adversaries caught up to them. His shoulder injury had diminished his ability to fight and, with no weapons, the two antagonists would overpower them.

Reed grabbed Euan's arm, and they retreated from their opponents, their feet trampling on the stones and soft mud. He scanned the area for a means of escape as they fled underneath Tower Bridge on foot. The explosion of a gun being fired and the clang of a bullet as it hit the metal stanchion above their heads redoubled his efforts. Sophia must have resolved the issue she had with the gun. Ahead of them were several large tourist boats and a couple of smaller speedboats, but no way of utilising any of them. Then he spotted the solution. A wooden pontoon stretched into the river had jet skis moored to it, with a small shed-style building at the shore end.

As they reached the building, Reed whipped out his crowbar and cracked open the metal door. Keys for the jet skis hung on hooks behind the reception desk. He grabbed them all as Euan shouted from outside.

"They're getting close, hurry."

"I've got the keys," he said.

Reed burst through the doorway and bundled the keys into Euan's hands, but unfortunately, one dropped and bounced away.

"Leave it, let's go."

They rushed to the nearest jet ski, and Euan tried three keys before one fitted. The engine fired. Euan threw the others into the river, then grabbed the handlebars, and Reed jumped on behind him. Another shot rang out from the shoreline, but fortunately, Sophia missed them again. The rain poured onto his head from the heavens, like a waterfall from a leaky gutter. He hung on as Euan twisted the throttle and they sped off from the wooden pontoon, away from their chasing opponents.

As his mate accelerated into the centre of the river Thames, the brown water churned up behind them. Reed glanced backwards, spotted Sophia and Jakob scrambling aboard another jet ski. Damn, they must have found the key he had dropped. He shouted above the roar of the engine and the incessant storm.

"They've grabbed the key I dropped and are chasing us."

Euan spun his head to view their pursuers and inadvertently wrenched the handlebars simultaneously. The jet ski lurched left and nearly flipped them off into the river. Euan let go of the throttle as they ground to a halt.

"You drive, I'll watch," shouted Reed.

His mate nodded his head, righted the jet ski and zoomed off once more. Reed checked on their pursuers, who had now gained on them. He saw Jakob at the front whilst Sophia peered from behind the Polish lad, her blonde hair flowing in the wind. Their jet ski cut through the water effortlessly as another bolt of lightning lit up London's skyline. The dome of St Paul's cathedral prominent on one side of the river, whilst The Shard dominated the south bank with its rainbow of night lights still acting like a beacon. They raced past HMS Belfast, a World War II warship permanently moored on the Thames.

Reed wondered how to escape with only a gap of a few feet between them now, as Jakob had thrust through their wake at full pelt. They rushed underneath London Bridge, and then two other bridges whizzed past as Euan desperately tried to outrun the other jet ski. He spotted Sophia draw her gun one handed as her other hand gripped the pillion. The blonde girl fired off another round, but it went hopelessly wide. He heard Jakob shout at her, presumably to stop her from wasting ammunition. He counted up her shots. That was four bullets she had used. If it was a standard gun, she would only have two remaining. Hopefully, she had no more ammunition with her.

His shoulder wound hurt as he gripped onto the pillion handle so swapped to the other hand to ease the pain. He felt the ruby bounce around in his jacket pocket and wished he had taken a few seconds more to secure it inside his backpack. Suddenly, the two pursers had drawn level, and Jakob twisted his handlebars to smash into them. Euan took evasive action, but with Reed holding on with just one hand, he wasn't ready for the sudden turn of direction. He lost his grip, flipped off the jet ski and hit the water as Euan raced away.

Reed plummeted into the icy cold water head first, dropping some ten feet below the surface. His backpack filled with water as he desperately fought to right himself. This wasn't his strong point, swimming. He had to fight against the increase in weight, his clothes now fully laden with water. Another bolt of lightning allowed him to become orientated as he struck out for the surface. Two shadows raced across the surface. Hopefully, Euan could rescue him and he didn't pop up in front of his opponents. He stroked forcefully to reach the surface and gulped in lungfuls of air.

A jet ski skidded to a stop several feet away as Reed wiped water from his eyes. There was only one person on it. Phew. He clambered aboard and Euan twisted the throttle once more to race off just as Jakob was about to bring the other jet ski alongside. They headed towards Millennium Bridge as Euan weaved to throw off their pursuers. It didn't work, as their opponents kept pace with them. He remembered the ruby in his pocket and felt for it. It wasn't there! His heart sank. It must have dropped out when he landed in the river. He glanced back and made a mental note of the location between two bridges.

"I've lost the ruby," he said. Euan didn't respond. Perhaps he didn't hear him?

As they headed towards the next bridge, Reed peered around his mate at several barges moored on either side of the river. He pointed towards them so Euan could manoeuvre the jet ski in that direction. They zipped under two bridges and headed straight for the wooden barges.

Sophia clung onto the pillion handle as Jakob chased down their opponents. Two bridges flashed above them as they sped towards the riverbank. Maybe they were about to quit? Or had run out of fuel? She had seen Hascombe fall into the river a few moments ago, so perhaps he was suffering from hypothermia? Either way, she didn't care, she just craved the ruby in her possession. With Bernie and Ryan incapacitated, she and Jakob would go to the meeting and split the reward between them.

Moored barges loomed as another bolt of lightning flashed above them. Water erosion had ravaged the coloured barges as paint peeled off their hulls. Jakob swept alongside the other jet ski as it slowed, but then it whipped right amongst the barges. Her friend abruptly turned, but without easing off on the power. Jakob completely flipped the jet ski, and they both landed in the river. As Sophia plunged downwards, her thoughts strayed to the ruby disappearing into the distance. Her annoyance created a red mist, so she didn't detect the rusted metal spike that loomed in front of her before it was too late. Even with a twist to the side, it still pierced her jacket and drilled into her lower abdomen.

The sharp pain caused by the spike overwhelmed her. It took precious seconds before she realised what had happened. Blood pooled around her as it seeped from the wound. Sophia grabbed the spike and pushed away hard, but it wouldn't budge. The spike had embedded itself in her side. She unzipped her jacket whilst her legs thrashed around in the dark water. The pain seared through her brain as she frantically tried to remove her jacket. The dark pool of blood increased the more she fought against the metal spike. She scanned the water for any sign of Jakob, but the water and pain impaired her sight. Darkness crept into her vision as her life slowly ebbed away. She hadn't envisaged this ending when she had come to London six months ago. Her struggles waned as blood flowed into the river. Seconds later, everything turned black.

Reed swivelled to check on their pursuers and saw their jet ski had flipped over, discarding both occupants into the river. At last, they could escape. He waved his hand at Euan to slow down.

"They're in the river," he said.

"Thank goodness."

"Head to the bank."

They motored slowly to the shoreline and disembarked the jet ski. Reed needed to update Euan on the ruby's whereabouts. He found a seat to recover and sat himself down on the wooden bench. The water drained from his backpack.

"I've dropped the ruby in the river," he said. Euan's face dropped.

"Oh shit. Whereabouts?"

"When I fell off. It was in my pocket until then. I felt it bouncing around."

Reed felt Euan's disappointment, which matched his own. He cast his mind back to the first gunshot and hoped Brian was okay. The ex-SAS soldier would require immediate hospital treatment. They should hurry back. He wondered about the jewel's fate. Was it lost forever?

Chapter 70

PENTONVILLE PRISON
FRIDAY

MADELEINE FELT AS THOUGH her world had fallen apart. Since she had learned of her husband's arrest, time passed in a blur of confusion mixed with anger. How had he duped her? Whilst she never knew of the thoughts in his head, his actions showed nothing sinister. Or had she misinterpreted everything? The police had only given her scant detail, but now, as she waited to enter the visitor's room, she wanted full disclosure from her husband. A bell rang, and she stepped forward.

She glanced towards the steel bars that separated her from Richard, his head bowed. Unwashed hair hung like a grey curtain, obscuring his murderous features. Madeleine sat on the metal chair facing him.

"What the fuck Richard!"

No movement, but she caught a whisper of an apology. "Sorry."

"Sorry, doesn't cut it. Look me in the eye, you coward," she spat as anger overcame her.

Slowly, he lifted his head. Madeleine glared at his drawn face etched with guilt. His brown eyes were vacant, lacking the normal sparkle, but she felt no compassion. What her husband had done was beyond comprehension.

"Why? No, that's a stupid question. Those poor people you murdered, don't you feel any remorse?"

"I wasn't thinking straight, Maddy."

"Seriously Richard! You make it sound like you stole something absentmindedly. Oh wait, you did. Their lives."

"I didn't mean to. My mind clouds over and I lose all rational control."

"That's bullshit, Richard, just a feeble excuse. The police said you kept a scrapbook," she said.

"My great-great-grandfather was Francis Tumblety, a doctor. I just kept some notes."

"That's not notes. That's an obsession. You lied to me so many times."

"I didn't mean to," he said.

"How can you say that? Of course you meant to. Those nights at the art gallery crashed on the sofa were just a cover for your vile acts."

He didn't answer her. She realised he hadn't taken ownership of his actions, still deflecting the truth with excuse after excuse. How could she have loved this man? All she saw now was an evil killer, wrapped in his own crazy world.

"The detective told me you had served a prison sentence in America for GBH. So you've always enjoyed hurting people?" she asked.

"Sometimes I can't think straight."

Angrily, Madeleine pointed her finger through the bars at her husband. "That's no excuse, Richard, own your crimes!" He lowered his head and the grey curtain obscured his eyes once more. She knew then their relationship was over. He wasn't the man she thought she had married. This person in front of her was inherently evil. With total disgust, she stood and ran into the corridor, away from the vile monster that had been her husband. She burst into the toilets, pushed a cubicle door open, and threw up into the pan. She felt sick to her core. The life they had built together was based on lies. She would instruct her lawyer to dissolve it immediately.

Chapter 71

NORTH LONDON

FRIDAY

THE THUNDERSTORM HAD SUBSIDED and the remnants of rain clouds drifted away, with puddles left on the pavement as the weak winter sun tried in vain to evaporate the rainwater. After their jet ski chase, Reed had hurried back to Tower Bridge, searching for Brian Morgan. The gunshot wound had left bloodstains on the road. He caught up with him in Royal London Hospital. Fortunately, the bullet had only pierced soft tissue with all his organs still intact. Brian was adamant he'd be out in a few days. Reed and Euan had returned to the hotel and relayed their exploits to Emily before crashing out for a solid eight hours of sleep.

Refreshed from his slumber, Reed awoke to find Emily had devised a plan to recover the jewel. With his injured shoulder strapped up, he checked the news online and discovered that Sophia had died in the river. An early morning dog walker had seen blood on the river bank who alerted the authorities and then they had recovered her body, but no mention of Jakob. Reed had made a quick call to Madeleine and promised to update her fully later in the day. She seemed strangely absent on the phone, then he discovered why. The police had charged Richard, her husband, with the copy-cat murders. He would need to tread carefully when they met later.

Reed ushered Euan and Emily through the tube station ticket

gates as they arrived in North London.

"This way," he said, after consulting directions from Google maps on his phone.

Reed weaved around the crowds of people, entered a side street, and spotted the blue banner that declared the name of the shop he sought.

"Here we are. Let's buy the equipment we need and return to the hotel."

"Are you carrying the tank?" asked Emily.

"Yes, I'll take it."

They entered the shop, and Emily wandered over to the racks that contained wetsuits. She chose a medium-sized navy one, while Reed examined the air tanks and picked a twelve-litre model. Emily could dive for at least an hour with that size of air-tank. Reed couldn't dive because of his shoulder injury, plus it may become infected in the notoriously polluted water. Emily, a certified PADI diver, was a more skilled diver than him. He gathered all the equipment and settled the bill with the shopkeeper.

Reed struggled with the pain in his shoulder as he carried the air tank, so Euan offered to take it instead. On their way back to the hotel, they stopped at a cafe to eat and recap their plan. Reed ordered his favourite sandwich, tuna mayo without cucumber, the only food he really disliked. He matched that with a Columbian coffee. The cafe wasn't too busy, which gave them a chance to discuss the plan.

"You'd rather dive at low tide?" he asked Emily.

"I think it gives the best chance of locating the ruby. There'll only be eight feet of water."

He pulled up the tide times for the Thames at Millenium Bridge and identified the optimum time was five thirty. That presented another challenge as twilight begun at six o'clock.

"Looking at the tide times, Em, start a tad earlier, say five."

"Okay. We need to head back shortly. I hope we can dive

discreetly without being reported to the police," she said.

"We'll find a suitable place. Once you're in the water, no-one will spot you."

They finished their sandwiches, grabbed their equipment and strode off towards the tube station. Whilst the underground train whistled through the tunnels from one station to the next, Reed's thoughts drifted to the ruby. It would be hard to spot on the riverbed, amongst the mud and tangle of plants. The brown hessian cloth would make it especially hard to spot. He felt annoyed that he wasn't able to dive and hoped Emily could find the Black Prince's Ruby.

Chapter 72

MILLENIUM BRIDGE

FRIDAY

EMILY SAT WITH HER back to the wall facing the river Thames as Reed pointed out roughly where he fell off the jet ski. At low tide, the river revealed a stoney beach which the lads had already searched in case the river's tide had washed the precious ruby up onto the shoreline. They didn't find it. Millenium Bridge thronged with pedestrians crossing the river, but as the sun slipped behind buildings, Emily hoped no-one would spot a lone diver. She made her final safety checks, set twenty minutes on her waterproof watch, and entered the icy water.

Sightseeing boats and passenger ferries would continue to operate throughout the evening, which meant Emily had to be extremely careful. She felt the sharp stones through her thin diving shoes as she waded further towards the centre of the river. She plunged into the brown-coloured water and dived to the riverbed. Daylight helped her survey the area without the aid of a torch for now. The river bed was a mass of mud that was littered with rubbish that moved with the tide, aluminium cans and plastic water bottles were the most prevalent. She identified varied metal shapes, some dangerously poked from the riverbed as she edged her way around.

From the surface, the water didn't appear to sustain much life, but the constricted river channel at low tide brimmed with aquatic life. A shoal of smelts drifted past, closely followed by a hungry pike.

Amongst the mud, she spotted a pair of grey eels weaving around, which caused clouds of mud to rise and impair her search. How could she locate a jewel the size of an egg in the murky water? Her fins caused more mud clouds to drift upwards. She mulled over what was the best way to search when a mechanical noise and dark shadow above reminded her that boats would pass overhead. The wash from the boat caused further turbulence and a current that whipped her backwards. She timed how long it took for the mud cloud to settle, which was less than expected at thirty-six seconds. The timer on her watch beeped. Twenty minutes was up, time to exit the water for a break.

Back on shore, she spoke to the two lads. "It's really difficult exploring, as anything that touches the mud causes clouds to rise. I need to devise a method of searching without disturbing the bottom."

Reed handed her a cup of tomato soup to warm her and draped a foil blanket over her shoulders.

"Do you think the ruby's sunk into the mud?" asked Euan.

"It's possible. Then we'd have to dredge the riverbed."

"Crikey, how would we do that?"

"We can't without proper equipment."

"Then the authorities would stop us!"

Emily finished her tomato soup and prepared herself to re-enter the water. She grabbed the powerful underwater lamp that Reed had purchased at the dive shop. She would need this now as the winter sun had disappeared totally. Twilight would soon give way to total darkness. Streetlamps were lit and The Shard's upper floors beamed their colourful lights across London's skyline.

"Are you sure I'm searching in the correct place?" she asked Reed.

"Closer to Southwark Bridge. What to do you think, Euan?"

"I agree, although it's hard to remember exactly as it was dark and we were in a mad panic."

"Okay, I'll try there."

She completed her safety checks and headed back into the water. This time, she would try a different approach. She reached the deepest point of the river and hovered above the riverbed. She powered on the underwater lamp and swept it ahead of her, backwards, forwards and side to side. The lamp highlighted everything on the riverbed. Aluminium cans glinted as eels raced away from the bright light. The beam cut through the mud clouds with ease as she edged towards Southwark Bridge. The loud engine of a passing ferry boat interrupted her concentration as the undercurrent whisked her back beyond her start point.

Emily groaned inwardly. This could prove annoying. Nevertheless, she continued with her approach and swung the lamp across the riverbed. Suddenly, a large eel burst from the riverbed about five feet in front of her that created another mud cloud. As the lamp's beam strobed through the suspended particles, a glint caught her eye. It could just be another aluminium can. She slowly approached the area, but once the mud had dropped to the riverbed, it had gone. Damn. She refused to be defeated and rooted around the top layer of mud with her hands. Her fingers touched a polished surface, she grasped it and brought the object into the light. A red object reflected in the lamp's beam. She had found the ruby. What a stroke of luck. Relief flooded through her body, followed by exhilaration. She stroked upwards, raced out of the water and, in her haste, narrowly avoided being hit by a small tourist vessel.

She waved her arms and launched out of the water towards Reed and Euan, brandishing the ruby.

"I've found it!"

She received a massive hug and kiss from Reed, even though she dripped mucky river water on to his clothes.

"You're amazing Em. Well done."

"Thanks. We need to get the ruby to Madeleine straightaway."

Whilst Reed called Madeleine, Emily dried herself off and grabbed another warm drink from the thermos flask. The tide had changed, the current flowed inward as tiny waves rippled across the river's surface. They had triumphed once again. She sat on the stoney beach and basked in her achievement before Reed ushered her towards the stone steps to meet Madeleine now.

Chapter 73

The Shard

Friday

REED PRESSED THE ELEVATOR button in the entrance lobby of The Shard, then turned to his girlfriend and best mate.

"Act surprised if Madeleine mentions Richard being arrested. She mustn't learn we were involved."

"He deserved to be arrested," said Emily.

"I agree, but she owes us ten per cent of the ruby's sales value."

"That's true."

A ping alerted them to the elevator's arrival. They stepped inside and rode it up to the seventeenth floor. The office had closed, so Reed rapped on Madeleine's office door and stepped in to greet her. He immediately noticed her blackened eyes, drawn face and sad expression.

"As I said on the phone, we have some excellent news."

"I'm in desperate need of something positive," she said. "I guess you've heard about my husband?"

"No. What's happened?"

"The police arrested him for the recent copy-cat murders. And he has made a full confession. I saw him this morning at Pentonville Prison. He won't get bail because of the horrendous crimes. You think you know someone and then they turn out to be a completely different person."

At that point, the tears spilled down her face, so Emily jumped up to comfort her. After a few minutes, she continued.

"He committed the murders on nights when he slept at the art gallery. According to the police, he has a criminal record in America. They found the murder weapon and other evidence at the art gallery."

"Why did he kill those poor people?" Reed asked.

"He said his great-great-grandfather was Francis Tumblety, a suspect in the Jack the Ripper case. He was also an American doctor. How that justifies what he did is beyond my comprehension. I won't see him ever again."

"So sorry."

Madeleine's bottom lip quivered before she reined her emotions in.

"Enough depressing talk, let's talk about your positive news?"

Reed unzipped his backpack, reached in for the Black Prince's Ruby and laid it on the table in front of his client. Madeleine's hand grasped the jewel and spent ages studying it.

"This is incredible. I can save my company with this. You've done an amazing job, all of you," she said. A reluctant smile broke across her face.

"We enjoyed it even if it was dangerous at times," said Euan.

"How do I go about selling it?"

"I can put you in touch with Alistair Edgeworth. He'll find a buyer for the ruby."

"I want a quick sale, so that's probably the best course of action."

He gave Madeleine Alistair's email address and phone number. They said their goodbyes and trooped off to celebrate at the local pub.

With her office now empty, Madeleine wandered over to the floor to ceiling window, absorbing London's skyline. She held the ruby in her hand, rotating it as her thoughts drifted off. Three weeks ago, she had a husband, failing company and no money. Everything had suddenly flipped. The ruby provided the opportunity to solve her financial worries and save the company. Tears trickled down her cheeks as she thought about her soon to be ex-husband. Until six months ago, everything had been fine between them, but on reflection, the letter had changed everything. Clearly Richard had an evil core, re-brought to the surface by all her talk about the letter. If only she hadn't found it. She rebuked herself as he had committed crimes in America, so his personality had severe flaws.

Madeleine wiped away the tears, her body drained of energy after two days of heartache mixed with anger. She had loved him but now felt only contempt. How could he have killed three innocent people and not shown one glimmer of remorse? He not only took his victim's lives but also damaged the souls of their families forever. She resolved to move on, but needed some space first. She recalled the holiday planned in the Canary Islands and vowed to go alone, allowing her time to process everything that had happened and come back refreshed. Her inner steel came to the fore, and she made an instant decision. She grabbed her phone.

"Hi Alistair, it's Madeleine Robinson. Reed Hascombe gave me your number," she said, dropping the second part of her double-barrelled surname. That was history to her. Just plain Madeleine Robinson from now on.

"Hi, Madeleine, Reed messaged to say you would call at some point."

"It's about the Black Prince's Ruby. As amazing as the jewel is, I need to sell it quickly. Can you help?"

"Of course. Since I spoke to Reed two days ago about the ruby, I've been putting some feelers out. I have two interested buyers already."

"Excellent."

The conversation continued and concluded with plans to meet.

Madeleine put the phone down, opened up her computer, and made travel plans. No need to dwell, life moved on and whilst the next few weeks would be emotionally difficult, she felt positive about the future. Then the realisation hit her. The letter had brought to light the hidden character of her husband. She was better off without him. Now, thanks to Reed and his team, time to save her company.

Inside the local pub, the three friends sipped their drinks as Reed mulled over the past three weeks and felt totally vindicated in his decision to quit his job six months earlier. This quest had been demanding, dangerous, and challenging, which was everything he had hoped for. With their share of the sale, he would have plenty of money to continue with his donations to help homeless charities. A notification on his phone snapped him out of his reflections. It was an email from someone in Utah that required some help to locate missing Aztec gold coins. His reputation had spread across the pond. He looked up.

"Who fancies a trip to Utah?"

About the Author

I hope you enjoyed The Ripper's Legacy. Please leave a review by heading over to the website you purchased the book from, as it helps other people to decide to buy the book.

This is the third Reed Hascombe adventure and hopefully you enjoyed it enough to want the first two books – Paradox of The Thief & Enigma of The Sword – available on Amazon in Kindle, paperback, hardcover and audiobook formats.

I've written a short story called Downfall that sits alongside the other books in the series. An unexpected twist concludes one of Reed and Euan's Peak District day trips. It's available for free on my website. Head over to www.unearthedquill.com/free.

I've planned the outline for the fourth book in the Reed Hascombe series – The Aztec Pursuit - it will be available around Christmas 2025. If you sign up for my newsletter, you will get notified when it's published. I promise not to bombard you with loads of emails, just one a month. You can join at www.unearthedquill.com/newsletter.

Don't forget to tell your family and friends if you enjoyed my book, maybe they will too.

Thanks Nigel

Printed in Dunstable, United Kingdom